Mind & Music

Originating from heart, MUSIC gets expression through MIND

Mind & Music

Demystifying The Thumri Maestros

Meenakshi Prasad

MLBD PUBLICATIONS

Motilal Banarsidass Publications

MOTILAL BANARSIDASS
PUBLICATIONS
4741/23, Ansari Road, Daryaganj, New Delhi - 110002 (India)
Email: *mlbd@mlbd.com* | *sales@mlbd.com* | *exports@mlbd.com*
Website: *www.mlbd.com*

Mind & Music:
Demystifying The Thumri Maestros
by
Meenakshi Prasad

2nd Reprint Edition Published in 2024
First Edition Published in 2023

Published in India by Motilal Banarsidass Publications

ISBN : 978-93-91759-67-4 (HB)

Printed and bound in India

V

Mind & Music

In Bhagawad Geeta, The First counsellor lord Krishna says:

सत्त्वानुरूपा सर्वस्य श्रद्धा भवति भारत।

श्रद्धामयोऽयं पुरुषो यो यच्छ्रद्धः स एव सः।।

Man is made by his belief. As he believes, so he is!

Bhagawad Gita 17.3

Dedication

To the legends who inspired me to achieve what I never ever dreamt.

"Mind and Music" is not merely a book. It's a heritage of the legends passed on to me. It was my duty to preserve it carefully for our coming generations.

This book was launched by the very revered Dr. Karan Singh ji, one the greatest public intellectual of modern India. He remarked that it's a deeply researched book and that It's beneficial not only for music lovers but also for all readers. He further stated that It's not merely a book, it's an encyclopaedic work. A must read book, lauding the efforts of the author Meenakshi Prasad.

Launched by
Dr. Karan Singh
India International Centre
New Delhi 110003
30th July 2023

FOREWORD

Pt. Birju Maharaj

Padma Vibhushan

मुझे बड़ी खुशी हो रही है, मीनाक्षी प्रसाद एक ऐसी किताब लिखी है जो कि अभी तक नही लिखी गई थी संगीत एवं मनो विज्ञान के ऊपर, यह उनका अभूतपूर्व प्रयास है। हम चूंकि नृत्य के कलाकार हैं जिसमे शरीर के हर अंग का सांगीतिक विकास कर पाते है। जो कि इनके पुस्तक मे इसी विषय से सम्बन्धित बहुत से कलाकारो ने अपने विचार प्रकट किये है। मेरी हार्दिक शुभकामना और आशीर्वाद इनके ऊपर रहेगा, और ईश्वर से कामना करता हूँ कि इस पुस्तक को ज्यादा से ज्यादा लोग अध्ययन करे और लाभ उठाये।

शुभ आशीष

[signature]

(पंडित बिरजू महाराज)

D-II/33, Shahjahan Road, New Delhi-110 011 | Tel.: Res. 011-23782889, Off. 011-41555434
Email: kalashrambirjumaharaj@gmail.com, kathak.birjumaharaj@gmail.com

ACKNOWLEDGMENT

This book would not have been possible without the immense contribution of musicians, musicologists, scholars of psychology, music lovers and the young brigades (struggling vocalists), who gave me their time and cooperation for in-depth interviews. I am personally thankful to all the legends for their participation.

I owe my deepest gratitude to my *guru* Vidushi Savita Devi, a renowned exponent of *Thumri*, who hails from a legendary musical family of *Banaras Gharana*. She was my constant support and guide not only through the journey of the book but in my life as well. Without her support this book would not have been possible. I would like to register my gratitude to Pandit Govardhan Mishra, a renowned *khayaal* and *thumri* singer of Gaya *Ang*. I consider him to be my *Shastra Guru*.

I am grateful to Shri Mohinder Sareenji, who taught me the nuances of light music and supported me in most of my endeavors. He would often ask me about the progress of my book both in terms of quantity and quality, which pushed me to strive harder.

I owe thanks to Dr. Gyantosh Jha, Principal of ARSD College, for permitting me to conduct a workshop on *Thumri*, with the students and the staff of ARSD College. My heartfelt gratitude to Dr. Ishita Bhardwaj, Associate Professor, Department of Psychology, at the University of Delhi for giving important insights at crucial junctures. She introduced me to various scholars, who gave me their precious time and rich inputs. I am thankful to Ms. Vrushali Pathak, Assistant Professor at Jesus and Mary College, University of Delhi, for assisting me and accompanying me throughout the journey.

I am grateful to Professors, Scholars and senior students of of Faculty of Music (Delhi University) for sparing their precious time and actively interacting with me on issues related to this book.

My parents deserve credit for shaping the soul of a precocious child. I am also indebted to my both brothers, who have helped me discover and understand the world, which really enabled me to expand the scope of this book. My in-laws and all the family members were also a strong source of inspiration. My special thanks to all the support systems. I am thankful to my sister Pallavi Sinha for editing the manuscript.

I am really indebted to my elder daughter Darshita Neeraj who has helped me throughout my journey with her novel and productive ideas. She is a published author in her own right and thus could guide me with technical details. My younger daughter Vartika Neeraj, a graduate student and a very good writer herself, turned my ideas into a meaningful activity through her encouragement and editing. In fact, she was the first person, who encouraged me to write a book, at a time when this was not even on my mind. Her belief in me endured throughout the journey.

I would also like to thank Motilal Banarsidass for turning my dream into reality.

Last but not least, my husband Neeraj Prasad, who was my guide from the beginning down to the last of this journey. His library of books served me as a treasure trove of ideas and reference materials for this book.

*****

AUTHOR'S NOTE

There are some books that refuse to be written. Some stand their ground year after year. This book relies on personal interaction with stalwarts of *Thumri* genre. The base year of the study starts around the early 20th century (from the period of Ustad Bade Ghulam Ali Khan Sahib in 1902 to today's living legends like Pandit Ajoy Chakrabarty and Pandit Rajan-Sajan Mishra). It approximately covers a period of 118 years. The surprising findings of the study is the relative consistency of their outlook toward various psychological dimensions over many decades. The chapters deal with the following issues:

Chapter 1 deals with how the ideas for the book germinated in the author's mind.

Chapter 2 deals with the different flavors of Indian music, especially a brief introduction of *thumri* genre with a collection of some old and beautiful *thumries*.

Chapter 3 dwells on methodology and a brief introduction to stalwarts (how the author found them personally) based on their biographies and personal interaction with living legends.

Chapter 4 deals with how Indian aesthetics study the capacity of music. From sensual attractiveness to spiritualism and showing innovations in embellishment of *bandish* (song) while maintaining its originality and so on.

Chapter 5 tells the understanding the special integration between emotions & music to understand the fundamental nature of both.

Chapter 6 deals with the relevance of *Guru-Shishya parampara* in present time. How a *Guru* plays the role of sculptor, counselor and guide?

Chapter 7 explains the idea of being innovative, i.e., this explains how Indian-thought views creativity as a process of understanding and enlightenment, different steps of creativity and so on.

Chapter 8 is about the flow experiences of stalwarts while singing as well as creating something new.

Chapter 9 explains how legends see opportunity in every difficulty and deal with it, which would help the new brigades in developing optimism.

Chapter 10 deals with the role of stalwarts as a leader who are good at influencing and persuading others. This chapter tries to focus on their confident behavior, style of presentation, communication skills etc.

Chapter 11 deals with the issues and concerns of young artists of the future. After interaction with stalwarts, a need was felt to share these ideas with the upcoming artists through workshops and focused group interviews to address their problems, the prime objective of this book.

Chapter 12 deals with the concept of self. It's an idea we have about who we are physically, emotionally, and socially. This sense is developed early in life, but it goes through constant evolution and adjustment throughout the life span.

***

PROLOGUE

On a Sunday evening at 8:30 pm in 2016, the prestigious *Kamani Auditorium* of New Delhi was packed to the full with an excited audience. *Padma Vibhushan* Late Girija Devi, popularly known as Appajee, was glowing in her tastefully draped off-white silk saree and a matching diamond nose pin. I was sitting amongst the spectators who were present there. Appajee was singing a *dadra,* a sub-branch of *Thumri,* in *raag kaushikdhwani, 'shyam tohe nazariya lag jaaegi'* (Oh, Krishna! Evil eyes might hit you). The exhilarating response Girijaji was getting from the audience inspired me to start working on an idea which had been haunting me for several years.

This book has been written to introduce readers to *thumri* as a musical genre and to present the insights I gleaned from many of its stalwarts on their journey, navigating their musical careers. *Thumri* is a semi-classical genre of Indian music which is generally sung from a female perspective. It's a beautiful way to engrave the emotions and various forms of women. There is usually a confidante in *thumri* with whom the *nayika* (heroine) shares her inner thoughts. It's a journey from materialism to spiritualism; so the text explores various themes ranging from romantic to devotional. The lyrics are usually in *"Brij Bhasha"* an Uttar Pradesh dialect generally derived from the theme of eternal bonding of Radha and Krishna. This style of singing is also used as a generic name for some other light forms music such as *Dadra, Hori, Kajri, Savan, Jhula, Chaiti* and *Barahmasa.* Even though each one of them has its own structure and content—either lyrical or musical or both—exposition of these forms vary. The present volume is an attempt to underline the predispositions of eminent vocalists of *thumri* genre. While working on this idea, several stalwarts were interviewed for the book.

The idea of this book couldn't have come without the contributions of a plethora of stalwarts, performers and eminent musicologists in the field of classical and semi-classical Indian music. Every artist's work has some untold stories behind it; the story of their ups and downs, of their great dedication and sacrifice, and how they dedicated their entire life to their art. Luck plays a big role in this saturated and challenging art field but is 'luck' everything? The answer is a emphatic 'No'. Training in the field of art and an undying dedication to *riyaaz* and *guru* are the keys to success. However, even when all factors work out favorably, only a few artists become successful. I believe that the role of psychological factors is very important behind this. In our country, 'psychology's impact on human life' is given very little attention while it is as important as good training and *riyaaz*. This book explores how these characteristics can mark the making of a legendary artist.

While reading legends' mind the readers will simultaneously paint the canvas of their own mind with vivid hue of psychological insights and predispositions of the stalwarts. They can relate themselves with many anecdotes narrated in this book.

Success can be an abstract word. What is success for you may not be how I view the subject. However, a common thread in its meaning is definitely self-satisfaction. The stalwarts interviewed for the present book were definitely satisfied with themselves and their art along with an urge to do more for their music and the society at large. They believed in growing as a musician and learning more every day, yet there was a sense of contentment. Through the interactions various aspects came up which I considered played an important role in 'making them an artist'. The present book is a humble attempt in this direction. I have tried sharing some of the factors which could play an important role in the making of an artist. I wanted to share these factors and anecdotes related to them (as shared by the legends) with upcoming artists, the future of music and the country's cultural preservation. These aspects could be used by upcoming artists as lessons to remember and inculcate in themselves to 'enjoy' their art to the fullest. The book is about the journey of some people who came to be known as the best in "thumri singing" in their times and our attempt is to learn from them, their stories.

Lastly, this book also aims at changing the outlook of society towards women involved in learning and nurturing classical and semi-classical music forms for generations. I have tried my best to share my experiences with you.

For all this brainstorming, debate and discussion, I had found a 'right' place, a Costa Coffee outlet at Green Park, Delhi and Triveni Kala Sangam. These places are special for me as I feel they helped nurture and fuel our discussions with the right ambiance and 'food'. The scholars felt at ease in these environments which helped them in sharing their ideas at length and kept them engaged for long hours. They were my '*adda*s' for anything and everything related to the book.

***

CONTENT

Dedication VII

Foreword by Late Pandit Birju Maharaj IX

Acknowledgment XI

Author's Note XIII

Prologue XV

Chapters

1 Ideas Flowing Into Words | 21

2 Flavors of Indian Music | 29

3 Meet the Legends | 65

4 Singers in Stylistic Form | 137

5 Understanding Emotions in *Rasa* and *Raga* | 155

6 Relevance of *Guru-Shishya Parampara* in Today | 179

7 The Idea of Being Innovative | 203

8 ...But Who Enters the Flow? | 221

9 See Silverline in Every Dark Cloud | 231

10 Behavior Says It All | 243

11 The Way Forward | 261

12 What A Man Can Be, He Must Be | 279

Epilogue | 299

Reference | 310

Glossary | 317

Index | 321

Disclaimer | 322

CHAPTER 1

Thoughts Flowing into Words

Don't limit yourself.
Many people limit themselves to what they think they can do. You can go as far as your mind lets you.
You can achieve.

- Mary Kay Ash

Thoughts Flowing into Words

"Now you are listening to Pandit Bhimsen Joshi Ji from All India Radio. In a short while, you will hear news from our Delhi Centre."

These were the common words we used to hear off the radio in our household. In a few years, televisions literally entered the 'picture' but this trend continued to ring day in and day out. Both my parents were interested in music, listening to news in the morning and classical music and film songs everyday at night was part of our daily routine. My two brothers Amit Mohan Prasad and Rakesh Mohan and I would eagerly look forward to this. There was no discussion on the subject of music *per se* in the house, but everyone listened with great passion. I do not remember when music started finding its way into my mind and influencing me. Years passed by and many famous artists of the country, including Kumar Gandharva, Pandit Jasraj, Siddheshwari Devi, Begum Akhtar, Ustad Bade Ghulam Ali Khan, Girija Devi appeared on the Indian music scene and became very popular. Among the instrumentalists, Pandit Ravi Shankar, V.G. Jog Ji, Baba Allauddin Khan, Pandit Kishan Maharaj, Lachhu Maharaj, Ustad Amjad Ali Khan, Pandit Shiv Kumar

Sharma, Ustad Bismillah Khan all used to linger on in our *zuban*. Slowly these names began featuring on my music palette and influencing the way I viewed Indian art forms. I am thankful to my parents, who made us aware of the great cultural heritage of our country. At the age of five, I could sing the banners of Sehgal *"Gum Dye Mushtakil"*, a couple of lines from Begum Sahiba's *"Aei Mohabbat"*. However, I did not understand the words or world of pure classical music but I could manage to sing the *thumri*s used in films. It can be said that music made its way into my life and my interest in music increased day by day.

Dussehra is a festival that brings a lot of enthusiasm among the people of Bihar, especially in Patna. Those who do not belong to Patna and are music lovers would visit their relatives to celebrate *Dussehra* from *Saptami to Vijayadashami*. The three-day *Nukkad Jalsa* of Patna was famous all over the country wherein great artists of the country would participate. The atmosphere of the entire city, especially the homes of cultural aficionados, used to be very encouraging. Fortunately, my grandmother's family was among its chief organizers, so I always had a chance to sit in the front row and enjoy listening to the maestros. There were at least ten to twenty-five thousand listeners coming in and out of the *pandal*. I took full advantage of this great opportunity that I had as a young girl. The manner of presentation of these artists, their way to connect with the audience, their dress sense and the way to talk to their co-artists were all watched carefully. In two or three years, I would get a chance to see those artists again. It's a delightful memory that I have of my childhood days. I noticed that while they kept repeating some of my favorite things, there was always something new added to it. The young girl I was at that time, I couldn't pay close attention to all these subjects. Years passed and I went on to get my honors in Psychology followed by my post-graduation in it. Studying the subject, my outlook and attitude towards various things and events started changing.

Eventually I got a job and after that, like most of the girls in our society, marriage came my way followed by family, children, and a beautiful life that lasted for about fourteen happy years.

One day I had a chance to hear the well-known singer Vidushi Savita Devi, who was the daughter of *thumri* Empress *Padmashree* Siddheswari Devi through one of her disciples, Mrs. Indira Mukherjee. My desire to learn music sprang up spontaneously in my mind. I met her backstage and asked her if she could teach me singing. She responded encouragingly, saying that I should learn from her *guru* Vidushi Savita Ji. "I will give you her phone number; you can talk to her and meet her."

I met Savita ji. I have watched her on *Doordarshan* before; the rich, soulful voice of an infinitely beautiful personality. It did not feel like I was meeting her for the first time. She asked me to sit, made me comfortable and told me to sing something. I was so nervous about singing in front of such a talented artist. I sang a folk song. As I finished singing, I saw two or three pictures of Siddheshwari Devi on the wall. I had read about her as the *thumri* Empress of *Banaras Gharana* when I was preparing for a competitive exam and had seen her picture as well, so I had no problem in identifying her. I asked Savita Ji with mixed surprise, "You know her?" She laughed and said, "Yes, I know, but how do you know these songs?" I said, "I have heard them on the radio and read about her during my exam preparations." Then she said, "She is my mother." I loved hearing this so much that I was unable to express my happiness and feelings in words. I kept looking here and there; then on one side I saw a picture of Savita Ji and the world famous *tabla* player Pandit Kishan Maharaj, on the other. Then I told myself, '*now there is no need to ask anything.*' I understood that Vidushi Savita ji is the wife of Pandit Kishan Maharaj. At that moment, I felt that these people are such great legends in themselves, so why would they want to have me as a disciple?! I was sitting quietly when she said, "I liked your voice. *Gangadashara* is just after two days. You can come. I will do your '*Gandabandhan*'." I had no idea about all these things but I agreed. Two days later, the *gandabandhan* happened and my music training started in good earnest.

The kind of music you have been listening to since childhood becomes your interest in your life. First, she taught me *raga Durga* in the class, then in *Yaman* and at the end of class. Sometimes we used to sing *Kajari*, sometimes *bhajan* because it was the rainy season at that time. I was a little familiar with all of this, so I began to enjoy learning music here. She used to sing so well that I would just keep watching her. As beautiful as she herself was, her voice was even more beautiful and compelling. At the time of teaching, she used to pay a lot of attention to discipline, sitting posture and maintaining the concentration of the pupils she was teaching. I thanked Indira Mukherjee deep in my mind. Due to her I had reached here. After that a music family was formed in which Vidushi Savita Devi became my 'mother'. I called her '*maa*' and Indira Mukherjee became my Indira *didi*. The *Siddheshwari Devi Academy of Indian Music* is a fantastic example of the *Guru-shishya parampara* (tradition), where all of us are called *Gurubahne* and live as a family by being called '*extended family*' *naa*. The families of all the disciples were also connected to each other. Only when you enter this tradition, you can understand the importance and its meaning.

I never thought in my life that I would learn *Thumri* but let's just call it a 'coincidence' and a happy one at that. *Thumri* is a difficult genre, a language full of emotions wherein the artist expresses different emotions or its different intensities with the same word. When I started learning, my health was not good in those days. So I took leave from my work. If I had a class two days a week, I used to get a lot of time to learn *Thumri*. I started training with all my heart and soul and tried to put in my best efforts. I even started reading about the artists associated with it and allowed everything to seep in. I found that there was a great difference in the social status of men and women even in the same profession with the same level of singing proficiency. Though *thumri* came into vogue a little later, women used to sing *Dhrupad* and *Khayaal* even before that. Historically, they were also singers at the royal courts and took part in charitable work. My master's great scholar, Maina Devi, was a singer in the court of the King of Kashi and was revered for it. After entering this field, I found that my lifestyle was also changing. I started attending and doing live concerts. I used to enjoy it a lot that I decided to quit my job. The decision to quit the job was not easy, but my family was extremely supportive.

There is a lot of difference between studying and imbibing a subject as a degree or getting a job. I have already stated that I had a Masters in Psychology. Although psychology is a subject, it proves useful to you in whatever field you are, but if you go in for such a field where you are emotionally connected, the joy of learning this subject with your experiences increases manifold. I started attending as many concerts as possible and started paying careful attention to the presentation of these artists, their expressions, their stage handling skills, and everything.

In this context, I heard *Padma Vibhushan Swargiya* Girija Devi ji singing at the Kamani Auditorium in 2016. Appaji's singing, which had won the hearts of millions of people for almost six decades, was equally refreshing that way and people were so excited about listening to her. By now, I had read a lot about *thumri*. It kept on occuring to me that this style of music has suffered the most harm and disdain in the patriarchal Indian society which perhaps artists of other genre did not suffer, especially of this magnitude. As long as *thumri* enjoyed the patronage of the royal court, its dignity was different; its contents revolved around the various sentiments of Radha-Krishna, but as the content, literature and manner of presentation of *thumri* dominated the society, it declined significantly. It played with its classicism to make it a medium of luxury. I want to applaud the male actors who brought it to the stage by singing this genre with care and giving respect to *thumri* and its content. However, there is a clear need for a campaign to include it in classical music forms. There is a need to bring it from the semi-classical style to the pure classical style gallery. The artists who have sung this genre have struggled a lot to pursue and uphold this genre. When a person goes through a period of struggle, sometimes he feels weak and disappointed, sometimes hurt, sometimes faces financial troubles. It was clear to see Girija Ji on the stage that day that she was a *master* of a very strong personality who had complete control over her mood. Perhaps that is why she had been ruling people's hearts for the last six decades.

After listening to Girija Ji's concert, I was eager to know the psychological facts which not only made her and other great artists like her successful, but was helping them to stay on this pedestal for so many years. This applies not only to Girija Ji but also to other veteran artists of the country like her. Everyone's circumstances and conflicts will be different. If successful artists with good voice had good training and *riyaz,* then perhaps this country would have been filled with successful and best performers like Vidushi Siddheshwari Devi, Ustad Bade Ghulam Ali Khan, Begum Akhtar, etc. However, the number of well-known artists in India today is deplorably low. So, psychology will definitely have a much bigger role in understanding what else lies behind their success. I thought about these characteristics before I met them and my learning continued to deepen after meeting them. I would like to share these findings with you through this book and highlight some common characteristics of their personality despite their different circumstances. If this effort of mine proves to be helpful for rising artists in the future, then I will consider this to be a successful project.

The findings in this book point towards the relative consistency of positive psychological factors of the stalwarts in areas like creativity, emotions, hope and optimism and spiritualism. This will be dealt with in detail in this book. Since almost all the artists are stalwarts of the '*thumri genre*' I will try to walk you through the interesting and informative journey of '*thumri*' in the next chapter.

CHAPTER 2

Flavors of Indian Music

Though music transcends language, culture and time, and though notes are the same, Indian music is unique because it is evolved, sophisticated and melodies are defined.

– Dayanand Saraswati

Flavors of Indian Music

Indian classical music has a hoary past. From the *Vedic* times, this music developed through the rhythmic and melodious chants of the sages. The discipline of music flourished amidst colorful and exotic surroundings in the Indian intellectual tradition. The four *Vedas* have been mentioned in the Indian tradition: *Rigveda, Yajurveda, Samaveda,* and *Atharvaveda.* It is the *Samaveda* that is specifically connected to music and contains hymns which are sung. Music formed an important part of the rituals which defined various sacrifices mentioned in the *Vedas*. Singing, instrumental music, and dance were described as divine in Vedic literature. The *Rigveda* relied on reciting hymns (*richa*). The musical chanting of the *Samaveda* employed more notes (finally settling on 7 notes from three) and is said to be the source of later classical music. The word *'sama'* itself means 'rich' in musical notes; *sa'* refers to hymns i.e. rich and *'ma'* refers to musical notes.

Indian music comprises, within its fold, a vast and varied

and rich tradition of classical, semi-classical, light and folk music, which have grown out of the different cultures and sub-cultures of India and their mutual sharing. Music basically involves the creation of emotionally pleasing effects by means of sound. It is not just a fabrication or manipulation of a few notes but an expression of human feelings and desires. Hope, pleasure, desire, sadness, joy, disappointment, love, faith and other emotions and feelings are the experiences that could be related to human beings and their lives and are the subjects of musical compositions.

Musical preferences are a good predictor of one's personality (Schwartz & Fouts 2003). Moreover, it has been found that musical preferences can often reveal a lot about an individual's lifestyle as there exists a similar relationship between musical preferences and lifestyle characteristics. Music is a good stress-buster and one should try to develop a habit of listening to music at least ten minutes every day. One can have strong emotional experiences. Music has the power to take control and can also carry one into spiritual realms. Bade Ghulam Ali Khan believed that music has the power to transport one to both the "spirit of God" and the "God of this world."

Indian vocal music has different categories, as stated before. Here we will focus on classical music and folk music because *thumri* stands like a bridge between the two.

Indian classical music is one of many forms of art music that has its roots in regional cultures. It has two major traditions. The North Indian classical music tradition is called Hindustani *sangeet,* while the South Indian music is called *Carnatic.* Their traditions were indistinguishable until about 16th century. Thereon, during the Mughal reign of the Indian subcontinent, the traditions evolved into distinct forms. However, the two systems continued to have more common features than differences.

The root of the classical music of India are found in the Vedic literature of Bharat and the ancient *Natya Shastra by Bharat Muni*, the classical Sanskrit text *Sangeet Ratnakar* of Sarang Deva is regarded as the definitive text by both the Hindustani music and the *Carnatic* music traditions.

Indian classical music has two foundational elements: *Raga* and *Tala*. The *raga* forms the melody structure while the *tala* measures the time cycle. But the uniting feature of both the systems of music is the *raga* system. Indian music has one of the most advanced and scientific systems of categorization of the melodic entities known as *raga*s and an equally sophisticated sense of rhythmic patterns called *tala*s.

The role of music in ancient India was to assist in the performance of rituals and other religious ceremonies. Being intimately connected with nature and its sounds, Indian music draws its seven basic *swaras* from the sounds of animals and birds. This system is known as *Raga Sangeet. Raga* is a special creation of sound in general which is beautified with *swaras* and words, having the power to reach the heart of the people. Ferand (1961: 5) describes *ragas* as "melody models that lived on in the musical sub-consciousness of a race or people."

When the glory of the Mughal Empire reached its peak in Delhi, and the celebrated *nawabi* era of Lucknow commenced, music was molded to please the lavish princely patrons. Awadh emerged as the cultural center of India; the *nawabs, wazirs* and the kings of Awadh gave full patronage to all types of fine arts, especially music, paintings and dramas.

One of the oldest forms of Indian classical music is called *Dhrupad*. A highly stylized, structured and complex genre, *dhrupad* compositions predominantly eulogize Hindu gods and goddesses. However, they were sung without any reservation by Muslim singers as well. Thus, *dhrupad* became a symbol of the unique Indian ethos of multiculturalism and it was very popular until about the 16th-17th centuries. With the consolidation of Muslim rule in North India between 12th-13th centuries the popularity of *dhrupad* slowly began to wane. Its place was taken by *Khayaal,* a genre not as rigidly bound by technicalities as *dhrupad* was. *Khayaal* means "thought" or "imagination." The emphasis was on the imagination of the artist who was free to expound a *raga* in a manner he or she wanted whilst adhering to the basic rules and norms. *Khayaal* in its present form owes its existence to the later Mughals and the *nawabs* of Oudh (Awadh). *Miyan* Tansen in Emperor Akbar's court and his descendants are credited with crystallizing this new genre from the earlier *dhrupad* and mystic *qawwali* of the Sufi saints of North India.

In this complex galaxy of Indian music, *thumri* serves as a bridge between the world of classical and folk traditions. Some musicians took an active interest in the local folk traditions'; some interests probably extended to *thumri* which itself was a part of a product of Braj Folk music. Several scholars say that *thumri* predates *Dhrupad* and *Khayaal,* for both of which we have more or less certain dates of inception. *Thumri* is originally a vocal form. Most commonly used *ragas* are *khamaj, jhinjhaunti, bhairvi, sindura, tilak kamod, peelu, desh, tilang* and *kafi*. It is understood that all the mentioned *ragas* belong to *Sampurna Jaati* (using all seven *swaras*) and due to this nature, they help in improvisation of *Thumri.*

Though often dismissed as semi-classical, *Thumri* has a rich past as attested by several scholars. Semi-classical music is derived from Hindustani classical music. It takes the basics of classical music but here the rules are allowed to be flexible as and when required. Musicologist Thakur Jaidev Singh traces the earliest form of *thumri* called *"chalithamnrithyaasathitam"* to the *Harivansh Purana* (L.200 A.D.). This was sung along with the dance. *Lord Krishna* is believed to have learnt in the celestial court of *Indra, the* King of Gods.

Some scholars attribute the creation of this romantic genre to Nawab Wajid Ali Shah. *Thumri* means to 'walk with gait' or 'dancing steps', which would make the *payal*s (ankle bells) tinkle. The form is thus connected with dance, drama (through gestures), mild eroticism, love poetry and the folk songs of Uttar Pradesh. Despite this general definition, regional variations exist in the lyrics, pronunciation and rendition of the pieces.

While generally concerned with unrequited love, *thumri* lyrics range from the mystical to the explicitly erotic. Their subject matter can be viewed in relation to both the traditional Indian aesthetic theory, as well as to contemporary Indian society. Towards the late 18th century, a concurrence of social, economic and political factors in the princely state of Awadh created a uniquely fertile atmosphere for the flourishing and extraordinary popularity of the *"Bandishi thumri"* which combines improvised rhythmic manipulations with a lively pre-composed refrain, set to fast tempo *teentaal or addha* (16 beat rhythmic cycle). *Thumri* began to emerge from its traditional role of accompanying dance to the status of an independent musical form. The process culminated in the mid-twentieth century with the blossoming of the mature *"Bol Banaao Thumri."*

Thumris are generally written in *Braj Bhasha,* a dialect of western Hindi spoken in the region around Mathura in Uttar Pradesh. The dialect was associated with *Krishna-Bhakti* movement that raged across North India in the medieval times. However, *Khari Boli* or the spoken Hindi of today and Urdu words also appear in *thumri*. Besides, there are entire compositions in dialects of Hindi, *Awadhi, Bhojpuri, Mirzapuri, Dingal,* to name just a few. The language employed is soft and tender and allows the usage of colloquial words to make them sound elastic. For instance, *"Paani"* becomes *"Paniya"*, *"Piya"* becomes *"Piyu"* or *"Piyarwa"*. Goswami

(1957) states that *'Braj Bhasha'* is employed in classical as well as semi-classical pieces, due to its supposed paucity in conjunct consonants, it contains more vowels than other North Indian languages and is therefore more suitable for singing. Similarly, Meer (1981) opines that "the softer and more open sound" of *Braj* and *Awadhi* are preferred over modern Hindi due to "the lack of long vowels and urgent consonants" in the latter. The following well known *thumri,* for example, would be distinguished as *Braj,* solely due to its use of vocative *"tori"* rather than *Khari Boli's "tumhaari".*

Piya tori tirchhi nazar laage pyari
Piya tori shyamsalonenaina
Jadu bhari ya katari

In this *thumri,* the use of *"tori"* is softer than that of *"tumhaari."* Apart from this, the above *thumri* can be easily understood by an Urdu or *Khari Boli* speaker because it is very close to the spoken language. In contrast, *thumris* composed in Bhojpuri and Awadhi may not be easily understood by an average Urdu- or Hindi-speaker. After *Braj Bhasha, Khari boli* or Urdu elements are slightly more common in *bandish thumri,* as most of these were composed by Urdu-speaking musicians based in Lucknow. As far as *Bol Banao thumri* is concerned, Avadhi and Bhojpuri occur somewhat more frequently. This is primarily because many of them presently originate from the provincial towns of Banaras and Gaya; thus were more subject to local influence.

Thumri texts represent a union of urban classical and rural folk traditions. The folk element in *thumri* lyrics is perhaps most conspicuous in the *Holi* songs celebrating spring times or other *thumri*-related styles like *Chaiti, Kajri, Dadra* etc. The standard themes of separation and Krishna worship also pervade the folk music, particularly of Uttar Pradesh and Bihar. *Thumri* and *Khayaal* lyrics have mutual influence overeach other and their themes are generally based on the different issues; view of life (*Nirgunas*), a patron (king or other), religious devotion to a deity other than Krishna, weddings, Krishna, union with lover (husband or other), separation from a lover (husband or other), and seasons particularly spring and monsoon.

Generally, the themes are predominantly erotic and sensual and these can be easily called obscene if seen at a surface level; but there is an inherent spirituality even in eroticism as the propounders of the *Madhurya Bhakti* tradition link it to a form of *Krishna Bhakti* (worship). They believe that all living souls are deemed feminine and the only masculine super soul is *Krishna*. It is this pining union with the man (Krishna in this case) that creates the body-text for these *thumri* compositions. *Thumris* are thus written from a woman's perspective as *ghazals* are generally written from a man's perspective.

Thumri has been classified broadly in two categories – the *Bandish Thumri* and the *Bol Banao Thumri*. Typically, both have a first part called *sthaayi* and is followed by single or multiple verses called *antaraa*. *Thumri* belongs to the semi-classical genre (as opposed to the fully classical genres of *Khyaal* and *Dhrupad*) and thus is not bound by the strict rules concerning *raga*s that apply to its classical counterparts. Rather, it provides flexibility and freedom to combine other suitable *raga*s for improvisation permitted in the genre. Nevertheless, many of the schemes and compositional principles applicable to the classical *genre* also operate in the semi-classical *Thumri*. Figure 1 is a summary of the structural units that make up *thumri*'s over-all forms, showing the different structural options available to perform.

The Structure of a *Thumri* Performance

In a performance of *thumri*, the performance might follow the arrows along any possible course. *Thumri* includes the composition, which is a pre-existing melody, the typical style of ornamentation expected in the genre and the *raga* and *taal* of the performance.

Bandishi Thumri: Most *Bandishi thumris* are composed by the Urdu-speaking, Lucknow-based poets and musicians and thus the dialect used was *khari boli* mixed with some Urdu. The word *'bandish'* means composition and hence in these *thumris* the lyrics assume a greater importance. *Bandish* is a fixed melodic composition. It is set in a specific *raga* performed with rhythmic accompaniment by the *tabla* and melodic accompaniment by *sarangi* and *harmonium*. The *Bandish Thumri* was the popular versions of *thumri* prevalent in the 19th century and many of these were composed by savants like Bindadin Maharaj. They are light, lively pieces and were generally written as dance accompaniments. Here the focus was seldom on leisurely musical improvisation but on fast *bol-taan* patterns or melodic thrills and intelligently rhythmic manipulation of the lyrics in fast tempo. They have long texts with multiple *antaraas*. Set mostly in medium or fast tempo, they stressed *bol-baant, bol-taan* and *layakaari* and these were largely *Kathak* centric compositions. They were set in *ragas* like *Kaafi, Piloo, Gara, Khamaaj, Sindura, Dhani, Manj Khamaaj, Des, Tilang, Jhinjhoti* amongst others. The *taal* employed in both varieties of *thumris* are *Deepchandi, Addha, Ikwayi, Sitarkhani, Jat* and some derived from folk music like *Keharwa, Dadra, Khemta, Chanchar* and so on.

Bol Banaao Thumri: As the very name suggests, they are about 'making or creating a conversation'. A musical conversation in this case dwells on the effective and detailed exposition of the text and the melody through leisurely improvisations. The *Awadhi* and *Bhojpuri* dialects occur more in *Bol Banao Thumri* that originated from the cities of Banaras and Gaya. Trivial and day-to-day pastimes of Lord Krishna, his flirtation with the *gopis* of Vrindavan, the festival of Holi, eternal love of Radha and Krishna – all lend themselves to a textual, dynamic and musical improvisation and form the core of these *thumris*. While the lyrics are not as sophisticated compared to *bandish thumris*, it is precisely this rusticity of the lyric, the free rhythmic character and its open-endedness which help create multiple patterns and gives the singer scope for improvisation. For instance, through this single verse *"Kaun gali gayo Shyam?"* (Which road has Krishna taken?), the singer can demonstrate a variety of emotions by shifting the emphasis in the lyrics and varying the rhythmic patterns.

Wajid Ali Shah had been taught the art of music by Basit Ali. Under his guidance, he evolved new *raginis* like *'Jogi'*, *'Juhi'*,' Jasmine' or 'Shah Prasad,' according to his predilections. It was the literary and artistic attainments of Nawab King Wajid Ali Shah which bear testimony to his skills as an artist and his patronage that resulted in Lucknow surpassing other centers as a cultural *center* of *'thumri'*, *'dadra'* and other forms of musical arts. He composed *thumri* and *dadras* under pen names *'Akhtarpiya'* which won instant popularity. He himself wrote three books - *'Dulhan'*, *'Bani'*, and *'Najo'* that deal with contemporary music and musicians. Nawab's most famous *thumri* in *Raag Bhairvi* has very close similarity with Hazrat Amir Khusro's compositions. An example of Nawab's most famous *thumri* in *Raag Bhairvi* can be found below:

"Babul mora naihar chhuto jay,
Char kahar mil mori doliyan uthaye."

This sad song is a depiction of the parting of a bride leaving her beloved parental home in a *doli*. It signifies a human being and his last journey into eternity when the body is carried on the shoulders of four bier-bearers. A very similar composition by Amir Khusro is as follows:

"Bahut rahi babul ghar dulhan chal tore Pi ne bulayi,
Bahut khel kheli sakhiyan se, ant kari larkayi,
Bida karne ko kutumb sab aye, sagare log lugayi,
Char kahar mil doliya uthayi, sung purohit aur bhai,
Khusrau chale sasurari sajni, sung nahi koi ayi".

Nawab Wajid Ali Shah's book *'Bani'* mentions his composition in its first chapter *'Sur'* as *dhamar, khayaal, thumri, dadra, tappa, sawan* and so on.

Kolkata's Romance with Thumri: On May 6, 1856, a steamer named General McLeod docked in Calcutta. Aboard was Wajid Ali Shah, the last Nawab of the Kingdom of Oudh who was later shifted to Matia Burj. He was the last of Nishapuri kings who had reigned over Oudh and he had held the title for almost nine years, just two days short of

Palace of Wajid Ali Shah, last King of Awadh at Mitiaburz, Kolkata

the of his nine-year rule. His reign had been cut short by the ambitions of Lord Dalhousie, Governor General of British India, who had deposed him under the pretext of mis-governance. Calcutta became his final stop, where he would live out the rest of his days in exile. It was at this agonizing moment of being wrenched away from his beloved city and subjects that Akhtar sang the unforgettable *thumri,* which he had composed – *"Baabul mora naihar chooto hi jaaye."*

The king used to live in Garden Reach, where affluent Europeans had built large mansions. Wajid Ali Shah can be credited with bringing *thumri* from Awadh and firmly planting it in the soil of Calcutta. Thus, began Calcutta's romance with light classical music, especially *Thumri.* His court had musicians like Ali Baksh Khan and Badal Khan, who trained many classical music exponents from the city. The *tawaifs* and courtesans too followed suit and settled in this city, finding patrons among *zamindars* and princelings, who were swept off their feet by the beauty of *thumri.* His *thumri* not only survived in the foreign environs of Calcutta, but inculcated a musical aestheticism among the listeners, leaving an indelible mark on the compositions of Atul Prasad Sen, Kavi Najrul Islam, and Rabindranath Tagore. Finally, the gentle *tehzeeb,* the mark of a true denizen of Lucknow – is actually the legacy of the last Nawab of Awadh, which lives on, and found in the all-embracing love and hospitality that Kolkata showers on all, irrespective of their wealth or lack of it. He is credited with stylizing *folk raas* into a more sophisticated form of dance drama which he called *raas.* He is famously known to have donned the role of Krishna himself and danced with his court dancers who were *gopis or* female cowherds.

The Mughal and Lucknow courts, and later on the Bengalis of Calcutta greatly patronized all these allied songs and dance forms. Wajid Ali Shah's reign was the Golden Era for the growth of *Thumri* and *Kathak*. He produced lavish dance dramas and operas himself and wrote exquisite *thumris* and *dadras* under the pen name, *"Akhtar Piya."* The most famous of his compositions is *"babul mora naihaar chhooto hi jaye."* He patronized many prominent musicians like Sadiq Ali Khan, who has been hailed as the King of *Thumri* and also about twenty-six *sarangiaas* and thirteen *tablchees* in his court. The credit for refinement of the *Bandishi Thumri* goes to Sadiq Ali Khan. He is also regarded as the pioneer of the *"bol banaaao style."* His disciples were great singers and composers of *thumri* and included the most famous names like Wazir Mirza Qadir popularly known as *"Qadir Piya"*, Bindadin Maharaj, Bhaiya Ganpat Rao and other stellar musicians like the Lucknowi vocalist Khurshid Ali Khan, *"Shaswan Gharana"* vocalist Inayat Hussain Ali Khan, *Khayaal* singer from Maharashtra Ram Krishna Bua Waze, renowned *tawaifs* from Lucknow like Haider Jaan and Nazma. The other male musicians who specialized in *thumri* were *"Lallan Piya"* whose *bandishi thumris* were extremely popular include Kalle Khan *"Saras Piya"* of Mathura (1860-1926), Nazir Ali *"Nazar Piya"* of Rampur, *"Sanad Piya"* of Bareilley and Rampur's *"Madho Piya"*, *"Chand Piya"* and others (Sampath, 2010).

Art is generally the reflection of the happenings of society. After the revolt of 1857, India saw the emergence of a new middle class consisting largely of educated civil servants, lawyers, teachers, doctors, and also merchants and landlords. They had enough Western education to serve their British masters and more than enough to feel superior to their people and look down upon all things Indians, especially performing arts. To them these activities were synonymous with a debased feudal set-up dominated by *tawaifs*, prostitutes, Lucknowi *nawabs* and *zamindars*. *Thumri* and *Kathak* were deplored as decadent entertainment and their accompanists labeled as pimps and social pests. *Nautch*es were believed to be attended only by *naies* and much less reputable Englishmen who had little or no character to lose. Herein was sown the seeds of the "anti-*nautch*" that raged across the country. This also led to the associated social taboo with music, especially *thumri* and *kathak.*

Meanwhile, the early 20th century saw the gradual disappearance of the *"bandishi thumri"* which had occupied a place of privilege in the courts and salons of oriental Lucknow. This sub-genre got subsumed in the *chota khayaal* format. On the other hand, the arrival and consolidation of the recording industry in India sounded the death knell to the *bol banaao* format in the early records. With time and technological advancements also taking place, apart from court presentations, private and public performances and concerts, there came gramophones. The gramophone discs had the inherent disadvantage of a limited time-span (2-3 min of disc time). As a result, the singer had to present fast, lively and crisp tunes that would fit the time slot and sell well. Thus, even though *thumris* were sang and recorded, the leisurely pace of the *bol banaao* was ignored for recording purposes. However, singers like Ganpat Rao sang *bol banaao* style and used harmonium to accompany the fast tunes in *thumri* as against the *sarangi* and his students like Mauzuddin Khan and Gauhar Jaan continued to render the *bol-banaao* in their private soirées and concerts (Sampath, 2010). During the same time the *Banarsi ang* of *bol banaao thumri* became popular. It involved singing the *thumri* in slower tempo and text elaboration, being strongly influenced by the folk forms and rich tradition of seasonal forms like, *kajri, jhula, sawaan, chaiti.* The Banarasi style was a beautiful amalgam of these varied sources. It was pioneered by Guru Jagdeep Mishra of Banaras who was Mauzzuddin Khan's first teacher. Unlike the Lucknow composers who used weighty and classical *ragas* like *Malhaar, Malkauns, Darbaari* for their *bandishi thumris,* the *Banarasi thumris* were generally set to the light *ragas* and folk *taal* like *Keharwa, Dadra* as against the classical *teentaal.* A rhythmic interlude of *laggi* was also a direct folk adaptation (Shukla, 1983).

With *thumri* slowly getting away from the *kothaas* of the courtesans to the gramophone records in the public domain, it lost much of its seductive function and transformed into a pure abstract form. The increasing number of male musicians took away the original *"nakhra"* and eroticism associated with the courtesan's rendition of the same *thumri.* The 1920s and later were considered the prime period of the *Thumri* era as the genre was rescued from the lascivious *tawaaifs* by male musicians who appropriated it as yet another component of their classical repertoire. This also ensured a longer social acceptability and respect for *thumri* and gave it an unprecedented degree of sophistication and expressiveness like the other classical genres. The *bol banaao thumri* continued to remain the mainstay of all live performances. *Thumri* and *Kathak* had a formal divorce (Sampath, 2010). The seated *abhinaya* in *Kathak* to accompaniment of *thumri* slowly began to wane. Musicians and dancers began specializing in one or two arts and seldom combined the two. *Thumri's* tempo is also noticeable in records as time passed. This was in a way linked to the introduction of new records with increased time span that were used for recording and in 1925 to the birth of electrical recording that replaced acoustic mechanical technique.

The celebrity status that the artists of the gramophone era achieved and their travels across the country singing for nobility was responsible for *Bol Banaao Thumri* becoming popular all over the country. Banaras continued to remain the citadel of the *bol banaao* style. Banaras and Calcutta were important cultural centers from the commercial and popularity points of view. By 1910, along with the Banaras style, another style that became popular was the *Purab Ang* or the eastern style (Eastern UP and Bihar). This style was mainly initiated and cultivated by many *khayaal* singers of that time.

Ramnidhi Gupta (1741-1839 AD) created a style known as Bengali *tappa*. Another musical stalwart of the 19th century was Sourindra Mohan Tagore (1840-1914). In the early 20th century Vishnu Narayan Bhatkhande and V.D. Paluskar (1872-1931 AD) established the first music college, introducing music as an institution.

Taluqdars, a new class of landowners of Oudh, replaced the *zamindars* of the time as the key patrons. They had little taste for complex *Dhrupad* and *Thumris* started gaining immense popularity given the sensuousness of the style. Most of the *tawaifs* were trained in both music and dance. However, some chose only to sing while others did both. This led to the classification of *tawaifs* into *Bai* (the *tawaif* who only sang) and *jaan* (those who sang and danced). The seated style was most suited for intimate gatherings in wealthy households.

It is fascinating to note the space *thumri* occupies in the scheme of things in Indian music. Much like a woman in a patriarchal society, a *thumri* is the voice of the female in the world of traditional classical music, largely dominated by men. However, it cannot be considered a feminine form merely because it was sung and propagated by courtesans and its theme is essentially from a woman's point of view. A subtler investigation shows that its interrogative, its wonderful ability to coexist in harmony with numerous ambiguities, multiple layers of meaning, usage of subtle humor in a way mirrors the variety of roles played by women in our traditional Indian society. Her role is ambiguous, undefined and lends itself to multiple definitions depending on the whim of the male patriarch. The woman creates space for herself within the limitations that are placed on her by traditional society. Quite analogously, *thumris* too operate within similar limitations of largely orthodox classical renditions, but manage to extend beyond the set patterns. They are set in *raga*s which themselves do not have fixed structure; they have lyrics which mean multiple things (Manuel, 1990).

The *thumri* singer negotiates and explores the ambiguities at several levels; the level of the text, the level of *ragas* and its malleable nature, the *tal* and the theme and also the emotion it is conveying because in any music form, especially so for *thumri*, emotion is of utmost importance. "A *thumri* singer would reveal the points of danger and explore just how far and how much otherness can be introduced into the body of the *raga*. A *swara* in the *raga* becomes the door that leads to another *raga*. A *swara*, as it is heard in one *raga*, is deliberately punned upon to give it a different meaning in another *raga*. It is not so much that *raga*s are mixed to create a third new *raga* with its own identity and personality. Instead the point of weakness, the margin and boundaries in the *raga* structure are used as points at which other *ragas* are allowed to enter into the body of the main *raga* very beautifully." (Sampath, 2010).

An analysis of any of the *khayaal* recordings of Gauhar Jaan shows a clear sense of shape and balance in the way she had structured an expansive form like the *khayaal* into the requisite time span of gramophone records. The improvisation part of her rendition was primarily through her *taans*. Blessed with a high pitched, flexible and highly plain voice, she could create stunning thrills at varied speeds to fit into the time span available before returning to a compressed version of the *mukhada* at the end of each phrase of *taans*. She concludes with singing the whole stage once and then with her customary flamboyance signs off with,

"My name is Gauhar Jaan" (Sampath, 2010).

Today, the world of *Hindustani* music has forgotten the pioneers of this genre. But it certainly goes to the credit of Gauhar Jaan's grit and her musical ingenuity that despite the criticism and scepticism, she showed her skills and courage to face her peers and evolved a style suited to the needs of a gramophone recording which was adapted thereafter by most artists. Her personal style i.e. her personality was perhaps akin to the genre of *thumri,* thus she could easily get into the character of the composition.

The Nukkad Jalsa of Patna, Bihar: In the 1940s, Mohd. Badruddin, a jeweler, had come to Patna from Bangladesh. He changed his religion to become Badrinarayan. He was an ardent fan of *Hindustani* music. Owing to his passion, he formed a small team of traders who were equally interested in the art and were ready to invest financially to promote the art form. Together, they used to organize *mehfils* during *Durga Pooja,* especially 6 to 9 days out of the ten-day festival. Later it became larger and took the shape of an open theater program. The number of audience now increased from twenty-five hundred to twenty-five thousand in one *pandal.* It was called *"Nukkad Jalsa"* by many of the artists. Initially, it used to be a nonstop 4-day program keeping in mind the time theory. *"Nukkad Jalsa"* covers almost six decades of the journey of *Hindustani* music.

Artists who performed from 1940 onwards in Patna: Siddheshwari Devi, Rasoolan Bai, Badi Moti Bai, Mahadev Prasad Mishra, Begum Akhtar, Bade Ghulam Ali Khan, Kanthe Maharaj *(tabla),* Sitara Devi (dance), Shambhu Maharaj, Ganpat Rao *(harmonium),* Bismillah Khan *(shehnai),* Gopalji Mishra *(sarangi),* Anokhe Lal *(tabla),* Ahmed Jaan Thirakwa *(tabla),* Ramoji Mishra and many more.

1950 onwards: Girija Devi, Shobha Gurtu, Nazhakat-Salamat Ali Khan, Kishan Maharaj *(tabla),* Pt. Samta Prasad

(Gudai Maharaj- *tabla*), Abdul Halim Jaffer Khan *(sitar)*, V.G. Jog (violin), M. Rajam (violin), Birju Maharaj (dance).

1960s onwards: Rais Khan *(sitar)*, Pt. Ramnarayan Mishra *(sarangi)*

1970s onwards: Savita Devi, Urmila Nagar (dancer), Ustad Rais Khan a Pakistani sitarist, Ustad Amjad Ali Khan *(sarod)*, a singer from Kabul and many more artists had started performing in that event by then.

Recent performers (1980s onwards): Kajal Sharma (dance), Nalini-Kamalini (dance), Pt. Channulal Mishra, Anup Jalota, Ghulam Ali, Pankaj Udhas.

These artists were not only performing in Patna but were considered *gems* throughout the country, performing at various places both in public, and private concerts. They were also representing the country on the international platforms

Some of the famous incidents of the *jalsa* that have been passed on orally were extremely intriguing and would be sufficient proof to determine the level of creativity and talent that was exhibited. It was also testimony to the kind of *maahaul* that would be created taking the performer and audience to experience bliss *(anand)*. Once Abdul Haleem Jaffer Khan *(sitar)* and Kanthe Maharaj *(tabla)* were performing, he was so deeply engrossed in the performance that his *tabla* broke in between while doing the *jugalbandi*. He was so into the moment that it took him quite some time to realize what had happened and had to wait till the organizers got a replacement *tabla* but that didn't dampen his spirit and he started his mesmerizing performance again.

In another performance, Rais Khan was playing *sitar* but was demanded by his audience to sing a few *ghazals* as well and spontaneously he sang many *ghazal*s that are cherished even today.

An ardent music lover of that time recalled an incident when Begum Akhtar was singing a *hori* in *Raga Peelu*. While improvising it started raining. Then she suddenly but very imperceptibly shifted to a *kajri* in *Raga Peelu.* The audience was also singing along and they also shifted to *kajri.* After a while when it stopped raining, *Begum Sahiba* addressed the audience and brought their attention to the shift. The audience was so mesmerized they didn't recognize the shift until Begum Sahiba herself pointed it out. And, then she again came back to her *hori* very smoothly showcasing her prowess and creativity. The gradual shift was the creation of the moment and was the result of her surrender to the performance and her total involvement.

Abdul Karim Khan who propounded *Kirana Gharana* was regarded as the most important *Hindustani* classical music singer. He had a major role to play in the journey of *thumri* and has contributed with his creative compositions.

Brief Introduction to the Music and Culture of India:

Indian folk music is diverse because of India's cultural diversity, although the arrival of movies and other kinds of private music albums has weakened the popularity of folk music. Folk music has many forms including *Bhojpuri, Bhangra, lavani, dandiya* and *Rajasthani,* wherein, saints and poets have large musical libraries and traditions to their name, often sung in *Thumri, Bhangra* and *Giddha.*

Bhangra is a form of dance that is originated as folk music of Punjab. The present musical style is derived from non-traditional musical accompaniment to the phrases of Punjab called by the same name. The female dance of Punjab region is known as *Giddha.*

Bihu Geet: Bihu is the most celebrated festival in Assamese culture. The festival is celebrated thrice in a year in different ways and amongst them, *Rangoli* or *Bohag Bihu* is the most celebrated, followed by *Bhogali* or *Magh Bihu. Bohag Bihu* brings a windful of the sound of *dhol-pepa* with melodious songs to every corner of Assam. They represent the joy of the colorful society of the place and are called *Bihu geet* which are performed through *Bihu* dance. The songs have themes of romance, love, native incidents. *Bihu geet* usually have a wide range of lyrics from nature's beauty to a lover's expression and stories of social awareness. It symbolizes the varied colors of Assam.

Lavani Geet: *Lavani* is a popular folk form of Maharashtra wherein traditionally the songs are sung by female artists. The dance format associated with *Lavani* is known as *Tamasha.* This dance format contains the main dancers (*Tamasa Bai),* the supporting dancer(s) (*Maavshi*), the Drummer *(Dholkiwala)* and the Flute boy *(Baasuriwala).* It is famous for its erotic and sensuous expression.

Uttrakhandi Music: *Uttrakhandi* folk music had its roots in the lap of nature. The pure and blessed music has the feel and touch of nature. The folk music primarily is related to the festivals, religious traditions, folk stories and the simple life of the people of Uttarakhand. Musical instruments used include *the dhol, damoun, turri, ransingha, dholki, daur, thali, bhankora* and *masakbaja. Tabla* and *harmonium* are also used to a lesser extent. The main languages are *kumaoni* and *Garhwali.* The songs are a true reflection of the cultural heritage and the way people live their lives in the Himalayas and its nearby regions.

Dandiya: *Dandiya raas* or *raas* is a traditional folk-dance form of Gujarat and Rajasthan, and is associated with the scenes of Holi and the *lila* of *Krishna* and *Radha* at Vrindavan. Along with *Garba,* it is the featured dance of the *Navratri* festival. In most of the cities of Gujarat and Rajasthan, people gather and perform Garba dance, an event that is becoming increasingly popular in countries with large Gujarati-speaking communities around the world, such as Canada, the United States and the United Kingdom.

Pandvani: *Pandvani* is a folk singing style of musical narration of tales from ancient epic *Mahabharata* to various musical accompaniments. This form of folk and theater is popular in the state of Chhattisgarh and in neighboring tribal areas of Orissa and Andhra Pradesh.

Rajasthani music: *Rajasthani* music originates from Rajasthan, the home of several important centers of Indian musical developments, including Udaipur, Jodhpur and Jaipur. This region's music shares similarities both with nearby areas of India and the other side of the border in the Pakistani province of Sindh.

Bauls: The *Bauls* of Bengal were an order of musicians in 18th, 19th and early 20th century India who played a form of music using a *khanak, ektara* and *dotara.* The word *baul* comes from Sanskrit *batul* meaning divinely inspired insanity. These are a group of Hindu mystics and minstrels who are thought to have been influenced greatly by the Hindu *Tantric* sect. *Bauls* travel in search of the internal ideal, *Maner Manush* (Man of the heart).

Bhatiali: This type of music was cultured mainly by the oarsmen and fishermen of the erstwhile Bengal. There are many views regarding the origin of the term *Bhatiali.* Most popular of them are:

- They used to sing in the ebb *(Bhati)* as in this phase it does not need much effort for rowing.
- It originated from the *Bhati* area (now in Bangladesh). One of the most eminent singers of this art form is Nirmalendu Chaudhary.

Veeragase: It is a dance form prevalent in the state of Karnataka. It is a vigorous dance based on Hindu mythology involving very energetic dance movements. *Veeragase* is one of the dances demonstrated during the *Dussehra* festival procession in Mysore.

Naattupura Paattu: It is folk music of Tamil Nadu. It

consists of *Gramathu Isai* (village music) and *gana* (city music). It is also sung in Rajasthan.

Dollu Kunita: This is a group dance that is named after the *Dollu* - the percussion instrument used in the dance. It is performed by the menfolks of *the Kurumba* community in North Karnataka. The group consists of 16 dancers who wear drums and beat it to rhythm while dancing. The beat is controlled by a leader who is positioned in the center.

Bhojpuri Folk Music: For centuries women in *Bhojpuri*-speaking peasant society of western Bihar and eastern Uttar Pradesh have been experiencing migration of their men.

Bhojpuri is a dialect of Hindi which is spoken in the eastern part of Uttar Pradesh and western part of Bihar. *Bhojpuri* dialect owes its name to the town of Bhojpur, a small village in the district of Shahabad in Bihar. The region's folk songs are associated with the various events in the life of ordinary people. The heroic deeds of freedom fighter Kunwar Singh have been immortalized through these folk songs. There are songs like *Sohar* performed during childbirth *Sumangali* associated with wedding, *ropnigeet,* performed during occasion of sowing paddy, *katnigeet* performed during the paddy harvesting season *Purbi, Fagua-Holi* festival song. *Ghato-chaita* and *chaiti* is very popular in the month of *chait* (Hindu Calendar), *Bidesia, Birha, Kajri, Birmi, Pachra, Jhumar, Jatsani, Aalah, Nirgun, Samdaun.* There is also the traditional song called *Beer Kunwar.*

The influence of Bihari music is seen in regions such as Mauritius, South Africa and the Caribbeans, where a large number of laborers from Bihar were taken during the 19th century as well as Pakistan and Bangladesh where many Bihari Muslims migrated to after Partition of India. Bhikhari Thakur, Mahadev Mishra, Radha Mohan Chaubey 'Anjan', Laxman Pathak, Pradeep, Sharda Sinha are some of the famous singers of Bhojpuri. *Dholak, sarangi, tanpura, majira, harmonium* are important instruments used in *Bhojpuri* Songs. *Jat-Jattin, Bhaktiya Kirtan* are also forms of *Bhojpuri* songs.

As described above, the role of *Thumri* as a bridge between classical music and folk music shows its vastness and comprehensiveness. Affinity with classical music makes it technically sound, robust, and artistic, whereas folk music impacts it with its flavor of simplicity, innateness, emotions and experience, making it relatable and popular to all kinds of audience.

In this chapter, we read that *thumri* is a language of emotions. The lyrics are usually derived from the theme of eternal bonding of Radha-Krishna and its infinite facets. There is usually a confidante, in *thumri lyrics,* with whom Radha confides her innermost thoughts, her joy, sorrows, anxiety, insecurity and other feelings. In the language of *thumri,* these intimate conversations between *Radha* and her *sakhi(s)* are expressed wherein *Radha* calls them, *"Sun Ri Sakhi."*

Some of the *thumris* which have echoed through the ages with their interesting appeal have been narrated in the following pages.

SPP-5390

THUMRI 1

राग: मिश्र खमाज

सथाई

जाओ वहीं तुम श्याम

जहाँ सारी रैना जगे हो।

अंतरा

हमसे कपट करत नित छैला

नित ललिता घर जाए।।

***

Raag: *Mishra Khamaz*

Sthayi

Jaao wahin tum Shyam,
Jahaan saari raina jage ho.

Antra

Humse kapat karat nit chhaila,
Nit Lalita ghar jaae.

Radha is upset with Krishna because he promised to come home by evening, but for some reason, he could not. An annoyed Radha entreats: "O Shyam, go back to where you stayed overnight". Then she confides in her sakhi that Krishna is deceiving her by lying that he could not come because of work but she knows that he goes to meet her sakhi *Lalitha every day. This thumri is very clear in its meaning, but the emotion expressed here is telling Shyam to stop now, and not leave her alone. It's a lover's quarrel where Radha is upset and asks Shyam to leave but secretly wants him to stay back and pacify her. To express this sentiment, if the singer is singing it while representing Radha, the word is to be sung like this – "Jaaaaaaaaavo!" to express the emotion of stopping Krishna, but Radha indeed implores him, "Aavo!" (come) in a subtle but delightful manner. After this elaboration, we will sing the word "javo" to justify the lyrics of the* thumri.

THUMRI 2

राग: जोगिया

स्थाई:

पिया के मिलन की आस

छिन - छिन बहत कजरो जोबनमा।

अंतरा:

धन - धन भाग सखी वा दिन मेरो

जो मै जाऊँ पिया पास री॥

***

Raag: *Jogiya*

Sthayi

Piya ke milan ki aas,

Chin-chhin bahat kajro jobanmaa.

Antra

Dhan-dhan bhaag sakhi vaa din mero,

Jo main jaaun paas rii.

The bhava of this thumri *expresses that the heroine in her endless wait for her Shyam is shedding tears and complains to her* sakhi *that while endlessly waiting for Krishna, her youth is being wasted away with every passing moment. She is just waiting for the day when she would go to her beloved, her most valued moment of her life in its spiritual or devotional sense. Here, the devotee wants to subsume her soul with the Divine. She says, "I am shedding tears for the grace of God in the evening of my life, my dear friend. I will consider myself blessed the day I will be at the lotus feet of the Almighty.*

THUMRI 3

राग: सिंदुरा
स्थाई
आए ना श्याम ना लिनी खबरिया
कबकी खड़ी मै तो जोहती डगरिया।
अंतरा
कहत छबीले सुनो मोरी बतिया
वेग करो प्रभु गहो मोरी बइयाँ॥

***

Raag: *Sindura*
Sthayi
Aaye na shyam na lini khabaria,
Kabki khadi mai toh johti dagariya.
Antra
Kahat chhabile suno mori batiyaa,
Baig karo Prabhu gaho mori baiyaan.

Radha, in her anxiety, confesses to her sakhi *that neither Shyam has come nor has he sent any messenger inquiring about her well-being. She says she does not know how long she's been waiting for Krishna. It is so late that Radha does not have the time now to understand. Radha is sending her message to Krishna through* Chhabile Ji *(the signature singer of the Banaras Gharana, who is the creator of the presented* bandish*) that Lord, now you should come soon and hold me and save me. 'Gaho' Mori Baiyan means to hold the arms tightly. There is a difference in literary terms between 'Dharo' and 'Gaho'. Dharo means 'to hold' and Gaho means 'to hold very tightly' so that you need not get caught again.*

THUMRI 4

राग: माँझ खमाज
स्थाई
जाग पड़ी मै तो पिया के जगाए,
भोर होत सैा घर आए।
अंतरा
इन नैनन मे नीद कहाँ
है जिन नैनन मे आप समाए

Raag: *Maanjh Khamaz*
Sthayi
Jag padi main to piya ke Jagaae,
Bhor hoat saiyaan ghar aaye.
Antra
In nainan mein neend kahaan,
Hai Jin nainan mein aap Smaaye.

This thumri *presents a beautiful piece of conversation between Radha and a gopi. The literature of this* thumri *is seen from the perspective of a young woman, and then the scene of a playful woman who is the beloved of her husband, comes out. Here Radha confides to her* sakhi *that when Krishna/her husband came early in the morning and woke her up, then only I got up. In the Antra though, it's not mentioned but it's clear from the lyrics that the* sakhi *says that Radha is saying that she can't sleep in the absence of her lover, then how can she sleep when Krishna has not come yet. Then Radha replies that yes, sheis right, she was just pretending to be asleep as how can a person sleep when her lover all the time dwells in her eyes. I am always awakened in his absence. Interpreting it on another plane, the devotee says that I have awakened from my sleep as darkness of my life is over by receiving God's blessings.*

THUMRI 5

राग : मिश्र काफी

स्थाई

जब से श्याम सिधारे

तड़प - तड़प जिया जाए।

अंतरा

बिन प्रीतम के प्राण जात है

ना आए प्रीतम प्यारे ।।

Raag: *Mishra Kaafi*

Sthayi

Jab se Shyam sidhare,
Tadap-tadap Jiya jaae.

Antra

Bin pritam ke praan jaat hain,
Naa aaye pritam pyare.

In this thumri, Radha is talking about Krishna's departure from Brajbhumi to Dwarka. She feels like a gambler, who has lost everything. She had never even dreamt that Krishna was meant for Rukmini. What is fated cannot be avoided. Radha confesses to the gopis that without Krishna her life is lifeless and soulless, but Krishna has no worries about her anymore, he would never go back to Radha. She says, without him my heart will ache forever.

THUMRI 6

राग : मिश्र किरवानी (दादरा)
स्थाई
दिवाना किए श्याम क्या जादू डारा।
अंतरा
उन गलियन में आना रे जाना
हमसे करो ना बहाना मोरे श्याम
क्या जादू डारा॥

Raag: Mishra Kirwani (Dadra)
Sthayi:
Deewana kiye Shyam kya jaadu daar.
Antra:
Un galiyan mein aana re jana,
Humse karo na bahaana more Shyam,
Kya jaadu daara.

This is an example of a Dadra. In comparison to thumri, dadra is sung at a faster pace, although the themes are almost the same. In the present dadra, Radha calls Shyam a beguiling character for driving everyone crazy in Braj bhumi by his charming spell. In the Antara, Radha goes on to tell Krishna don't make excuses as I know that you go to meet other gopis. This dadra is a beautiful example of accusing someone romantically.

THUMRI 7

राग : मिश्र गारा
स्थाई:
पानी भरे कौन अलबेले की नार
झमाझम - झमाझम।
अंतरा:
हाथ ले जुरिया सिर पे गगरिया
तिरछी चितवन से मोहे घायल करे री कौन॥

Raag: *Mishra Gaara*
Sthayi
Paani bhare kaun albele ki naar,
Jhamajham-jhamajham.
Antra
Haath le juriya sir pe gagariya,
Tirchhi chitwan se mohe ghayal kare ri kaun.

Mostly thumri or dadra is written from a woman's perspective but the above dadra is written from a male's perspective. It is an alluring dadra. A person is describing a beautiful woman who is taking water from a well with a rope in her hand. In the literature of Thumri presented, the voice of water is very beautifully described as jhama jham. The person thinks that this woman is so beautiful, and then her husband must also be a very attractive man. So he uses the word albela for her husband. He further says that now this girl has filled up the water and holding a matka full of water on her head and holding a rope in her hands, she walks towards her house and in this sequence she looks at the person with her beautiful slanting eyes which injures him (romantically); here, injured means he gives her his heart.

THUMRI 8

राग : मिश्र तिलंग
स्थाई:
अँखियाँ रसिली तोरी श्याम
मोहत ब्रज की बाम।
अंतरा
नवल त्रिभंग कद्म तले ठारे
मोल लेत बिन द्ाम
ये ब्रज की बाम॥

Raag: *Mishra Tilang*
Sthayi
Ankhiyan rasili tori Shyam,
Mohat Brij ki Baam.
Antra
Naval tribhang kadam tale thare,
Mol let bin daam,
Yeh brij ki Baam.

This thumri describes the enticing eyes of Lord Krishna. Radha blames Krishna that these beautiful eyes have captivated the hearts of all the gopis. *Everything has become Krishnamayi – fully drenched in Krishna's colors. Lord Krishna is hearing her accusation with the flute to his lips in his standing in his cross-legged* tribhang *posture under the* Kadambha *tree. He provides his love to anyone who wishes to receive it. Krishna's love and blessings are considered priceless and one can receive it only by devoting and surrendering oneself to Krishna. No money or valued possession can buy it.*

THUMRI 9

राग: मिश्र तिलक कामोद
स्थाई:
सजनी छाई घटा, घनघोर
अंतरा:
बादल गरजे बिजुरी चमके
पपिहा मचावे शोर
रामदास के गोविंद स्वामी
छैल - छबिले चितचोर

Raag: Mishra Tilak Kamod
Sthayi:
Sajani chhayi ghata ghanghor
Antra:
Baadal garje bijli chamke
Papiha machave shor
Ramdas ke govind swamy
Chhail – chhabile chitchor.

In this Kajriv, Ramdas Ji [vocal signature of Banaras Gharana], while representing Radha, is saying that it is a rainy season, black clouds are appearing in all directions in the sky and it is evident that Radha is feeling lonely in this difficult environment. He further describes the scene and states that the clouds are thundering, there is lightning in the sky and papiha is chanting pihu-pihu. Ramdas ji further says that his master is Govind and the other name of Lord Krishna is also Govind. He further beautifully describes his form and nature and explains that his Lord Krishna appears to be a handsome young man and this appearance of his automatically attracts the people en-mass. In this kajri, the Papiha appears to tell Radhika, by chanting pihu-pihu that she should remember her Master Govind who will discharge her either from this deadly situation or would relieve her from this mortal world.

THUMRI 10

राग: मिश्र देश
स्थाई:
मोरा सैय्या बुलावे आधी रात नदिया बैरी भई,
गहरी नदिया नाव पुरानी,
केवट मतवारो ना माने
मोरी बात, नदिया बैरी भई ।
अंतरा:
सुन रे मलहवा मै तेरी चेरी

Raag: *Mishra Desh*
Sthayi
Mora saiyaan bulawe aadhi raat Nadiya bairi bhayi,
Gehri nadiya naav purani,
Kewat matwaaro na mane
Mori baat, nadiyaa bairi bhayi.
Antra
Sun re malhawaa main teri cheri

In this thumri, the heroine is desperate to cross the river to meet her lover but it is quite late in the night, the river is very deep and the boat is also rickety. Kewat *(the boatman) is not willing to take the heroine across the river. The heroine implores the boatman (also known as* Mallah*), O* Kewat*, I am ready to be your slave, but make me cross the river. There is deep spirituality imbibed in the* thumri*. God is calling the devotee to himself, but in the form of a deep river, worldly responsibilities and bondage are hindering his path. When the devotee says that the river is deep, he is referring to the endless burden of responsibilities and the body is being compared to rickety wearing 'boat'. The devotee accepts the boatman as his master. The boatman here is the symbol of 'Guru' who will take that devotee away from this worldly attachment - Maya and help him to meet God i.e. to attain salvation.*

THUMRI 11

राग: मिश्र तिलक कामोद
स्थाई:
सजनी छाई घटा, घनघोर
अंतरा:
बादल गरजे बिजुरी चमके
पपिहा मचावे शोर
रामदास के गोविंद स्वामी
छैल - छबिले चितचोर

Raag: Mishra Tilak Kamod
Sthayi:
Sajani chhayi ghata ghanghor
Antra:
Baadal garje bijli chamke
Papiha machave shor
Ramdas ke govind swamy
Chhail – chhabile chitchor.

In this thumri, Ramdas Ji *[vocal signature of* Banaras Gharana*], while representing Radha, is saying that it is a rainy season, black clouds are appearing in all directions in the sky and it is evident that Radha is feeling lonely in this difficult environment. He further describes the scene and states that the clouds are thundering, there is lightning in the sky and papiha is chanting* pihu-pihu. *Ramdas ji further says that his master is Govind and the other name of Lord Krishna is also Govind. He further beautifully describes his form and nature and explains that his Lord Krishna appears to be a handsome young man and this appearance of his automatically attracts the people en-mass. In this kajri, the Papiha appears to tell Radhika, by chanting pihu-pihu that she should remember her Master Govind who will discharge her either from this deadly situation or would relieve her from this mortal world.*

Ustad Abdul Karim Khan was a classical as well a great thumri singer, the founder of Kirana gharana. His famous thumri was "*Jamuna ke teer*". His period was 11.11.1872 to 27.10.1937.

Gauhar jaan was a veteran thumri singer (26.06.1873 to 17.01.1930). She was one of the first performers to record music on Gramophone. Popularly known as "the Gramophone girl" and "the first recording superstar of India". Her famous thumri was- "*Ras ke bhare Tore Nain*" in raag bhairavi.

CHAPTER 3

Meet The Legends

Please find a suitable Quote

– Xoxoxo xoxoxo

Meet The Legends

Sixty musicians were contacted for an interaction. They were chosen across four levels: stalwarts (15), biographies (3) renowned artists, young students (12) pursuing music and amateurs (30). Fifteen seasoned artists were chosen as they are considered illustrious figures of Hindustani music ,especially *thumri shaili* due to their prowess, rigor and zeal for the art. Three biographies that were chosen were of accomplished artists with immense contribution to the *thumri* genre. It is believed that they changed the face of *thumri*. All the biographies belonged to the different *ang*s of *thumri*. Twelve young students were considered as it is the young brigade who would become the future of the lineage.

In this book I have used in-depth interviews of the participants (stalwarts and amateurs), focus group discussions with young students, and analysis of biographies.

In-depth interviewing was chosen as the method for collecting data from the participants. This method is influential in collecting rich and detailed information about how individuals experience, understand, and explain events in their lives. In-depth interviews involved conducting intensive discussions to explore the participants' perspective on a particular idea or situation (Boyce *and* Neale, 2006).

Focus group discussions are considered useful to obtain detailed information about personal opinions, and also feelings, perceptions and opinions of the group. It helped me in getting to know the view of the young students as a group and their concerns about the field.

Biographical text analysis was used because it helped in closely analyzing the content of the communication more than the structure of it. It's a good tool to understand the meaning and ideas expressed through written words. Text analysis uses the perspective of the writer of a document to interpret the data. In the present case, the authors of all the three biographies are the disciples of the stalwarts. Along with being a disciple, one of them was also the daughter of a stalwart.

I had detailed discussion with all the artists on various aspects of music. The data from the three biographies and maestros were discussed at length with scholars of psychology and music. These biographies were read carefully and the data was studied rigorously. Since the participants were both male and female, their response was also noticed from gender perspectives. After a 'one-on-one' interview of all the living legends, they were also contacted telephonically when required.

All artists are arranged in decreasing order by age. So, first of all in this sequence, we remember the eldest *Padma Bhushan,* Bade Ghula Ali Khan Saheb.

*****

The Legend - Ustad Bade Ghulam Ali Khan

Bade Ghulam Ali saheb is a priceless gift of god to this nation. Before reading Bade Ghulam Ali Khan Sahib's biography, I used to think of him as a fantastic singer. My father, who was an ardent listener of Khan Sahib's singing, had painted a picture of a generous and devoted artist. I always wanted to know more about him and his personality in detail. He was a reservoir of a rich heritage; a naturally creative artist with high emotional adjustment traits and a tender heart. His kind-heartedness is reflected in his singing which also gave his rich voice a spiritual touch.

On April 2, 1902, there was much rejoicing and celebration all around held to welcome a new arrival in Kasur, Punjab. Mai Buddi, wife of Ustad Ali Bux Khan gave birth to a child, who was named Ghulam Ali – the slave of Ali, the son-in-law of prophet Mohammad. Elders of the town prophesied that the child would bring joy to millions and make a name in the field of music.

The child grew up in the small-town environment of Kasur. He was brought up by his mother in a simple way as his father had remarried and neglected his first wife. Ali Bux Khan was a court-musician in the state of Jammu & Kashmir.

Ghulam Ali Khan was Ali Bux Khan's eldest son. He was trained both by his father, and uncle. While singing a *taan* pattern, he showed the style of his uncle Kaale Khan and when he did the *sargams*, he presented his father's style. Thus, he was a beautiful synthesis of various styles of classical singing but he got his *taleem* mainly from his uncle, who became his *Ustaad.* Kaale Khan Sahab had only one child, a girl child, and in those times, the daughters in musician families were not taught to sing, because when it came to women, singing was associated with courtesans and dancing girls. So, he showered his love, affection and technical knowledge of music on his nephew Ghulam Ali. He adopted him, taught him and groomed him as he would his own son, to be his successor. The child used to fetch water, clean and cook food for his *ustaad*. Kaale Khan was a hard task master and strict disciplinarian. This is a beautiful example of *guru-shishya parampara,* where the *guru* was a family member himself.

In 1911, when a "Dilli Durbar" was held to welcome King George V, Ghulam Ali accompanied his uncle to Delhi, as Kaale Khan Sahab was invited to sing before a select gathering of connoisseurs and was gifted a bagful of gold sovereigns. This visit had a deep impact on young Ghulam Ali. He saw and experienced the challenges for a singer to perform in front of large audience and that too before Rajas, Maharajas and Nawabs. After which he started observing his uncle more closely. His *ustaad* believed in *"sudh mudra-shudh vaani"*, which means "purity of expression-clarity of voice".

Ghulam Ali was very much influenced by the sounds and

moods of nature. When he practiced the *aalaaps* of a *raga,* he would feel himself to be attuned to the cosmic music. His *taan* would flash like lightning, the *gamak* of *riyaaz* would resound like a thunder followed by the sonorous rainfall. All this diligent practice went into his development as a singer par excellence.

When Ghulam Ali was just 16 years old, his *Ustaad* Kaale Khan died in Kanpur in 1918. So, the responsibility to carry the family lineage fell very early on his shoulders. Then his mother persuaded him to take further training under his father, Ali Bux Khan. So, Ghulam Ali had to shift to Jammu. His father was very glad to see him. His training started under him. Once Ali Bux placed his hand on the boy's head and said, "*Puttar* (my child), nobody like you has appeared in seven generations of our family nor is there any possibility of anyone matching your excellence in the future." This compliment from his father greatly encouraged the young man. For someone as gifted as Ghulam Ali, it was not difficult to become popular in musical circles.

I must mention that his father's and uncle's *(Ustaad)* credentials in this field also helped him become popular at a very early age. Extraordinary merits too require good opportunities and platforms to showcase and evolve. So, apart from getting perfection in the field, maintaining good interpersonal relations is also a must to become an artist. He was recognized as one of the most successful young singers of his time. He made a lot of money and lived lavishly. He stood out as an exceptionally gifted artist. The musical instrument *Sur Mandal* is his contribution to Indian classical music.

In 1932, when young Ghulam Ali had just started his family life his wife, Allah Jiwai suddenly became ill and died. His two young sons, Karamat and Munawar were barely four and, two years old respectively at that time. Music was his only solace and savior in this hour of grief. One day he picked up his beloved *Sur Mandal* and poured out his grief into the melody and the words came spontaneously, *"Yaad Piya Ki Aaye, Yeh dukh Saha na jaye, Hai Ram!"* (Remembering my beloved is a pain unbearable, oh Ram!). Another *thumri* he sang which became famous, *"Aaye Na Baalam, Kaa Karoon, Sajni"*. This means, "My beloved has not come; what should I do, O friend?" This shows that crisis, grief and struggle are also *'conducive'* to creativity.

After the death of his wife, Khan Sahib's sister took care of his sons, but Khan Sahib himself felt very lonely. Fifteen years after the death of his first wife when his sons were almost adults in 1947, Khan Sahib married again. His second wife's name was Allah Rakhi. They lived a happy married life. Even after the Partition of India, they were still in Pakistan. When in 1954 he got his visa to move to India he immigrated to Bombay India with his family, An Urdu newspaper in Bombay headlined the event as "The Gem of Pakistan Becomes the Kohinoor of India." At that time Bombay had a galaxy of famous singers like Pandit Omkar Nath, Kesarbai and Ustaad Allah Deeya Khan, Kale Nazir Khan, Amaan Ali Khan, Moghubai Kurdikar (mother of Kishori Amonkar), Ustaad Latafat Khan, Pandit Vishu Digambar etc. So Khan Sahib's house always had a festive air around it.

Once he sang for Mahatma Gandhi who wrote to him a postcard in which he expressed his great appreciation for Khan Sahib's music. *"Sabrang"* was his pseudonym he used in his compositions.

Khan Sahib played the role of singer Tansen, a singer in the court of Mughal Emperor Akbar, in K. Asif's legendary film *Mughal-e-Azam*. Around that time, he suffered a paralytic attack on the left side of his body and it affected his throat too. But due to his strong will power, he resumed his *riyaaz*. People who had heard him earlier said, "Earlier the Ustad's singing was like the sound of a waterfall striking against the mountain side and rushing with great force to mingle with the ocean. Now it resembled the vast ocean whose might and depth was unfathomable." In 1962, Khan Sahib was awarded the *Padma Bhushan*. In 1963 Khan Sahib moved to Calcutta with his family. At that time Sangeet Natak Academy had made a documentary on Khan Saheb. Kolkata warmly welcomed the *Ustaad* and he was invited to sing before a highly appreciative audience. The appreciation and exuberance which the people of Kolkata showed was characteristic of their emotional and artistic nature. In one of the concerts Khan Sahib said, "My throat is like a paint brush and I paint on the waves of air with my voice. The *swaras*, notes of my *raga*, are my colors; it is like a painting created in the air, which is my canvas." To me this detail is an excellent employment in music of the psychological principle of figure ground propounded by Gestalt psychologists.

He was never secretive or guarded about his vast knowledge. He generously shared his thoughts and experiences with his *shagirds* and listeners. He was like a fountain of knowledge ready to shower gifts on whoever he felt was worthy enough to appreciate it. He was a real *fakir* who shared whatever he had with others and infused his own knowledge with spontaneous ease and generosity into his *shagird*s. He used to say that in our *shashtra*s our *raga*s are classified according to different mood, emotions, feelings and aesthetic delight. The Sanskrit word *'rasa'* cannot be translated effectively as it means the various moods of human beings such as *shringar* or romantic, devotional, sadness, renunciation, *veer rasa* or martial melodies, fear, peaceful and *adbhut rasa*. One of the greatest qualities of Khan Sahib was that he could infuse his innermost emotions into his singing.

It was in November 1967 that Khan Sahib went from Calcutta for a concert in Visakhapatnam. There was great excitement over the arrival of Khan Sahib. In the South, like Bengal, music and dance is a way of life. When the concert took place that night, Khan Saheb took his listeners on a journey of musical understanding and fulfillment, leaving everyone spellbound. The five days in Visakhapatnam were quite rejuvenating for Khan Sahib. Then they left for Hyderabad. Khan Sahib's train arrived at the Hyderabad station. Begum Zaheer Yaar Jung had come to receive him. He stayed in Basheer Bagh for almost five months. December passed peacefully. In January 1968, Khan Sahib had a severe asthma which created difficulty in breathing. Throughout the month of April he was extremely weak. On 22nd April he was cheerful, drank his fruit juice and even ate a little. On April 25th 1968, as the rooster crowed, the legend breathed his last in the wee hours of the morning.

*****

Born:	2 April 1902, Kasur, Pakistan
Died:	25 April 1968, Hyderabad
Spouses:	Allah Jiwai, Allah Rakhi (remarried after the death of his first wife)
Children:	Karamat Ali Khan, Munawar Ali Khan
Grand Children:	Raza Ali Khan, Mazhar Ali Khan and Jawad Ali Khan
Album:	Classical Vocal, Ustad Bade Ghulam Ali Khan, Mehfil, Hindustani Vocal, more
Awards:	Sangeet Natak Akademi Award (1962), Sangeet Natak Akademi fellow (1967), Padma Bhushan Award (1962)
Genre:	Hindustani Classical Music

The Legend - Maa Siddeshwari Devi

MAA SIDDESHWARI DEVI

Maa, as she was affectionately called not only by her children and disciples, but also by her admirers all over the world, used to dream of a world where people with a thirst for music could not only learn it but also breathe it, and feel it in their veins. That was *Maa*'s love for music.

When I was a student, I used to read about Siddheshwari Devi, a wonderful *thumri* exponent, in the art & culture section. I had never ever dreamt that one day, I would become a part of her family. Her daughter Vidushi Savita Devi is my *guru* and not only my *guru* but my *mother* in the field of art. Almost every day we used to talk about my *Nani guru* (grandmother, Maa Siddheshwari), especially during discussion around *thumri* singing. So, I have known Siddheshwari Devi not only by reading her biography but also I always feel that I have lived in those times. Perhaps I have lived with *Maa* through my *guru*.

Siddheshwari Devi's mother Shyama Devi was the younger sister of famous singer of that time, Rajeshwari Devi. The grandmother of Siddheshwari Devi was a courtesan at the court of King of Banaras. During the last part of the 19th Century, and the first part of the 20th Century, the court of the King of Banaras and the people of Banaras were captivated by the melodious voices of Maina Devi and her daughter Rajeshwari Devi.

Being of frail health, Siddeshwari Devi's mother died very young. Her father Shyamu Mishra was unable to take care of his two daughters and requested Rajeshwari Devi, elder sister of Shyama Devi to take the responsibility of his daughters. Unfortunately, the younger child could not survive.

The elder child, nick-named Gogo, who later became the renowned Siddheshwari Devi, grew up uncared and neglected in her aunt Rajeshwari Devi's house. Two or three years later, she also lost her father, becoming an orphan in this world.

Even in the richest homes of Banaras, it was customary for cooking to be done by the women of the house. Serving food and snacks was the duty of younger women. It was not unusual that all these chores became Siddheshwari's responsibility. Rajeshwari Devi received guests at all times of the day, so the days were never at Siddheshwari's disposal, but the quiet nights belonged to her. During her rest at night, she used to sing what she listened during day time from her aunt's rehearsal or her cousin Kamleshwari Devi's (daughter of Rajeshwari Devi) music classes. Kamleshwari Devi was almost of Siddheswari's age. Her tutor was the famous *sarangi* player of Banaras, Siya Ji Maharaj. Music had been running in his veins for generations.

Siya Ji Maharaj spotted Siddheshwari's musical talents, and expressed his wish to Rajeshwari Devi that he would adopt her as his student. He even refused to take any fee to teach her. Rajeshwari had refused this proposal, to which Siya Ji Maharaj said firmly, "I will be sinning against *Goddess Saraswati* if I do not teach Siddheshwari. I cannot destroy what Saraswati herself has created." Thus, Rajeshwari had to allow her to attend Siya Ji's classes in his house. It was a Thursday, the auspicious day for Saraswati, when a simple *ganda* ceremony strengthened a life-long bond for Siddeshwari. It was the day when she got a *guru* who saved her from a life of endless drudgery.

Siddheshwari's training in music began in all earnestness. She could go to her *guru's* house only after finishing all her household chores. He taught her whenever she came. Her *guru* Siya ji Maharaj had no child of his own, so Siddheshwari stepped into that vacuum and filled it to the brim with her love and devotion. *Maa* used to remember, "I had been brought up on leftovers." But her *guru* and his wife used to take good care of *Maa*. Once she said, "He fed me, he taught me, he taught me everything."

Siddheshwari Devi got phenomenal exposure at Rajeshwari Devi's place. Rajeshwari Devi was a learned person in her own right and was well-versed in English, Urdu and, Persian. Her house was well-known for "*Baithkis*" where big musicians deemed it an honor to perform. In fact, *Maa*'s love for music came from being a part of such musical gatherings. Besides, since Banaras was the spiritual center of Hinduism, her aunt's house was frequented not only by musicians but also by various *pundits* and reputed scholars. These were the earliest inspirations and learning for *Maa* that left a lasting impression on her personality.

Siddheshwari Devi had undying optimism, and the ability to perceive hope in the most hopeless of situations.

She saw positivity even in the most depressing times. Life had never been easy for her. She had struggled hard for all that she had achieved. Experience had taught her that it was important to see silver lining in each dark cloud and then polish it until it lit up the cloud like a halo. She progressed quickly. She worked hard not just for recognition but to be economically independent. Her *guru* insisted on a little more training before starting formal performances. *Maa* remembers her first performance in 1925 at Ranka in Sargoja state in Madhya Pradesh when she was just seventeen and the number of performances grew longer each day.

She was a worshiper of Lord Shiva and Krishna. She always respected other religions as well and believed they are just different ways to connect with the Divine. Siddheshwari's training under Pandit Siya Ji Maharaj continued until his death. After which she learned from *Ustaad* Razab Ali Khan of Dewas and *Ustaad* Inayat Ali Khan of Lahore. She had also learnt from Pandit Bade Ramdas Ji of Banaras, whom she regarded as her greatest *guru*.

She saw the glories of the feudal world and also witnessed its decadence. She lived to see the emergence of India as an independent country and the largest democracy in the world. She soon became a recipient of royal patronage as invitations from highly regarded royal houses from all over India came her way. Her visit to Lahore was more significant than she had imagined at that time. It was here that she met a tall, fair gentleman named Pandit Iqbal Narain Pandey who became her future husband and she shared a large part of her life with him. *Maa* always loved to perform in Calcutta. She found the ambiance of the city very motivating. She considered it special because it had been home to singers who had been a source of inspiration for her in her formative years like Gauhar Jaan and Maujuddin Khan. There she was chosen to sing along with veterans like Dilip Chandra Vedi,

Pandit Omkarnath and Ustad Faiyaz Khan. She continued singing all over the country.

The struggle for independence had slowly taken the shape of an uncontrollable storm. Siddheshwari could not keep herself away from the storm. She provided shelter to the freedom fighters. She also extended financial help during the freedom struggle.

Soon her audience heard her singing a song that continued within itself. *Maa*'s hope for the future of India as well as her undying faith in God:

Mathura na sahi, Gokul hi sahi
Raho bansi bajate kahin na kahin
Deen bharat ka dukh door karo
Raho jhalak dikhate kahin na kahin.

(*This song urges Indians not only to pray but also to fight for their freedom*).

Siddheshwari Ji had a remarkable quality - that of counting her blessings rather than her misfortunes. She considered her children and her music as a gift from God. Her doors were open to all, but artists received that special warmth and hospitality which she felt was their rightful due. Lata Mangeskar, Bade Ghulam Ali Khan, Vilayat Khan, Gangu Bai Hangal, Hira Bai Barodekar, Patwardhan Ji and so many others visited Maa's house. *Maa* had also worked in films. She was closely associated with the late Shree S.D. Burman, Shree Guru Dutt, and Dev Anand, to recall a few.

M.S. Subbulakshmi learned *thumri* from Siddheshwari Devi. *Maa* used to go to meet Subbulakshmi, whom she affectionately called "Shubham". Siddheshwari Ji never forgot the two months she spent with her and the whole atmosphere: the large house, the beautiful garden and the "uncorrupted" people, as she described them.

In 1965, after the death of her husband, she shifted to Delhi. She taught music at the prestigious Bhartiya Kala

Kendra. Her public performances continued unabated and she would also record for All India Radio. Her lifelong homage to music finally won her formal recognition. She was honored with the *Sangeet Natak Academy* Award in January 1967. The same year saw her receive the *Padma Shri*. The Rabindra Bharti University of West Bengal awarded a D. Litt., in 1972, and *Sahitya Kala Parishad* awarded her in 1975.

She had an innate ability to strike relationships with people in minutes and to nourish them through years. She remained a warm hearted, simple and lovable person;

Legend Meets the Legend: Vidushi MS Subbulakshmi, along with her illustrious daughter Radha Viswanathan, and Vidushi Siddeshwari Devi with her legendary daughter Savita Devi.

an extraordinary amalgam of innocence, courage, humor, generosity, youthful zest for life and rare dignity.

She used to say that while training and practice are very important for the *thumri* along with the style of singing without which we cannot even take a single step, but *thumri* is a state of mind and without which there can be no *rasa* or beauty in our singing. *Thumri* requires a special attitude and aptitude on a singer's part-special sentiments, delicacy of feeling and the abundance of love in the heart. In the *pukaar* (she was famous for that) of her songs, the same word was repeated many times but each time it found a new expression. The special quality of Sddheshwari Ji's music came from her deep spiritualism. When she sang, she seemed to be singing not merely for her immediate audience but for some higher being. This mystic quality of her singing is what made her different from the other musical exponents. In my opinion, often through her music she tried to transform the poor and corrupt mentality of society towards female singers to a healthy and pure sphere.

*****

The Legend - Begum Akhtar

MALLIKA-E-GHAZAL - BEGUM AKHTAR

Akhtari Bai Faizabadi alias Begum Akhtar was born on 7th October 1914 in the Faizabad district of Uttar Pradesh. She had a twin sister, who died at the young age of two and a half. Her mother's name was Mushtari Begum and her father's name was Asgar Hussain.

I have been listening to Begum Akhtar's *ghazal*s on the radio since my childhood and looking at her beautiful pictures, sometimes in magazines, and sometimes in newspapers. Their world seemed very dazzling to me then. But as my eagerness to know about these *legends* grew, it seemed that the other side of the coin was rather painful.

Her father refused to accept Mushtari Begum as a wife and whatever arrangements he had made in return cannot play the role of a father in the development of a child. From a very young age, Akhtari Bai had to move from one city to another with her mother in the *jugad of rozi roti* (to win their daily bread). Since her mother was a professional singer, it is obvious that she also wanted to teach music to her daughter. Begum Akhtar's childhood was full of challenges and she became both a son and a daughter to her mother. Begum Akhtar had to face sexual abuse in her childhood and was raped as a teenager. These were all dark aspects of Begum Akhtar's life, but it is important to talk about them because these incidents had deep impact on her personality. These situations can ruin a human being and can also become a weapon to win his/her victory. But the pain cannot be denied. Akhtari Bai made this bitter experience of her life both as her armor and weapon.

At a very young age, she came with her mother to the city of Gaya in Bihar state with her mother and started learning music from the famous *Sarangi* player, Imdad Khan. She moved to Calcutta at the age of 11–12 years and began her training with the famous Ustad Ata Muhammad Khan of Patiala. Khan Sahab was a very strict *guru*. He lovingly called her by the nickname, *Bibbi*. Even at 3 o'clock at night, she used to singing *'Aalaap'* in her sleep. The first public performance Begum Akhtar gave was a fundraiser held in Calcutta after a massive earthquake in Bihar in the early 1930s. She was very young then; so her *guru* accompanied her. She sang so well that a hush fell over the audience and she was hailed as the new star, Akhtari Bai Faizabadi singer as well as patriot.

She entered film industry with *"Ek Din Ka Badshah"* and *"Nal-Damayanti"* (1933) and in the film *"Roti"* she got recognition for her famous song *"Phir se fasale bahaar aayi."*

During 1930s and 40s, she worked in many films and in the theaters of Calcutta. She also got a chance to work in a film directed by Satyajit Ray, *"Jalsaghar."*

She moved to Lucknow with her mother in 1943. In 1944, she married a distinguished lawyer from Lucknow, Janab Ishtiaq Ahmad Abbasi. This marriage paved the way for her to be connected to the prestigious section of the society and perhaps even the biggest dream of her life, probably the vengeance on her father for rejecting her mother for giving birth to a girl child. After her marriage agreement, she gave up singing. Until 1950, when her mother was alive, everything went well, but her mother Mushtari Begum's demise broke her completely. She started to get sick, she had a nervous breakdown. The doctors advised her to resume singing, which proved to be a miracle for her. There was a whole world of her fans who were probably waiting for her.

This time, the popularity of *ghazals* had also risen. Her husband also extended his support to her evolution as he hired an Urdu tutor for his wife. Many times, he used to organize *Mushaira* at his home for her exposure. He himself was also a great scholar of Urdu.

Begum Akhtar was strongly influenced by the couplets (*sher-o-shayari*) of Mirza Ghalib, Daag Dehalvi, Faiz Ahmed Faiz, Jigar Muradabadi, Shakeel Badayuni and Kaifi Azmi. Impressively, Begum Sahiba was as big a composer as she was a singer. She used to compose all the *ghazals* sung by her. She also used to sing *thumri, dadra,* but her *ghazals* definitely made her immortal. Famous poet Kaifi Azmi used to say that *ghazal*s have two meanings, one is *ghazal* and the other is Begum Akhtar. Begum Akhtar also made great contribution, putting *ghazal* and folk music on the world stage.

Her aesthetic sense was such that she would know which perfume to use in which month and season. Thus, like her *raaga* and *raginis* she would also choose her sarees and jewelery with care. For instance, fresh jasmine jewelery was deemed good during summers. She was also very particular about the decoration and arrangement of the hall, even the way food and something as simple as serving of *paan* was highly stylized and with a lot of care and dedication.

Begum Sahiba's generosity and charm made her legendary. If someone were to comment, even casually upon the beauty of a shawl or diamond that she was wearing, it was not uncommon for her to offer it on the spot as a gift. She never requested or accepted any fee from her disciples and believed in passing her knowledge on the basis of the pure merit, talent and dedication of the student.

The journey to read her biography was very interesting and at the same time it showed the other side (the darker) of a strong and successful personality, the bitter truth of her life. Begum Sahiba did not oppose the society but through her *ghazals* she registered complete resistance. She was conscious of the dignity of her femininity. On occasion, she used to force her front to be silent.

Birth: 07.10.1914, Faizabad
Death: 30.10.1974, Ahmedabad
Mother: Mushtari Begum
Husband: Ishtiaq Ahmed Abbasi
Award: Padma Bhushan, Sangeet Natak Academy Award

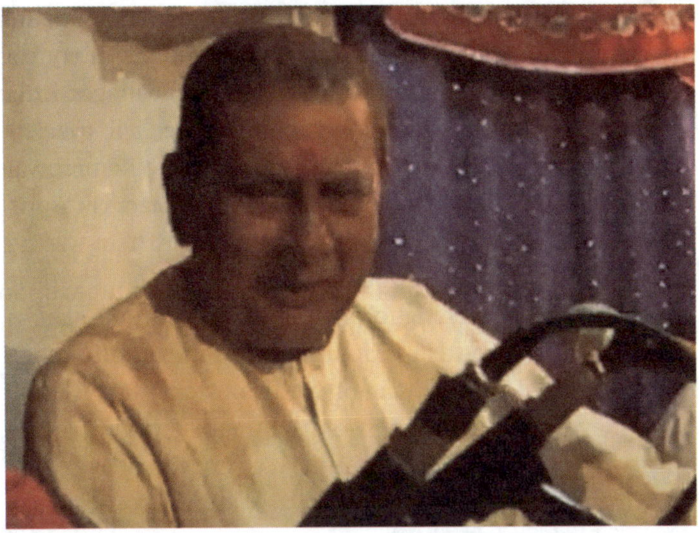

The Legend - Pandit Kameshwar Pathak

PANDIT KAMESHWAR PATHAK

Pandit Kameshwar Pathak Ji was the signature artist of *Gaya ang* of *thumri*. Music has been ingrained in his family for four or five generations. His great grandfather was a royal priest (Raj *Purohit*) in the court of the Maharaja of Tikari. He was an excellent singer as well. Legend says that once when the king's elephant died, the king was very upset and on that day he did not accept the offering (*prasad*) of the priest (great grandfather of Pandit Kameshwar Pathak Ji).The priest fed the prasad to the dead elephant, and the elephant sprang alive (apparently the elephant was certainly not dead and the whole incident was a fortuitous one). The King was very happy and took the royal priest on the elephant and said that as far as this elephant would go, the whole land would be yours. The elephant traversed three villages, and then stopped. Thus, Pandit Kameshwar Pathak Ji's great grandfather became the landlord of these three villages. After some time these three villages were consolidated and the new village was named 'Iswarpur'. This is how Pandit Kameshwar Pathak Ji's family trace their origin to the village 'Iswarpur' of Gaya district. His father was also a singer. There was an atmosphere of music throughout the village. As a child he used to wake up listening to the melodious sound of *sarangi* from one house and Harmonium and *Israj* from the other. His father used to do *riyaaz* of vocal music with *pakhawaj*. In all they were four siblings—with three sisters, he was the only son. He began to study music at a very young age.

A major pilgrimage center, Gaya is known for *'Gayawal Pandas'*. In the good old days they were fond of music and wrestling. There were a plethora of rich and influential people who patronized music. Great musicians like Ustad Moijuddin Khan, Bhaiyya Ganpat Rao (Harmonium), Soni Babu (Harmonium), and even Begum Akhtar, practiced and perfected their art by staying at Gaya, on the invitation of *'Gayawal Pandas'*. Ram Prasad Mishra alias Ramu Ji of Banaras Gharana also settled here and later emerged as one of the pillars of Gaya gharana.

When asked to explain the nuances of *Gaya Ang* and about other musicians associated with this *Ang*, Pandit Kameshwar Pathak Ji mentioned that there were several renowned singers like Siyaram Tiwari, Jairam Tiwari, Surya Pathak associated with *Gaya Ang*. The singers of *Gaya Ang* had a great influence on the singing of Dhanrang Ji. Speaking of Ramu Ji, he mentioned that he was a very intelligent and accomplished singer with a charismatic personality endowed with a polite mannerism. Ramu Ji used to sing from *Banaras Ang* and when the *murkies* (nuances of music) of *Gaya Ang* were included in his style of singing, the amalgamation became very attractive.

Pandit Kameshwar Pathak Ji explained that the Gaya and Banaras style of singing were not very different, improvisation is very similar in both the *gharanas*, the subtle difference is in the use of notes. In *Gaya Ang*, two or three notes are selected for improvisation on a relatively slow rhythm, the rationale being that the *bhava* (emotion) you want to evoke must be justified. The notes are the same but a proper combination of notes are essential for expressing required emotions. To evoke emotions, the *raagas* should be selected according to the literature of the *Bandish* (song). *Gaya ang* uses beautiful *Murkis* that helps in reflecting emotions. In this *ang* four to five harmoniums *Israj, Sarangi, Tanpura*, etc. were used while performing *thumri*, however, such elaborate usage of musical instruments have declined with over time.

Recounting his journey towards becoming a full-time musician, Pandit Pathak Ji mentioned that he was an officer in the 'Caltex Company' in Calcutta and had the life of a typical executive dressing formally in shirt, pant and tie and functioning from an air-conditioned office. Then one day his senior Mr. A.K. Banerjee invited him to a dinner party where he had also arranged a musical *baithak*. Pandit Kameshwar Pathak Ji sang a song to the accompaniment of violin and tabla. Pandit Gyan Prakash Ji (later a Padma Bhushan awardee) was also present there, after his performance Pandit Gyan Prakash Ji asked him to stop selling oil and start practicing music again as soon as possible. He asked, "You have learnt music from whom?" to which Pandit Kameshwar Pathak responded that his father had taught him music. Mr. Banerjee and Pandit Gyan Prakash advised him to quit his job, go to his hometown and do rigorous *riyaz*. The next day Mr. Pathak resigned from his job and rushed back to Gaya. He started his *riyaz* of vocal music and was immersed in it for five years. Sometimes he used to feel discouraged because he was habituated to lead a comfortable life, but whenever he remembered the sage advice of Mr. Ghosh and Pandit Gyan Prakash he used to feel inspired. Pandit Kameshwar Pathak Ji made his first appearance in the All India Music Conference five years later, he mentioned that he met Pandit Gyan Prakash in this program, he was very happy at my rendition. Pandit Gyan Prakash in effect had changed his life. Pathak Ji mentioned that music gave him wealth, respect and fame, for which he pays his obeisance to Goddess Saraswati. Blessed with a melodious voice, he was always very keen to learn new things and meet people.

I asked Pandit Kameshwar Pathak Ji that did he ever feel becoming fully immersed in your singing, in complete unison with music, and the world seemed to be cut off from you? He exclaimed, "Meenaskhi Ji! Let me tell you, once I was singing the morning *raga "Ramkali"* of *Bhairav Thaat,* unknowingly I struck a particular note immediately and felt that my body had levitated from his place, losing complete realization of myself." When the spell was over, shocked and mystified he tried umpteen times to touch that note again but could not do it. He exclaimed that a stage comes in this musical journey when one experiences the union of soul with almighty. I found Pandit Kameshwar Pathak Ji to be a very optimistic person with sophisticated manners.

*****

Birth: 1925.

Death: 17. 10. 2017.

Award: Takshshila Award-2007, Swar Samman-1988,

Sangeet Ratan-1977, Maharani Ahilyabai Samman-2009.

Genre: Hindustani Classical

The Legend - Padma Vibhushan Vidushi Girija Devi

VIDUSHI GIRIJA DEVI

Padma Vibhushan Vidushi Girija Devi was famous as "Appa Ji" among her followers. When I approached her for an interview with my *guru* Vidushi Savita Devi, despite her ill health she agreed to meet me enthusiastically. I was waiting for her in her living room with my *guru* when she entered with her daughter Sudha Dutta and the first thing she said to my *guru* was. "After *Maa*'s demise (Mother- Siddheshwari Devi, who is fortunately my *guru's* biological mother), I have taken care of everything, now Savita it's your turn to take the responsibility to further the art form. I do not feel healthy now-a-days." Savita Ji, nodded ever so politely as if she was saying that she would try her best but would require *Appa Ji's* blessings and wishes.

When *Appaji* was entering the room, I was keenly observing her, and to me it was as if *Banaras* came alive in front of me. She was wrapped in a light *Banarasi Saree, paan* in her mouth and *Bhojpuri and Banarasi thumri* was running in her blood. She had a few words with us and then moved to the next room with me. The interaction began and I just can't describe the sea of love that was embedded in her. The interview lasted for almost three hours but she neither appeared to be exhausted nor bored, she replied to all my questions very patiently.

In her interview, she highlighted some of the very important aspects about *thumri* as a genre and the artists as well. First, the singer may do anything to improvise the *bandish* but the originality of *thumri* has to be maintained, for *appa ji* that was imperative. While replying to every question, she also explained them with additional facts and anecdotes of herself and other artists. She quipped that she doesn't like to be alone, and wishes to befriend a number of people. She mentioned that she enjoys preparing food and serving the guests irrespective of their numbers.

I was surprised to see her level of energy even at the age of 85 years. Her followers and students told me that if *Appa Ji* met anyone once, they remained with her forever. She was an ocean of knowledge. I had several conversations with her on the phone even after the interview, with respect to the book and she was ever so enthusiastic about it.

When I met her for the first time, she told me that she had seen my *guru* in her childhood and that my *guru* had played in her lap. I could imagine the scene and that maternal warmth that oozed out of Appaji. When we met Appaji, she asked me, "Have you brought *rasmalai* for me?" (Rasmalai is the name of a sweet). Your *guru* knows that I am fond of *rasmalai*." I said, "Yes, yes! We have brought it for you." We all broke into laughter.

Once she shared some of her childhood memories with me. She fondly recalled her father and told me how encouraging he was and how she gave a lot of credit to her father for who she was as a person and also as an artist. She shared how she thoroughly enjoyed her childhood which was perhaps different from other girls of her age. She learnt swimming, horse riding, and would often wear pants and shirts. She believed that her parents didn't raise her as a 'typical girl' was raised in those times. Perhaps this was the reason for the immense confidence she had in herself and her capabilities. She was a strong personality who could make way for herself in any kind of situation.

Prior to this interview she seemed an introvert to me, but in my very first meeting, it did not appear to be so. In fact, it seemed as if I was not really meeting her for the very first time but had known her for agest.

Birth:	08.05.1929, Varanasi.
Death:	24.10.2017, Kolkata.
Husband:	Mr. Madhusudan Jain.
Daughter:	Mrs. Sudha Dutta.
Father:	Late Ramdev Rai.
Awards:	Padma Vibhushan, Padma Bhushan, Sangeet Natak Academy Award
Tenure:	1949–2017.
Genre:	Hindustani Classical Music (*thumri* Singing Specialty).

The Legend - Pandit Chhannulal Mishra

PANDIT CHHANNULAL MISHRA

The legendary Padma Vibhushan Pandit Chhannulal Mishra, a great exponent of the Banaras *gharana* as a colossus is simplicity personified. Though his great grandfather lived in Banaras, his father relocated to Azamgarh district of Uttar Pradesh. I was curious to know why he chose Banaras *gharana,* to which he responded that it was never a question of choice, Banaras flows in his blood! He shared that he is related to Bade Ramdas Ji of Banaras whose only daughter was married in the family of his paternal grandmother. Pandit Chhannulal Mishra had spent eight years of his life at Muzaffarpur, learning the nuances of music from *Kirana gharana's* maestro Abdul Ghani Khan. His *shastra guru* was Thakur Jayadev Singh, a scholar par excellence. Pandit Chhannulal Mishra has a firm belief that the devotion and commitment to the *guru* is everything and for a student nothing should be more important than that. He believed that if one has a good fortune of being under the tutelage of the right *guru,* then everything is possible in life. He considers himself very fortunate to have found *gurus* who inculcated a lifelong love for music in him. At the same time, he also shared his belief that "it's rare to meet a good teacher." According to him, a good artist emerges only when he/she masters both rhythm and melody, which, according to Pandit Ji, is a lifelong process and journey. His spiritual *guru* was 'Mauni Baba' whose presence gave him the feeling of being in the divine company of Lord Sankara. Pandit Ji was convinced that the mind should shed its restlessness and focus on the Divine, which is the path to all our goals. His curiosity to expand his knowledge allowed him to explore even the uncharted territories of creativity in music and his philosophy and knowledge provided depth to his endeavours.

Pandit Ji firmly believed that an artist of Indian Classical music must know Sanskrit as it helps in understanding the depth of knowledge and wisdom that *shastras* provide. He had said, "Knowledge of *shastras* would allow us to expand the horizon of music in limitless ways." He remarked that *Valmiki Ramayana and Srimad Bhagvat Gita* are all in Sanskrit, thus knowing the language becomes important. Pandit Chhannulal Ji expressed a longing to perform some of the *thumris* of *Ram Charita Manas* and compositions of his uncle SaJile Ji.

An important aspect that he highlighted in our interaction was about humility in an artist, which he believes is pivotal. He opined that arrogance clouds an individual's talent and thus requires patience along with confidence to succeed, but at the same time, one should be mindful of one's shortcomings as well. He stated that "eventually success comes by *guru's* grace and disciple's devotion only." Elaborating it further, he said that a real 'artist' is one who can simplify the nuances of classical music. He said that unlike film music, it's wrapped in some degree of complexity. He seeks to make this accessible to the audience through his performance thereby giving them the joy and pleasure of classical music. Applause and pleasure of the listeners is the touchstone of a successful musical performance and for all of this to fall in place, an artist should have in-depth knowledge of literature, especially on which the music is based. He said that many doyens of the yesteryears lacked the understanding and appreciation of literature. Literature by its very nature is meaningful and thus should be accessible to the audience; in the process the artists should not hesitate in improvising literature, especially to make it clearer and understandable to the audience. In this journey, Pandit Ji has been showered with many accolades. He has been felicitated for his rendition in the movie *'Aarakshan'- "Laage tose naina, naina rey"* which is an improvisation of the *Bol Banaao thumari, "Jaag pari mai to piya ke jagaaye".*

Pandit Chhannula Mishra said that music has brought him closer to God. He narrated an incident when one day, past midnight he felt that Lord Sankara was standing right in front of him. Musing further on this unique experience and encounter, he shared that *gurus* are a reflection of Lord Sankara and he was in the divine company of his own *guru.* Thinking aloud, he said that Banaras or Kashi is associated with Lord Sankara so why should Banaras *gharana* be not known more appropriately as Lord Sankara *gharana* and then what is the identity of Banaras? Answering it himself he said, "the identity of Banaras is Banarasi *thumri,* Banarasi

Paan, Banarasi *Sari."* "Those having affinity with the music of Banaras should know its *thumri* also, after all it's one thing to know the name of Rama and another to have an understanding of his essence." His affection for Banaras was evident when he said that living in Banaras and knowing what Banaras is all about is completely different.

In the end, Pandit Ji said that he enjoys every aspect of music. Rhythm and rendition should be continuously perfected by complete devotion to music, if one has an unhindered focus on this, his music would be appreciated everywhere whether it's a city or village. He concluded the interview with the following sloka:

Karm Pradhan Vishwa Rachi Raakhaa
Jo Jas karhi So Tas Fal Chaakhaa.

Every person has to bear the fruit of his own good and bad deeds. Those who put in their effort, God blesses them.

*****

Born:	03.08.1936
Children Son:	Ram Kumar Mishra (Tabla player)
Spouse:	Smt. Manorma Mishra
Awards:	Padma Vibhushan, Padma Bhushan, Sangeet Natak Academy Award for Hindustani Music-Vocal.

The Legend - Padmashri Dr. Shanti Hiranand

DR. SHANTI HIRANAND

Padmashri Dr. Shanti Hiranand Ji was the strongest link that truly sustained the rich legacy of Begum Akhtar's *thumri, Dadra* and the ghazal's repertoire. Dr. Shanti Hiranand was of a gentle and calm disposition and a *bon vivant*, born in an affluent and culturally alive Lucknowi family. Being a highly educated woman, her *lingua franca* was Hindi laced with Urdu.

My *Guru* took the time with her to set the interview for me. I was carrying a small gift for her, when I reached her house. After paying my respects the traditional way, I handed over the gift with some trepidation. She straight away shot back, "Why have you brought this?" Tongue-tied, not knowing what to say to a legend of such high stature, I said feebly, "M'am, there is a saree in it." On hearing this, a broad smile floated on her face and she said excitedly, "Show me!" I happily opened the packet for her, and she exclaimed that I had brought a beautiful saree. It was a cream-colored *jamdani* cotton saree. She spread the saree on the couch and remarked that she likes such sarees very much. Moving ahead, she said, "Savita ji called ahead for you; tell me what all you want to know about me."

Known for her simplicity, which overwhelmed me, I asked her if she would wear this saree. She eagerly replied in the affirmative! Being a student of psychology, my way of seeing people is different. I have discovered invariably that truly great personalities have an ingrained humbleness in them; they never let you feel belittled in their presence. People who succeed in life are large hearted from within.

Recounting some excerpts from the interview, when asked if she also held the belief that *thumri* originated in Lucknow? she disagreed, but added that it is certain that WaJid Ali Shah greatly increased the appeal of *thumri*. Continuing further she said that Bindadin Thakur Ji (fabled ancestor of Birju Maharaj) danced while singing *thumri*. Dr. Shanti Hiranand mentioned that there used to be *'Haveli Sangeet'* in which hymns of gods were sung. Those hymns were sung in the overarching bounds of the morning and evening *ragas* of Hindustani classical music. She was of the view that *thumri* started with Radha-Krishna's *rasa*, and she considers *Haveli Sangeet* to be the origin of *thumri*.

Moving ahead with the interview, I said that essentially, as we know, *thumri* is sung in Banaras, Patiala, Lucknow as well as Gaya *gharana*. So how is rendition of *thumri* in Lucknow *gharana* different from other *gharanas*? She said that it's true that *thumri* is sung in Banaras, Lucknow, Punjab, Gaya and other provinces. Kale Khan Sahab from Punjab came to Lucknow to learn *thumri* and made it popular in Punjab. Mashook Ali Khan Sahab used to sing *thumri* in the *tappa ang* with a prolonged *taan (phirat ki taan)*, a speciality of *tappa ang*. This became the identity of *thumri* of *'Punjab Ang'*. In Banaras, *thumri* is sung with a longing ('hook'), and is slow churning with perceptible halts, an effect of the weather in that part of the country. The *thumri* of Banaras was worth learning from Siddheshwari Devi, who knew how to share and how to construct a song, as an exalted artform. While in the Lucknow tradition the throw of voice and triangulation of *taans ('Khatke - Murki')* is its distinguishing feature, the lyrics of *thumri* in this *gharana* are delicate, a consequence of Urdu in Lucknow. In the Gaya tradition, it is customary to initiate with two-three notes and then move with a slow pace.

She mentioned that though Begum Akhtar was a resident of Faizabad, she had the influence of the eastern part and since her master Ata Muhammad Khan Saheb was from the Patiala Gharana, she was also influenced by its style. Essentially the singing of Begum Sahiba was a confluence of different styles with a predominant mix of *poorab ang* and patiala *gharana*.

As the interview progressed, I asked at what age did she start learning from Begum Akhtar Sahiba? Reminiscing, she said that she started learning music from a very young age of 12, and also sang on the radio. Subsequently, she started learning from Ustad Aizaz Ali Khan Sahab. She mentioned that he was an extraordinarily good singer, but fame eluded him. In her early years, she used to live in Lahore, where a music teacher taught her to have command of *sur* and *taal*s. She was the one who introduced him to the radio. After Partition, they came to Lucknow and got introduced to Begum Akhtar Sahiba, whom she used to call *'Ammi'*. Thereafter, she never learned from any other *guru*. Begum Sahiba taught her

Ragas, Thumri, Dadra and Ghazals and used to say that just sing with me. At that time, many things were not understood by young Hiranandani, but kept on practicing and as experience progressed, things became understandable and she also fixed errors in her renditions.

I asked her about a memorable moment she spent with her Guru. She recounted once she went to Pakistan in connection with an event with *Ammi*. While returning, the Immigration Officer's eye on the 'Wagah Border' went on the passport, the name written on it was – "Shanti Hiranand Akhtar", the officer found something 'wrong' with the name; he wanted to do some questioning, but then Begum Sahiba asked that officer, "What are you looking at? She is my daughter!" There was no questioning after that. Actually, when Shanti Ji's passport was being made in Lucknow in 1950, Begum Akhtar Sahiba had associated her name with Shanti Ji's name, so the passport had Shanti Hiranand Akhtar written on it. Begum Sahiba had no children of her own.

Shanti Hiranand Ji mentioned that there was no one in her family who was into music before her, but she had a good voice and thus started singing. She received a lot of support from her parents. In those days, music was not seen as an honorable vocation, but her family used to cooperate a lot. She used to stay for many nights with Begum Sahiba learning and practicing, but her parents never objected nor allowed anyone else to say anything.

I asked whether her marriage had any impact on her career. She said that her husband lived in America at the time of her marriage. Pandit Jawaharlal Nehru had called him to India on a government job. When he came here, he heard about me. When he proposed marriage to me, I said that I will marry on the condition that it will not affect my music. I will continue to meet 'Ammi' (Begum Akhtar Sahiba) and continue with music. Ammi used to come to Delhi. I stayed in a hotel for five-six days with Ammi but my husband never objected. The truth is that it is very difficult for Indian women to sing without family support. She got support, got a guru, got the opportunity, and worked hard to become a singer.

She said, "Ammi's personality was such that Shanti Ji could not go anywhere else. There was a lot of attachment to Ammi. Most people profitted from Ammi. I wrote a book on Ammi called, *'The Story of My Ammi'*. I wrote everything in this book from 1952, until the end of Ammi. I wrote down what all I experienced in this book".

This interview lasted about six hours spread in about 2–3 days. It emerged from the interview that Dr. Shanti Hiranand maintained and adhered to the guru-disciple tradition. Dr. Shanti Hiranand had a very deep knowledge of classical music and nuanced understanding of various traditions. She was a woman of great poise, a quality that is rare among artists. It was apparent that she had a hunger for lifelong learning and was a very optimistic person by nature.

*****

Birth:	29.10.1933, Lucknow.
Death:	10.04.2020, Gurugram.
Father:	Hiranand Mansukhani.
Mother:	Sita Mansukhani.
Husband:	Jagannath P. Chawla.
Son:	Nischint Chawla.
Singing style:	*thumri*, Dadra, Ghazal (Ghazal of Begum Akhtar were her specialty).
Award:	Honored with Padma Shri in 2007.

(She has also written the book "The story of my Ammi" on Begum Akhtar).

The Legend Vidushi Savita Devi
with her disciple Indira Mukherjee

VIDUSHI SAVITA DEVI

The signature singer of Banaras *Gharana* Vidushi Savita Devi is my *guru*. I interviewed her for several hours, spread over several sessions. Savita Devi was the Head of the Department of Music at Daulat Ram College, Delhi University. She used to teach *sitar* and was the *gandabandh shishya* of Pandit Ravi Shankar. Given her knowledge of both singing, and playing musical instruments, she had an in-depth understanding of music.

In an interview, I asked her what was more difficult – singing or playing sitar on the stage? She said, "singing". She had played the *sitar* several times with her husband Pandit Kishan Maharaj, the world renowned *tabla* maestro, before switching to *thumri*. She recollected that she sang well in her first performance but in her second performance, she was stuck while improvising some phrase in *antra,* and could not find her way back. She got nervous wondering what to do next but she tried to make the most out of the moment, finding cues around her and she stopped singing for a few seconds and started listening to the accompanists. Soon, she found her way back. She believed that such mental blocks could happen to any artist at any time, but what matters most is the ability of making the most out of it. Basically, to solve problems through intelligence and presence of mind, rather than succumbing to the pressure is the most important thing.

She was an honest artist who always shared her musical experiences with her disciples. For me, she was a reflection of *Goddess Saraswati,* in many ways: her fair complexion, a beautiful and serene face, her melodious voice, and her sophisticated dress sense typified her. She was very polite in her demeanor; an introvert in her personal life but interestingly, an extrovert as an artist.

As she was my *guru,* I was aware of various aspects of her personality. I had seen how she dealt with things in day-to-day life and what it was like to spend a day or many days with *maa* (I called her *maa* - mother). Your personal front can differ from your professional front. But it is important to mention here that both have an important influence on each other and that was evident in *maa's* case as well. There were two very distinct traits of her personality, her rich aesthetic sense and her ability to listen to others very carefully and attentively. She gave others their due.

I used to watch her on television or on stage. She had a charismatic personality. As I have mentioned, she was a mother to my artistic life, besides being my *guru.* In a way, my birth as an artist took place in her hands.

Maa once told me that whenever she felt skeptical about her performances, her *maa* Siddheshwari Devi would often appear in her dreams as if to guide her. Once when she had to perform alongside the great *Ustad* Bismillah Khan *Sahib,* she got very nervous. That night she saw her old Banaras house in her dream. She saw her *mother* standing near the top of the wooden staircase in the house, smiling at her daughter Savita Ji, looked up and felt her mother's loving gaze with outstretched arms ready to embrace her loving daughter. Savita Ji said, "I awoke to a promising day, full of contentment and confidence." She recollected how her performance went so well that Bismillah Khan *Sahib* applauded her. She believed that her mother Siddeshwari Devi showered her blessings upon her and assured her that everything would be alright.

She had a difficult and traumatic life. Her relationship with her husband could not last long, an inevitable consequence of confrontation between two towering personalities. The death of her elder son left her shaken. Her eldest son Sanjay Maharaj died at the age of 17-18 in a road accident which left an incredibly painful mark on her life and personality. He was fast emerging as a promising *tabla* player like his father.

In the field of music, the recognition to which Savita Ji was entitled eluded her, due perhaps to her introverted nature. She was hesitant in opening up to others, especially when it came to her personal life.

*****

Birth :	07.04.1940, Varanasi
Death :	20.12.1919, Gurugram
Husband :	Pandit Kishan Maharaj
Son :	Ajey Maharaj, Sanjay Maharaj
Mother :	Padmashree Vidushi Siddheshwari Devi
Awrd :	Tansen Award, Sangeet Natak Academy Award
Genre:	Hindustani Classical Music

The Legend - Padmashri Dr. Rita Ganguly

DR. RITA GANGULY

Endowed with a rich and mellifluous voice, Dr. Rita Ganguly evolved her own distinct style of singing *thumri* and *gazal*. She is known as one of the foremost performers of the light classical forms of Hindustani music. She received her training in vocal music from Gopeshwar Banerjee, Shambhu Maharaj, *thumri* legend Siddheshwari Devi, Begum Akhtar and Pandit Mani Prasad. Born in 1940, in Lucknow, Uttar Pradesh, she belongs to a reputed family which has been very active in public life.

Apart from music, she is an accomplished dancer of *kathakali*. She also received training in Manipuri,

Manipuri, Bharatnatyam and modern dance under eminent *Gurus* and also received training in Manipuri, Bharatnatyam and modern dance under eminent *Gurus*. She has been teaching movement and mime as a professor at the National School of Drama in Delhi for over three decades and has made notable contributions to theater. She has also researched on India's musical and theatrical traditions. She was a brilliant student. After her senior Cambridge, she studied at Shanti Niketan. There she learned *Dhrupad* in *Gauharbani* style. She went on to graduate from the prestigious Columbia University. As far as performing arts is concerned, Dr. Rita Ganguly has left her lasting imprint on many dimensions of the Indian cultural landscape.

In our very first meeting at Indira Gandhi National Centre for the Arts (IGNCA), New Delhi, I found her to be very affectionate with an aura of knowledge and self-assurance wrapped around her. And why not! After all, she has a lifetime legacy of achievements. She smiled and said, *"Kaisi ho?"* I touched her feet in greeting and said, *"Teekh hun."* She said, "You had phoned me up for an interview. What do you want to know?" I said I have been working on a book for the last two years. Through this book I am intending to write about the nuances of *thumri gayki* and would like to discuss some psychological factors as well as the experiences of stalwarts in this field. She showed keen interest and said that we still had half an hour at hand before the seminar began. She said, "Your project sounds interesting. *Poocho kya poochna chahti ho!"* (what do you want to know?). Then I started the interview and after that session, I interacted with her on three or four other occasions. Sometimes in person and sometimes on the phone. She is an ocean of knowledge.

When I asked her about the age of her initiation in the field of art, she said that she had started performing dance on the stage when she was just two years old. I became curious to know why she chose to dance at that age. She narrated a very fascinating incident. When Sarojini Naidu became the first Governor in Lucknow. After her taking oath of office, she sponsored a major concert to raise money for some public cause. That program was conceptualized by the daughter-in-law of Rabindra Nath Tagore and in that concert her sisters and mother also participated. After three months of rigorous practice, the day of the final performance arrived. She was not a part of it but was taken to watch the program. Carrying on with this fascinating narration, she mentioned that unexpectedly she was in shiny bow frock, her mother requested some government official to take care of her as she was just a little kid. The program started with Tagore's music. The next performance was of the Maihar band organized by Baba Allauddin Khan in which Ali Akbar, Pt. Ravi Shankar, V.G. Jog, and Pannalal Ghosh were taking part. Baba Allauddin Khan was conducting that program and it was decided that after three bells the curtain would be raised. The bell operator rang the bell thrice but no one raised the curtain. Thereupon the official who was taking care of her, tugged her along and went on the stage to raise the curtain. He left her hand for a few seconds and within that seconds, she ambled on to the center of stage, greeted the audience and started dancing with the band of Baba. Next day *Times of India, The Pioneer* and *National Herald* started by her father, all of them printed her photograph with headlines that Mrs. Tagore arranged an excellent concert, where a two-year-old child stole the show by her dance and it was the best item of the program. After that Sarojini Naidu began to take her along to every program she went to. She used to say that the baby would perform first. Thus, she started performing with the name of Baby Rita. She said that happenstance always played a significant role in her career.

It is evident that she started discovering the artist in her from a very early age. Despite not being professionally involved, there was a cultural atmosphere in her family which was also very supportive and had the financial means for getting her the best possible education.

At a young age she had become a recognised and acclaimed danseuse. Once she was presenting Kathakali in a concert, the accompanying singer forgot the lyrics, she had to sing the song as well as dance on the stage. Shambhu Maharaj was present on that day. He heard her singing. Enthralled, he remarked that she has an artistic element and offered her an opportunity to learn music from him. In this manner, she started learning from Shambhu Maharaj as his *Ganda-Bandh shishya*. Coincidence again played a role. Once Siddheshwari Devi, the *thumri* legend, came to visit Shambhu Maharaj at his place. At that time she was learning from Guruji. She liked Rita Ganguli's voice so much that she immediately took out eleven rupees and a ready beetle from her purse, tied a *ganda* on her wrist in a *Ganda-bandhan* ceremony. Although then *Gandabandhan* tradition was not allowed for female gurus (According to Prof. Rita Ganguly), it shows that Siddheshwari Devi was very progressive and a trend-setter of "*Ganda bandhan* ceremony" among female *Guru-shishyas*. It also reflects her keenness to carry forward the lineage not only in her family but also among talented sparks of society even from non-musical family background. In this manner she started learning *thumri, Daadra* and other *Poorab-Ang gayaki* from *Amma* (Siddheshwari Devi).

In this series of fortuitous coincidences, she narrated that once she went to meet Begum Akhtar Sahiba who had come to Delhi from Lucknow with her husband, Keshav Kothari. They had gone to invite her for a major concert organised by Sangeet Natak Academy, as her husband was the Secretary of

Academy. Begum Akhtar accepted the invitation to participate in the concert and told that she would sing on the stage with her as a co-singer. She took it lightly but Begum Akhtar Sahiba was serious and thus Dr Rita Ganguli accompanied her on stage. Begum Akhtar Sahiba liked her singing immensely and once again she got an opportunity to sing under the mentorship of Ghazal Queen Begum Akhtar. Begum Akhtar Sahiba went to meet Siddheshwari Devi and told that she wanted to teach her. That was how Dr Rita Ganguli's training started under Begum Akhtar. Since her childhood, Rita Ji had an aptitude for Urdu language. Her family was closely attached to the family of poet Majaz Lakhnavi who initiated her to the basics of Urdu. He also happened to be the uncle of famous writer and poet Javed Akhtar. Thus, her knowledge in Urdu came handy in learning Ghazal from Begum Sahiba and she excelled at learning Ghazals.

When asked if an artist could become a complete artist by learning only one art, she said a resounding no. When you learn other arts, your vision becomes very wide and you understand how one art influences the other and how they are related to each other. When you are open to other art forms, the scope of doing something new in your field grows. And it plays a big role in the creativity of an artist. Because no art and artist can flourish in isolation. She was also asked what was the role of academics and education in the evolution and growth of an artist? She stated that a good academic background played a very crucial role in the evolution of an artist, as it made an artist more complete. A person who is better equipped to live in harmony with his or her art, gets more out of it and gives more to the art, and here education plays a very important role.

When she was asked about flow in music, she smiled and said that she thinks this helps in creative thinking. You can't create something new without entering flow in music. I asked her about the message she would like to convey to the upcoming artists. She said, "My message is that whatever art field they want to learn, they should gain complete knowledge of that and give their best. They will certainly be successful."

Born: In 1940, Lucknow, Uttar Pradesh
Genre: Hindustani Music
Spouse: Keshav Kothari
Children: A son and a daughter [Meghna Kothari Actor)
Parents: K.L. Ganguly, Meena Ganguly
Awards: Padma Shri (2003), Sangeet Natak Academic Award (2000) for her contribution to Hindustani Vocal Music, Sahitya Kala Parishad Award, Priya dasrhi Award, RaJiv Gandhi Shiromani Award and many more.
Books: "Ae Mohabbat... Reminicising Begum Akhtar", and "Bismillah Khan & Benaras, the seat of Shehnai"

(She is the founder of Kaladharmi BAAG)

The Legend - Pandit Govardhan Mishra

PANDIT GOVARDHAN MISHRA

While many vocalists sing *thumri and dadra,* only a few could measure up to the excellence of Pandit Govardhan Mishra in singing *'Tappa'* (a style of singing which expresses emotion through *taans*). Although Pandit Govardhan Mishra was a resident of Gaya in Bihar, I first met him in Delhi when he came to Delhi to perform at an event. My *guru,* Vidushi Savita Deviji, introduced me to him. The first meeting and the interview lasted two-and-a-half hours. Sensing my curiosity, he answered all my queries patiently.

When I asked Pandit Govardhan Mishra to tell me something about himself, he said that his father was a famous singer of classical music belonging to the *Banaras Gharana*. His name was Pandit Ramprasad Mishra *aka* 'Ramu Ji'. His mother's name was Annapurna Devi. Pandit Ramprasad Mishra moved to Calcutta from Banaras in 1939. He was born in Calcutta at the height of the city's cultural renaissance. Due to his father's singing performances, he made acquaintances with almost all the major artists of the country. Pandit Govardhan Mishra mentioned that he used to meet senior artists, listen to them, talk to them, and perform along with them.

After a few years, the '*gayawal panda*s' of Gaya district of Bihar urged his father to come to Gaya. The '*gayawal panda*s' were deeply involved in cultural activities, and were very rich. His father eventually moved from Calcutta to Gaya. With the arrival of his father Pandit Ramprasad Mishra in Gaya, almost all big artists of the day started coming to perform in Gaya, and also for the purpose of pilgrimage. (Gaya is a major pilgrimage center for Hindus and Buddhists).

Pandit Govardhan Mishra resumed his studies at Gaya. He reminisced that during those days, the World War II had erupted and it had a major impact on Bharat. There was a financial crisis all over the world. Artists were also affected by this major upheaval. They used to travel all over the country to earn their livelihood. In 1947, when all the big artists converged on Gaya, they all sang the same *dadra* and *thumri* in different variations. Once initiated, the session lasted from dusk to dawn. Despite being a student of Commerce, he took great interest in music and studied classical music under the patronage and guidance of his father. His knowledge of music kept increasing with age.

When asked to elaborate on some distinguishing features of the '*Gaya Gharana*', he said that there is a lot of stress on every note in the tradition of *Gaya Gharana*. A lead of two or three notes is taken while initiating the performance. The rendition is selected according to the lyrics. Sometimes the lyrics are crafted keeping in mind the nature of the audience. These lyrics are made very thoughtfully. Six or seven harmoniums, sarangi, israj, sarod, tabla and others were used in Gaya Gharana tradition. However, nowadays, so many artists are not available.

I asked Pandit Govardhan Mishra whether he had spent all his life in Gaya, he mentioned that he in fact, used to live in Patna. Later, he was a visiting professor at Khairagarh University in Madhya Pradesh for five years. In his cultural journey, he performed in almost all major music forums in the country.

I asked him about his training and whether it was only under the patronage of his father. He said no. He used to live with his grandfather 'Bade Ramdas Ji' in Banaras and trained under him as well.

Pandit Govardhan Mishra was a very emotional person. Remembering his father, he had tears in his eyes. Talking to him, I felt that there was a burden on his mind. I asked him if there was anythng special about his father. He got very emotional about his father, while talking about him. He opened up, saying that I was of his daughter's age. Sharing his heartfelt sorrow, he mentioned that he could not take care of his father, as expected from a son, who was also his disciple, despite the fact that his father gave him all the comforts of life. Because of this he always carried a burden of guilt. I was fascinated by his honesty. I said, "Sir, you are an emotional person, which makes you feel so much. Otherwise, no one knows what many children in this world do; they don't even bother to think about their parents. When I thanked him for his love, affection and time, he said that I had freed him from a lot of guilt today. He mentioned that the knowledge he has accumulated in his journey, he wishes to share; whenever I want to talk by phone, on any facet of music, I could speak to him. From that day onwards, he became my *Shastra-Guru.*

Birth:	10.05.1941, in Kolkata
Death:	06.06.2019 in Gaya
Father:	Pandit Ramprasad Mishra urf Ramu Ji
Singing style:	Hindustani classical music, *thumri,* Dadra, Tappa etc.
Award:	In 2007, he was awarded the Sangeet Natak Akademi Award by the Government of India.

The Legends - Pandit Rajan-Sajan Mishra

PANDIT RAJAN-SAJAN MISHRA

I met Pandit Rajan-Sajan Mishra Ji for the first time at their abode "*Swarangan*". Stepping into the courtyard, I found there was such an aura in this temple of music that I could feel a sense of serenity and love. It was a special and a unique experience in a place where *swara* is worshiped. Jolting me from my reverie, Pandit Rajan Mishra Ji asked with much affection, "How are you? Where are you coming from? From home or somewhere outside?" It felt as if I had known them for ages! I could only mumble, "Not from home. I am coming from somewhere else." Sajan Mishra Ji also ambled into the meeting, and joining the conversation, he asked me what I would like to have. I couldn't have ever dreamt of such an encounter and that too for the first time, laced with warm hospitality and concern. My *guru* Vidushi Savita Devi, whom they had intimately known from childhood, had given me some message to deliver them. I conveyed the message and then settled down for an interaction at '*Swarangan*'.

It would be completely superfluous to state the obvious. The stature, name, fame, acclaim and achievements of Pandit Rajan-Sajan Mishra have come their way by their single-minded devotion and commitment to the art form. These legendary siblings were formal disciples of the famed progenitor of Banaras *gharana,* Pandit Bade Ramdas Ji. They had also learned music and understood its nuances from their father Pandit Hanuman Mishra and uncle Pandit Gopal Mishra. Their father and uncle were *sarangi* players who had carved a niche for themselves as accomplished Hindustani music artists. The famed duo added that the genre which they had listened to in their childhood gradually morphed into an abiding interest. This transformation was ably assisted and nurtured by their *gurus* who imparted learning in a way that they never felt weighed down or burdened by the demands of learning growing up.

The timeless city of Banaras, Varanasi or Kashi (different names used for it) is considered as the most cherished dwelling of *Lord Shiva* on Earth. It would not be an exaggeration to call it the primordial fountain of literature, music, art and spirituality. This place where these attributes of human civilization have been nurtured is the birthplace of the famed Mishra *Bandhu* (brothers). They believed that an individual's knowledge of different languages and literature is important for an excellent grasp over any art form. Very much like other legendary artists, they were convinced and seemed to have an unwavering belief in the purity of language and art ⊠ *Shaastra-Shuddhta*.

When asked what is their innate feeling about music? They remarked in unison that music is like worship to them. Further they said, we sing *khayal,* which literally means imagination and when imagination elevates from its level to meditation, it becomes spirituality. Through this succinct yet profound understanding of music, one could easily sense their devotion and dedication to their artform.

Indian society has always been known for its joint family tradition and Pandit Rajan-Sajan Mishra Ji's family is no different. They have carried the nurturing environment of the 'Swarangan' family together even today. It is believed that the happiness of the family members flows in the sense of satisfaction and state of joy reflected in the head of the family. Those who have had the privilege of knowing and/or interacting with Mishra brothers often vouch for their penchant for lacing their conversation with jokes and banter. Looking at this aspect of their personality from a psychological perspective, it was apparent to me that they were in a mental state wherein they were 'at peace' with themselves, as if they had discovered inner joy and happiness. It is obvious that only a happy person can share happiness with others.

At the time of birth of the Mishra *bandhu,* the country had barely been independent for around over four years. Decades of colonialism and the World War II had left the country terribly impoverished. At that time the patronage of kings and feudal lords, which had been a major source of sustenance, had almost dried up. Due to this, many traditional artists and their families diverted their children towards education and taking up a job rather than keeping them at home to impart knowledge of music through the traditional ways and techniques. This is how the Mishra brothers started going to formal schools and colleges to gain a formal curriculum-based education. This formal education proved to be a blessing in disguise for Mishra brothers, especially in the longer run. They believe that it helped them better appreciate music in the larger context of society and also enabled them to disseminate their music across the length and breadth of the country and abroad. Pandit Rajan-Sajan Mishra's mother had a deep understanding of music and a good vocal ability, she too contributed immensely in nurturing her sons' musical talent. Rajan Mishra Ji who had started learning music at a tender age recollected that when he would forget something in a *bandish* or skip some of its parts, his mother would tell him to pay attention and listen to it carefully, like a *lori* (lullaby). During interview Pandit Goverdhan Mishra also said when he was a 4-5 years old child, her mother used to wake him up early in the morning and sometimes also used to tune and play his *tanpura* for him. It is important to note here that women folk in all these traditional families have significantly contributed in keeping alive the music tradition and furthering its education, albeit this contribution has remained hidden in the shadows. Cultural empowerment of women folk is a theme worth exploring as it would most certainly enrich the field of music, especially traditional music.

The stalwart duo kept on sharing their understanding of music and its nuance in a very simple and elegant way. During the conversation, Pandit Rajan Mishra Ji said that the ultimate stage of singing is "reaching out to the Maker i.e. God/Almighty". He elaborated further that no one can reach this stage of oneness with a mind that is full of himself or ego, "it will forever elude you". To attain unison with the creator one has to shed his ego and strive to become completely egoless. The perfect stage of surrender helps one achieve this and paves the way to the Almighty. They believe that worship or penance cannot be done with a state of mind that is full of ego. Surrender is the state of mind where all doubts cease and this dedication gives rise to reverence. The nature of love varies with relationships, but reverence is something that has to be there in equal measure in all relationships. Explaining his point Pandit Rajan Mishra Ji stated, "If I have reverence for my mother, it will be there for your mother as well". That is, when reverence for the biological parents transcends to reverence for the *Guru* and the *Gurumata*, having reached this stage a person can truly expect to attain enlightenment. What Pandit Rajan Mishra Ji stated could be sensed and perceived by me and everyone else, in the relationship between the brothers; the unwavering bonding between Mishra brothers, emanating from the younger brother's reverence for the elder brother and elder brothers unqualified affection for his younger brother, never allowed the feeling of competition or comparison to ever cloud this deep spiritual bond between brothers, very much akin to the unwavering bond of *Bharat* and Lord *Rama* .

Pandit Rajan Mishra Ji has been an avid devotee and a life-long student of music, an attribute he shared with his brother. Both of them have closely observed various aspects of different *raga-raaginis* and have developed a profound understanding of them. Giving a glimpse of the breadth and depth of his knowledge, Pandit Rajan Mishra shared nuanced exposition on topics such as *rasa*, flow, contemplation and structuralism in classical music. The brothers have a great faith and commitment to the *guru-shishya* tradition. They have strove to create a *gurukul* for furtherance of the art form within this tradition. The *gurukul* is named 'Viram' and is situated at Dehradun-Mussoorie road. Every year the brothers converge here with their disciples, and for a month or two they are completely immersed in the practice of music. Renowned artists are invited during this period as resident scholars and the disciples thus get a rare opportunity to interact with these learned scholars. They get to watch their rendition/performance from close quarters. Such exposure to upcoming artists besides being essential is also invaluable from the point of view of honing and shaping their talent.

Inspired by Shri Shri Ravi Shankar Ji's *Brahmanaad* program *'Antarnaad'*, a similar program was organized in Pune in which thousands of disciples sang under the guidance of *guru* Pandit Rajan-Sajan Mishra. The program was received very well among the audience and music aficionados. Most of them described it to be a unique convergence of rhythm, sound, and *swaras that conveyed* a sense of oneness and unity with the Universe. In the process, it emanated vibrancy and positivity for everyone involved. From the unique and beautiful effort of 'Bhairav to Bhairavi', to spreading awareness of Indian classical music, their efforts and art has been rapturously received by the world. Over the years, both of them have worked tirelessly and ceaselessly to introduce Indian classical music to different cultures and societies and brought it to an international platform.

Pandit Rajan Mishra's first overseas trip was to Sri Lanka back in 1978 where he also learnt Sinhala language from the composer Amardeva Nayak and gave a performance in Sinhalese, unraveling yet another facet of his personality. This stands testament to his belief about unity and oneness of language, literature and music across the world. It not only reflects his care about the sensibilities and happiness of local listeners, but is also an evidence of his vast and expansive talent. After that, both the brothers got various opportunities to perform in many countries and spread the beauty and bliss of Indian classical music.

It is believed that with time true artists immerse themselves more and more in this infinite ocean of music and by the grace of almighty are blessed with salvation. Pandit Rajan Mishra Ji, who is no longer amidst us physically, certainly achieved this transcendental state in life. My first interaction with them ended on a very profound note and a message that I would perhaps carry throughout my life and would want to share it with everyone around me. They said that "*dharma* entwined with humanity and beyond, that is oneness of nature liberates us humans." Subsequently, the discussion continued on many other occasions, where I was the blessed recipient of their knowledge and wisdom.

To all their meteoric rise to fame, a lot of credit goes to their wives, whose support, encouragement, wisdom and dedication, allowed the Mishra brothers to explore the field of music and share it with the society at large. It is a matter of great pleasure that their children have emerged as acclaimed singers in their own right, committed to furthering their unique tradition of performing in unison just like their fathers.

*****

Born:	Pandit Rajan Mishra (1951) and Pandit Sajan Mishra (1956), Banaras.
Father:	Pandit Hanuman Mishra
Award:	Padma Bhushan (2007), Sangeet Natak Academy Award jointly (1978), Gandharwa National Award for (1994-1995), National Tansen Samman (2011-2012)
Film Songs:	"Sur Sangam" song "Aaye surke panchhi aaye" Children: Ritesh Mishra and RaJinish Mishra (Pandit Rajan Mishra), Swaransh Mishra (Pandit Sajan Mishra), all are vocalists and performers.

Disciple with tanpura is learning stage presentation by his Gurus Doyen Pandit Rajan-Sajan Mishra ji.

Rare Jugalbandi by Ustad Zakir hussain (Tabla), Pandit Rajan-Sajan Mishra (Vocal), Pandit Birjoo Maharaj (Kathak dance)

The Legend - Prabhati Mukherjee

PRABHATI MUKHERJEE

The Culture Ministry once organized a program at Vigyan Bhavan in memory of Begum Akhtar Sahiba. This was the first time that I heard Prabhati Ji. And one could make out even from a distance that she is a disciple of Begum Akhtar. There are very few disciples who are a close imprint of their *gurus*. Prabhati Ji appears to be one. After listening to her, I had an urge to meet her. I went straight to the Green Room. I made a request to Prabhati Ji for an interview. She said that she was staying nearby in the state guest house at Chanakyapuri and I could meet her at 5 o'clock in the evening. And I was there in time for the interaction.

Prabhati Ji's outward personality appeared to be that of a

rich, traditional, ebullient woman with a big bindi, vermilion, bangles dangling, adored in a beautiful silk sari, wearing gold jewelery with the air of Bengal surrounding her. There was an aura of tremendous self-belief and confidence which left a lasting impression on me.

Prabhati Ji offered me coffee and after a brief hiatus, the interview started. When I asked her to say something about herself, she said that her father's name was Badal Chandra Mukherjee and mother's name was Shubharani, and they were residents of Tollyganj area of Calcutta; situated very near to her house is the house of Gurudev Rabindra Nath Tagore. Her elder sister Chandra Mukherjee used to learn singing. It was she who inspired her to learn singing from Meera Bandopadhyay. She started training in classical music under Meeraji's guidance. Once an elderly person came to Meeraji; listening to her singing, he said, "I will take you to Bade Ghulam Ali Sahab." He continued, "if he liked your singing, he would take you under his wings." I went to Bade Ghulam Ali Sahab and became a *gandabandh* disciple. I continued to learn from him from 1961 to 1967. Then in 1968 Khan Sahab went to Mumbai. Mr. Khan used to call me a 'little bird'. I used to go to his place at 8 o'clock in the morning and Khan Sahab himself used to leave me at night. Throughout the day, I used to eat and drink, and sleep there. I remember *ammi* (Khan Sahab's wife) and Khan Sahab's son Munawar Ali Bhaiya's wife used to call me *'Aali'*. Sometimes, Munawar Ali Bhaiya's wife, *ammi* and I used to go to the cinema. Babhi used to cover me in the traditional burqa, saying that it won't give people an opportunity to gossip. Prabhati Ji asserted that no one can sing like Khan Sahib, he taught her to sing in his own style and he wanted her to sing just like him. That is why when I sing *"Yaad Piya Ki Aaye"* or *"Kya Karoon Sajni"*, people say that they are reminded of "Bade Ghulam Ali Sahab". She reminisced that he was quite fond of eating good food.

Prabhati Ji mentioned that she has also learned to sing from Begum Akhtar Sahiba and was a *gandaband* disciple of her as well, after Khan Sahab went to Mumbai. After her marriage, whenever she visited *Ammi* with her husband, *Ammi* (Begum Akhtar Sahiba) used to lovingly make *kebabs*; Prabhati Ji said that *Ammi* was just a beautiful doll. Prabhati Ji's husband Mr. Bahaduri used to say that *Ammi* was not an ordinary human being; she is so affectionate that she is like a messenger of God.

Prabhati Ji mentioned that whatever song she sings, she believes in singing in the original style. *Ammi Ji* always used to say that she sings very well, but cautioned her to be modest about it. *Ammi Ji* and Khan Sahab were like two colossuses of music, and it's impossible to mention one, leaving the other. Khan Sahab was paralyzed, which caused him a lot of agony, but he still used to sing even after the doctors warned against it. This is how Prabhati Ji said she imbibed the famous *thumris* and *dadras* of these two legends.

When asked about the difference between the singing of her two *gurus*, she said that Begum Akhtar used to sing in the style of *Kirana Gharana* and her singing had that imprint. Khan Sahab was from the *Patiala Gharana*, and he used to use lots of complex notes (*firat ki taan*), in his singing. The singing of both of her *gurus* was out of this world and heavenly. The foundation of her classical music was ushered in by Bade Ghulam Ali Khan Sahab. There was a difference between the introduction of lyrics and notes of musical phrases, embellishment techniques, and the *Murkis* (use of three notes) were differently used in the singing of Bade Ghulam Ali Sahab and Begum Akhtar Sahiba. She said it was the blessing of her gurus that she had acquired a modest ability to sing.

Prabhati Ji said that to capture the mood and attention

of the audience while singing on the stage should be the prime objective, but it was a challenging task. Sometimes while performing, she was so lost in the lyrics and the notes of *Bandish* that she didn't even know where she was singing. Sometimes she gets so emotional while teaching her disciples that she starts weeping, oblivious of the fact whether anyone is watching her or not. Such is the emotional appeal of music to her.

When inquired about her thoughts on creativity, she mentioned that when she went to Khan Sahab, she was a child and he used to improvise a song in a hundred ways. At that time, even if she wanted to, she could not have learnt more. But when you listen continuously, it is stored somewhere within you and you unconsciously start using it. It is very important to listen to the songs because your brain starts filling up like 'storehouse'. All this learning and listening emerges in good times like during performance. This is the essence of creativity. Singing is a god's gift, but one certainly will have to take the training of *sur-taal* and the *guru*'s blessings in this field is crucial. She mentioned that whenever there was an occasion to perform, she is always foremost in the remembrance of her *Guru*.

When asked if she was asked to sing songs of her choice, and what song she would select, she stated that she liked to sing what her husband liked. She mentioned that her husband whom she lovingly called "Sahab" always inspired her to sing.

She mentioned that to be a good artist you have to be a good human being. One should never indulge in pettiness. Artists should be in continuous practice, they should have a versatile oeuvre, as one has to sing from varied forms in different platforms with a good sense of *'sur-taal'*, as audiences vary. An artist has to work hard to connect with the audience. Prabhati Ji felt that it is the Almighty's blessings that her singing is liked and well-appreciated; and those disciples who respond well, she reaches out to them to bring out their best in them. She mentioned that she was a traditionalist and did not like improvisation in established notations.

At the end of the interview, she said that some of her disciples were singing very well. Her wish was that her daughter measured up to the standard of excellence she expected. Prabhati Ji extended her best wishes to all new artists and appreciated my efforts, which she felt would help new and upcoming artists.

*****

Born: 11th December in Kolkata

Parents: Badal Chandra Mukharjee, Shubharani

Spouse: Pradipta Shankar Bhaduri

Children: Tanaya Bhaduri, daughter

Book: "Yaaden" authored by Prabhati Mukherjee

Award: President Award and many other Awards.

The Legend - Pandit Ajoy Chakrabarty

PANDIT AJOY CHAKRABARTY

EMERGING FROM ITS SOURCE AT GANGOTRI, RIVER GANGA MEANDERS through the plains of UP and Bihar, before entering Bengal with its beautiful gift of *thumri*. Accordingly, Bengal has embraced *thumri* with tremendous affection, personified in legends like Pandit Ajoy Chakrabarty.

Pandit Ajoy Chakrabarty is a doyen of Indian classical music belonging to the Patiala *Gharana*. His father, Pandit Ajit Chakrabarty, was his first *guru*, who imbibed in him the mantra of perceiving music everywhere, in all animate and inanimate creation of the Almighty. Subsequently, he learned music from legendary Guru Pt. Gyan Prakash Ghosh and Ustad Manawwar Ali Khan, son of Ustad Bade Ghulam

Ali Khan. Pandit Ajoy fulfilled his father's dream to dedicate his life to music and to have that constant yearning for knowledge of music.

Pandit Ajoy Chakrabarty remarked in his interview that good voice and humbleness are key to excellence in this field. He further said that while singing, we should be focused on *Raaga*-literature and rendition. Espousing further, he said that your cultural moorings and education invariably impact your perception towards everything in life.

We asked about his views on creativity. With a smile he remarked that creativity has a multitude of dimensions but the crux of it is that it's a function of the depth and span of your knowledge and your open-mindedness towards others. Accepting the learnings offered by others without inhibition or ego, all this enables an artist to grow further and beyond sharpening his innate creativity. Pandit Ajoy Chakrabarty emphasized equal command on both music and literature.

Being a trend setter Pandit Ajoy Chakrabarty is a man endowed with a very generous personality. He says that it's not inappropriate to think about one's own family and career, but one should not be limited by such restrictive thoughts or approach; one should reach out to talents beyond the confines of family and try to contribute to their growth, too.

On *Gharana* tradition, he acknowledges its uniqueness while also delving on its limitations at the same time, stressing that one should always strive consciously to develop his or her own identity. On finding the path to growth and success, Pandit Ajoy Chakrabarty said that every artist, without exception, starts his/her career with struggle, pointing out to the severe financial crises his family suffered. High motivation and dedication to music was a constant in his family; these attributes sustained them and helped them forge ahead. Remembering his father, who one said, "if you are my son, you will have to become a singer; otherwise you are not my son," Pandit Chakrabarty emphasized cultivating an affection for one's profession.

While underscoring the importance of continuous *riyaaz,* Pandit Ajoy Chakrabarty made this profound observation that practice makes an artist and intelligence sets the artist apart. He further says that it is very important to train and strengthen your voice in order to make it a durable vehicle for sharing one's art with the world for a long time.

He is a gold medalist from Rabindra Bharti University and a very good table-tennis player too. After doing his Master's from Rabindra Bharti University, he joined ITC Sangeet Research Academy in March 1978 as its first resident scholar. This association with ITC-SRA allowed him to flourish and explore his own identity as an artist. For the first time, he got to perform on stage in 1978. At the age of 27, he went to America for a performance.

In 1979 Pandit Ajoy Chakrabarty married Chandra Bose. Chandra Ji created a world of love, harmony, and happiness with the help of the modest amount of stipend that her husband received. Thus, she became the greatest support of his life. He admitted with pride that his wife is the backbone of *Shrutinandan*.

"Shruti Nandan Institute" established by Pandit Ajoy Chakrabarty in Tollyganj is a center of excellence for learning and training in music and a manificent labor of his love. This highly acclaimed institution was bound to have a sterling presence given the thought behind establishing it and the persona guiding it. The first and foremost artist to train and impart the knowledge of music to students, helping them emerge as budding artists. Simultaneously, he also sought to make the rendition of classical music of a certain genre accessible to the general public. This institution, dreamt and conceived by Pandit Ajoy Chakrabarty, is a thriving place serving the founder's objectives.

Pandit Ajoy Chakrabarty is a doyen of Indian classical music belonging to the Patiala *Gharana*. His father, Ajit Chakrabarty, was his first *guru*, who imbibed in him the mantra of perceiving music everywhere, in all animate and inanimate creation of the Almighty. Subsequently, he learned music from legendary Guru Pt. Gyan Prakash Ghosh and Ustad Manawwar Ali Khan, son of Ustad Bade Ghulam Ali Khan. Pandit Ajoy fulfilled his father's dream to dedicate his life to music and to have that constant yearning for knowledge of music.

On being successful in life, he is of the view that 'success' is a gift that we give to ourselves with hard work. No one can push anyone into becoming successful because success is a journey that one eventually undertakes on the strength of one's own merits and commitments.

He expressed his views on lifestyle and how the relationship of *Guru-shishya* bond should be nurtured. On the traits of a good artist, he said that correctness of musical notes reflects the purity of your heart.

When he was asked about how upcoming artists can overcome their fear and nervousness , he said that knowledge and hard work are the only ways to overcome one's fear and hesitation. Your family environment, upbringing and training all play a vital role in making you confident. He further said that some nervousness to a degree may be a positive trait as it helps the artist to focus and thus perform better.

Like her father, his illustrious daughter Kaushiki Chakrabarty is an outstanding singer of Indian classical music as well as *thumri* and *dadra* from Patiala Gharana, and his son Anjan Chakrabarty is an established sound engineer. The entire family is down-to-earth and committed to their passion of furthering the cause of classical music in their own unique way.

At the end of the interview, he said that a singer's quality of voice should be steady and uninterrupted with a smooth finish. IIT Kharagpur has conceived an Academy of classical and folk Arts, under the aegis of Pandit Ajoy Chakrabarty. He has started training the IIT students to develop scientific/technological research with the aid of Indian classical music and explore its varied dimensions.

Born:	25 December 1952, Kolkata
Spouse:	Mrs. Chandana Chakrabarty
Awards:	National Film Award for best male playback singer, Sangeet Natak Academy award for Hindustani classical vocal, Padma Bhushan and many more.
Children:	Kaushiki Chakrabarty and Anjan Chakrabarty
Year Active:	1977-Present

When I was trying to reflect upon my interactions with the various stalwarts, I realized that there were certain things that became very clear right at the very outset. Irrespective of the *gharana* they belonged to, all of them pointed them out. Apart from excellent guidance and thorough *riyaaz*, there were certain psychological factors they believed made them a healthy and balanced personality: a primary requirement for great artists. Hereditary, exposure, family support, and various developmental factors were some of the strong psychological pillars which helped them to emerge as successful artists in their lives.

Most of the stalwarts with whom I had an opportunity to interact had parents, either one or both, who were maestros themselves in their field. They said that all of them got a chance to listen to music from their childhood. Perhaps it would not be an exaggeration to say that most of them had heard classical music when they were in their mother's womb itself. Research has also suggested that genetics play a major role in the field of arts as well. Tan, McPherson, Peretz, and Berkovic (2014) overviewed behavioral and molecular genetic approaches (the ones commonly used in human genetic analyses). Literature has suggested different genes that have been implicated in music perception, music memory, and music listening.

Along with this, the role of environment and exposure is also extremely important. The stalwarts in the present case have also claimed that they were provided with a music friendly environment, regular interaction and guidance from various artists who would usually visit their parents. Thus, from childhood itself a lot of attention was paid to them.

It would be important to note here that most of the artists who have been interviewed here, come from the times when the country was not stable economically. Life was comparatively easy for those whose parents were singers in royal courts and thus had money due to patronage to support their families. Others had to face a lot of economic struggle while growing up, which they overcame to make their mark. Apart from learning music, all of them had a formal education in schools and colleges which, they believed, had an important role to play in widening their perspective towards things and life in general. They got the opportunity to meet other people and students from all kinds of backgrounds which immensely contributed to their personality and these experiences were reflected in their music as well. For those, whose parents were established artists themselves got an opportunity to perform both in the country and abroad. Even if they didn't accompany their parent abroad, they said that they had a lot to learn from the discussions after they returned. It opened them to a new world of experiences, which helped them immensely in their growth as an artist. Some of the artists also had the privilege of getting an opportunity to sing alongside their parents at the royal court or on a major, respectable platform. They believed that whatever be the circumstance, performing, not performing, whatever be the stage, these events and moments acted as an inspiration for them which kept the spark alive. They shared how some of them had a chance to witness a competition between two artists at the court and intellectual debates which nourished their young minds and became a part of their personality. Stalwarts acknowledged that they got inspired from their parents' fame, glory and respect. It motivated them to learn better and spend more time on their *riyaaz.* Some of their parents exposed them to audience and outside world gradually by initially allowing them to play *tanpura,* while the parent was preforming and gradually they would let their child participate in the performances subtly. This would also help them in dealing with stage fright, facing the audience and any other insecurity associated with it.

Some of the other artists that we interviewed are also extremely successful, but unlike some their parents were not musicians themselves. It was their interest in music due to which they would invite other artists to their home for *baithak*s and that would act as stimulation for their children. So, here it was very clear how the parents gave or created a conducive environment for their children. Very much like any other formal education, they would send their children to various artists to learn the art and its nuances. They would invite different artists so that their child would get an exposure of different tones, melodies, *raga-ragini,* styles, and presentations. These *baithaks* would satisfy their interest while strengthening the *artist personality* of their child. There were some who were not singers themselves, and did not know much about *thumri,* but they made it a point to focus on their children's *taaleem* and ensured that their child received quality education from eminent artists in the field. An interesting thing about learning from an eminent artist was that these artists would perform very often which would give their disciples an opportunity to accompany them on stage. This worked very well for their self-esteem and self-confidence as budding artists.

Irrespective of the family background – musical or non-musical – a conducive, encouraging, and stress-free family environment is important for a child to work, make his own beliefs, and find a purpose in life. Family or parental support has been emphasized by almost everyone and they believed that they couldn't go ahead and be successful in its absence. Another significant aspect shared by the artists was focus and attention to detail that is required in music. They believed that in order to make full use of one's education, one needs to calm his/her mind. For instance, in order to combine two or more *ragas* for a *thumri,* attention to beat, time, emotion involved in it, and its literature, everything has to be looked at carefully.

Another interesting aspect to point here is the conscious effort of the parents in personality development of their child. The beliefs that are formed as a child go a long way. If the child feels inferior during his/her early stages in life, and has low confidence and esteem due to comparisons made with superiors or others, this impacts the personality of the child eventually. Although the development of personality is a life-long process but it is essential to have a healthy foundation which develops during the childhood (Soto *and* Tackett, 2015). For instance, a painful experience can impact the personality negatively but if channeled and dealt with properly, it can become strength as well.

Indian classical music also teaches that learning is never for an immediate gain or use. It gets stored in the subconscious of the individual and slowly along with various other experiences (mixed together) reveals itself and its colors to enhance the personality and experiences of the individual. For instance, it is not necessary that every practice culminates into something amazing or "new"; sometimes the repetition is also necessary to pave way for something "new". Our stalwarts have described it as a sort of creativity in itself. Sometimes, they do not prepare for certain conditions in their rehearsals but it comes up during their stage performance, and that happens due to the practice they have had over the years. The practice and listening to other artists also gave them the confidence to sing that new phrase or piece without any hesitation or fear of being "wrong."

Some of the stalwarts have also pointed out that respect and communication styles in the families are important in cultivating certain beliefs and values. They have discussed how gender equality is important not just for the girl child to flourish but also for the male child to help and develop a certain mindset and personality which respects all human beings irrespective of their gender, caste, class or creed. Some of them have also shared how in certain families, especially a few years back didn't allow their girl child to learn or perform despite their talent as it was considered a taboo. The women stalwarts, I interacted with highlighted this a lot and felt angry over the state of affairs. They shared that they always encourage womenfolk and their colleagues to further encourage women to step into the art and enhance it further. Parveen Sultana, Annapurna Devi, Sitara Devi and her sisters are some of the exceptional examples wherein, despite societal retaliation, they learnt the art, performed it and proved as an institution in themselves.

With guidance, *riyaaz*, family environment, support etc. (as mentioned above) one can become a very good singer but for an artist and to sustain or maintain the seat in the longer run, some more aspects are required which we would highlight and discuss in the following chapters. All the stalwarts, I have interacted about these aspects, know them and strongly believe in them. It's just that they may not have used the psychological jargons to explain these qualities. We will discuss their views on these traits in the coming chapters.

CHAPTER 4

Singers in Stylistic Form

Aesthetic matters are fundamental to the harmonious development of both society and individual

– Friedrich Schiller

Singers in Stylistic Form

"ART" IS A DISTINCTIVELY HUMAN INSTITUTION BECAUSE IT FULFILLS A vital need of human consciousness, there are biological necessities but there are other needs as well such as aesthetics. "Aesthetic" is the philosophy of art which is particularly devoted to the "art experience" and "art appreciation." Perhaps, its beauty and love which propagates the real frame of what is called aesthetic. The word Aesthetic was first used by Alexander Baumgarten (1735) followed by Kant, which means sensory perception. It has been believed that sensual attractiveness provides the aesthetic experience. The beauty with which aesthetics are chiefly concerned is that which gives delight to the senses, the beauty of the intelligible objects live forever, F.E. Sparshott says: "Beauty is relatively stable or real pleasure" (The Structure of Aesthetics; 78).

Indian aesthetics studies the capacity of music or any art form, to transmit and stimulate or induce an emotional state in the performers and develop the same state in the thinkers. Thus, emotions also play an important part in the aesthetic experience. Beauty is the perception which is perceived and translated by the emotions. The combination of color and sounds, the sight of objects are absolutely sensational experiencing the emotions which gives joy.

Beauty to express itself as a perception requires an object. This object might be a person or a thing, music, poetry or even an idea. When it is an idea, emotion arises at the bidding of imagination. Thus, aesthetic emotion can be satisfied purely by the play of imagination. Aesthetic experience with beauty, like other experiences, include an emotional excitement. The beautiful may please the eye or ear. Here, beauty exists on two different levels: physical and mental. On a physical level, beauty is the subject of decay, on the mental level, it is lasting. And joy is eternally related to beauty. Joy is the base of aesthetic beauty and is sometimes considered as a spiritual experience. Apart from the natural objects, beauty springs from the plenitude of the human aesthetic soul and man realizes the true self in beautiful objects; he realizes the joy. It is an inherent processing of the soul. The perception of beautiful objects gives unique energy - *Jivan Shakti Oorja* (force of life). Things become more beautiful when they are combined with spirituality, when the art experiences elevate it from the physical plane to spiritual.

The aim of this chapter is to show how the stalwarts explored the aesthetic in the wider context of originality - clarity, emotion, feeling, love and beauty in their dressing, selection of compositions, renditions and in their overall musical journey. It can be termed as their aesthetic behavior which plays an important part in the perception of aesthetic beauty. Here, we will study aesthetics in terms of its outlook on personal and musical aesthetics.

Like any other artform, the practitioners of Indian music and dance artists are at expressing emotions and creating the aesthetic and "beauty." Indian thinkers and musicologists have gone a step further in declaring that Indian classical music (*Raga Sangeet*) is the most appropriate means for attaining aesthetic experience and delight and the most suitable path towards self-realisation or realization of the ultimate reality or truth. So, aesthetics in the Indian context righteously follows the base of *Satyam, Shivam and Sundaram* (Truth, Tranquility and Beauty). To be able to perceive truth or beauty in creation, calmness is essential. An agitated mind can neither see the truth nor can appreciate beauty. That's why *Satyam, Shivam, Sundaram* go together. The whole of creation is nothing but "Waves of Beauty" and these waves create a thrill, they wake up the sleeping consciousness.

Aesthetic and spirituality make up the basis of the Indian arts in general and *Raaga Sangeet* in particular. *Raga* and *Sangeet* is thus considered a spiritual exercise. (*nada sadhna*) to attain salvation *(Moksha)* through sound. Pandit Rajan Mishra during his interaction emphasized on the importance of creating music that is not only grammatically right but also aesthetically profound and emotionally enriching. Such an approach will definitely influence the learning and teaching process of music. Pandit Sajan Mishra added that "we create *bandish* to preserve *raaga* and genre, so it is essential to compose them aesthetically rich with the essence of spirituality. In the end, the ultimate goal is to reach salvation through music. Only then our students will learn them with full interest and the audience will prefer to listen. Above all we can do justice with our *Raagas."*

In the Indian context, artforms like music, dance, drama, architecture, painting etc., are mentioned in the earliest available work like the *Vedas, Puranas, Itihaasa* etc. Thus, it is a tedious task to correctly identify the historical advent of art forms. The earliest treatises dealing especially with the art forms and mechanism of art - experience known as "*Natyashastra*" are attributed to sage Bharata. The period is roughly from 5th century B.C. to 3rd century A.D. By this time, the art form is classified into three parts namely., poetry (*kavya*) , drama or theatre, (*natya)* and music *(gana).* We find classification of arts that includes stringing flowers, face painting etc. but the identification of these three arts, seem to enhance the study of the art experience, elevating it from the physical plane to spiritual. Even among these three, Bharata in the *Natyashastra* shows that the highest form of art experience is poetry and it can be well brought out by acting. The *Natyashastra* deals with the three main arts and defines the art experience as *rasa* and provides the mechanism of what came to be known later as "*Rasa*-experiences (discussed in chapter 6 and 7)." The word *rasa* can be identified with the word "aesthetics" of Western origin.

In a live performance, the audience is first captured by the external appearance of the performer - his/her personality, dress sense, style and accessories. The external beauty attracts first the sensual acuities and it has its own importance. All the stalwarts make their own signature style. Begum Akhtar and Girija Devi used to wear a diamond nose-pin, Savita Devi would put a big *bindi,* Prabhati Mukherjee put broad vermilion and a big *bindi,* Pt. Rajan-Sajan Misra are usually seen wearing the same *kurta* and *dhoti* when they are together and prefer to present themselves as natural as possible. Prof. Rita Ganguly is usually seen dressing her hair with a simple flower, which enhances her stage presence and appeal further. It adds a calm and spiritual demeanor to her personality. She herself reiterated that the artists' aesthetic is reflective of their personality which is expressed in their performance and their presence on the stage. Thus, it reflects their preferences and lifestyle as well. Lifestyle is considered a product of interaction of heredity, environment and creative power. So, the external appearance reflects the innate feelings, desires and aesthetic emotions of the human. The aesthetic emotion makes the idea fixed. It associates and relates one idea to another by the virtue of beauty. Pt. Ajoy Chakrabarty emphasized that *"Aesthetic is like a habit, which one develops with life experiences and family background. If one learns music just as a subject, one can't embellish it. It has to become a part of life, something the individual loves the most and that would determine the aesthetic of the individual."* He himself has a very polished aesthetic sense and is often seen wearing a gold chain and specs with a golden frame which adds a different and pleasant dimension to his personality.

At times, the sense of aesthetic is also inspired by certain viewpoints and thoughts that can be seen quite well in their lifestyles or their performances. For instance, Siddheshwari Devi, Begum Akhtar, and Bade Ghulam Ali were highly influenced by the Gandhian ideology of simplicity and calmness which also reflected in their demeanor. Despite this, the three of them had a very different stage presence. Siddheshwari Devi believed in leading a calm, quiet lifestyle with only paying attention to basic necessities of life. Her signature style of keeping a hand over her ear while singing especially during her *pukaar* - calling out to God, which one could hear in her songs left one astounded. The beauty of Begum Akhtar's recitals would lie in the fact that there were no unnecessary frills and thrills in her performance. She would stick to the emotion of the melody and would carve out the emotion accordingly without making it dramatic. Additionally, she would always prefer her *harmonium* besides her. Bade Ghulam Ali Khan Sahab was seen with his signature *Sur Mandal,* which he had invented himself. This would add a lot of charm and authority to his stage presence.

Prof. Rita Ganguly said that the lyrics of *thumri* should be capable of expressing the emotions (romantic, spiritual, pathos, affection, etc.). The lyrics should be open ended. Pandit Govardhan Mishra said, "if the lyrics are governed by the rules of meter of poetry, the singer won't have the freedom for improvisation. *In bol-banao thumri* for expressing different emotions, a singer can't adhere to the details of *talas* lavishly. It has its own aesthetic demand and these have to be met."

The work on music is traced to the pre-Bharat period. Dattila, a pre-Bharat aesthetician, seems to have recorded about 18 *jatis* (species of melodies) while dealing with music. Bharata, in the *Natyashastra,* deals with the *jatis* in connection with *rasa* and *bhava*. The work *Brihadesh* by Matanga is considered as the fore-runner of works on music. Matanga for the first time introduces the term *"raga"* from the root *"ranj"* to please. Another important work on music is *Sangeet-Makrand* by Narada. Here, based on emotional feelings or *rasa,* the *ragas* are divided as masculine (*raga*) and feminine *(ragini*). Pt. Kameshwar Pathak said that we listen to *thumri* or any sort of music to get happiness from it and also to understand it. To enjoy and understand the beauty (*Ranjakta*) of *raga* and the purpose of the lyrics, one has to attain a certain level of understanding of classical music.

Nature is considered the most important driving force among all the beautiful objects of the universe. The aesthetic perception begins at the perceptual level in particular, with seeing, meaning, touching and moving. Perhaps, there is nothing more effective than flowers in developing a sense of form, grace and delicacy; or there is nothing more inspiring than rivers, mountains, the field and forests. Bade Ghulam Ali khan used to do *riyaaz* on the banks of the river Raavi. Listening to the sonorous waters of the river inspired him, uplifting his spirit. He used to spend the whole night by the river bank. During those days, young Ghulam Ali developed a remarkable ability to interpret the effect of natural "sounds" and "silence" into his singing. The changing colors of the sky, the sparkle of the stars and the golden rays from the moon - all joined together to infuse a unique effect into his thought and emotions. His sensitive intellect could focus on the *ragas* he sang.

The greatness and majesty of nature can be experienced at every juncture when the season turns. Thus, there is no better school for aesthetic education than Nature herself. In a famous *chaiti* of Banaras gharana, *"chait maas chunri ranga de O nandi Gulabi-Gulabi"*, a lady requests her sister-in-law to get her a pink color shawl because *chait* is the month of pink roses and the artist combines her feelings with the natural beauty of roses. During the Vasant season female artists prefer yellow sarees and males generally prefer white or off-white dhoti kurta or kurta and white sherwani in almost all seasons. The color of the kurta or shawl may change. A legendary singer of *thumri,* Late Mauzuddin Khan Saheb used to take four hours for dressing up before every concert. Two lady beauticians and one male beautician used to help him get ready for the concert and he essentially used to prefer to reach the concert venue in *a bagghi* (horse carriage). During chait month (after Holi festival in March and throughout April), females prefer pink sarees and men essentially wear white dhoti and kurta. Between July and September, that is, during monsoons, ladies prefer green sarees and men wear green kurta or put green shawl on them. There is a clear preference for red, purple, or any dark heavy silk sarees during autumn months. Further, artists essentially wear white dress when they sing to pay tribute to any person. According to Aananda Coomarswami, a veteran of Indian art- the scope of stylistic variation was indicated. Coomarswamy brings out the accidents of art and how it is by transcending it that art becomes universal. Style is contingent not intrinsic (Raghavan, 1982). *Rama* was beautiful, despite the style of his hair which was according to the trend of his times. *Thumri* singers especially from *poorab ang* sing seasonal songs too, apart from *thumri* and *dadra*. During spring they will sing *vasant, hori* and *chaiti* apart from *thumri,* and *dadra*. During the rainy season, they will sing *kajri, jhula* apart from *thumri* and *dadra. Baramasa* is sung throughout the year. These songs are adorned with the lyrics which clearly depict the scenes of that season. The selection of compositions expresses their level of aesthetic sense. Along with the lyrics, the techniques used to improvise these compositions and pieces are also carefully selected. For instance, we can't end an improvisation of a softer phrase with a very fast *tihaai,* or while singing a *jhula* usage of *taan* is avoided and rather *meend* is used to depict the to and fro movement. A popular *jhula* is:

Jhula dheere se jhulaao banwaari,
arre Saanwariyaa na....

Here, the word 'na' is just used to embellish the lyrics of the piece. Like any other *jhula,* this one also uses the technique of *meend* a lot. Although all these techniques, even the ones discussed here, are not used in certain cases but are not wrong but their usage in these situations may sound too abrupt and would not fit the scheme.

Prabhati Mukherji emphasizes on practicing the vocabulary of *murki, khatka, meend, jamjama, taans etc.* The aesthetic of *thumri* is based on the *mizaj* (a state of mind, an attitude) of the singer apart from other nuances of music. Years of training are required before the voice is even ready to begin attempting *thumri gyan.* You have to convey tremendous amounts of convictions and emotions through your voice. You should have command of each word of lyrics and the words should become a part of your being and it is only possible through experience and good *taleem* and *riyaaz* (training and practice).

According to Dr. Shanti Hiranand, "A *thumri* singer must learn *tappa* because it enriches your voice culture. A student must practice e, o, u vowels along with 'a'. When vowels are combined, they ideally become long sounds. In North Indian music, the vowels are elongated to as much as is required for musicality (pleasing musical effect). Training of *Kaku* (vibrato) is a must for *thumri* singing. It helps in expressing emotions and embellishment. The *kaku* means modulation of sound in the intonation." This word implies flexibility.

Aesthetics try to defend and yet expand, enrich and yet refine our awareness and taste of the beautiful. Beauty is the quality of perception. A *thumri* singer usually gives emphasis on the beauty of emotions. The traditional singers (the realists) try to explore the beauty in its original form. Once "AppaJi" during an interview said that you could experiment with improvisation or *bol banao* but you cannot fiddle with its original form. We should consciously sing the *bandish* in true and original form to make it really blissful and also to restore the traditional *bandish* intact.

Once, when I was interacting with Pt. Govardhan Mishra, during a conversation, he spontaneously mentioned that one should never forget the purity and honesty and how these are the two basic requirements of aesthetics. We should follow these requirements while rendering a composition. This is easier said than done. You have to be egoless to attain such a level. Without surrender and purity of soul, you cannot adorn your music. Purity of *swara*, clarity of language, understanding the theme of the composition. These traits make you confident and cheerful from inside, which reflects on the surface of your rendition. Here comes the philosophy of *"Sat Chit Anand"* or *Sachhidanand.*

Once Savita Devi said that, "the original tune and lyrics of a composition should exist unaffected by time and space." We can relate to her statement with the "Truth-*Satyam.*"

You have to be utterly *'absent'* for pursuing a traditional art. Your very presence may distort the originality of the art because your 'presence' means the presence of your mind, your prejudice, your conditioning, your past experiences and learning. We have to restore this valuable art. It means virtue- *shivam* - all that is good and precious. Shivam is the action of truth. The disciple who comes to experience the truth starts living truth immediately, i.e. starts pure *riyaaz.* Bade Gulam Ali Khan Sahab believed that good means *"suddha mudra, suddha vaani."* He believed that the repeated practice of a particular phrase with purity and clarity helps in revealing its inner or hidden beauty and meaning. It is important to go deep in *swara* then only its effect would be understood. Khan Sahib always emphasized that to achieve the perfect union with the cosmos or divine melody, one requires years of rigorous *riyaaz,* which becomes a kind of *ibadat* of divine worship. The singer finds the music of the sphere within the depth of his own being. He said, *"toh riyaz ibadat ban jaati hai."* Through *riyaaz* an artist not just refines and enriches his musical skills and prowess, but it is also about deep introspection and connecting with the inner I. Musical practice embellishes the soul with grace of meekness, self-control and lowliness of mind - his living truth is *shivam.*

One of the most distinctive and vital functions of art is to present itself in concrete form, which is essentially an abstraction. The most fundamental abstraction is the element of a worldview. An artist's deepest values are experienced most clearly in the emotional form of a sense of life. A compelling work of art can touch the deepest places in us, feelings we often have trouble defining, naming or perhaps making explicit.

A composition of recognizable tones is music, random noise is not. Once I was composing a song for a concert and my *guru* Vidushi Savita Devi was listening from a distance. She told me that my composition shows my artistic dimension but it is not a pleasant decoration i.e. it cannot be used for the function of concertizing the deepest values and experiencing directly the equivalent of a sense of life. The composition will be judged by the audience. It's lyrics and tune should appeal to the masses while showing your aesthetic quotient.

Similarly, selection of *ragas* also has a major role to play in enhancing the aesthetic quality of the composition, experience and even the performance. This is because selected *ragas* have a desired effect on both the psyche of the performer and the listener. For instance, the constellation of *swaras* in *raga khamaj* is such that it depicts both separation and union very well. To depict lively and youthful scenes, *Raga Sahana* should be used, *raga Piloo and Kafi* are best suited for *thumri* and *dadra* and *raga Jogia* is useful for spiritual and devotional themes. *Raga Bhairavi* is another one suitable for *shringara,* pathos and spiritualism, but due to the bindings of time theory it is generally sung in the morning or evening, especially at the end of any performance. *Raga Dhani* portrays the image and personality of a happy and empowered woman and *Raga Sohini* is used to express accusation or complaint.

Pandit Ajoy Chakrabarti says a *raga* blooms when the mind and speech are in perfect harmony. The *Shadaja* or *Sa* (Do) is the earth or the sub-structure that holds a *raga.* Fired by inspiration, the emotion of *raga* is its cosmos. *Raga* is life. Like God is the divine vehicle of man's faith, *raga* is the melodic vehicle of man's imagination. A *raga* happens best when there is perfect communication between notes and thoughts between lyrics and melodic structure.

So *raga* has a vast kingdom. It has infinite colors to offer you to match your mood and fulfil your requirement for composition of song according to time, season and occasion. To do justice to the *raga* on aesthetic grounds, one has to understand the content and value of lyrics, the relationship between the mind and the *swara* and the aesthetic of melody, word and intonation.

There should also be some objective standards for the art. "Aesthetic objectivism" is a must when you compose something for listeners. Its beauty should be eternal. There should not be much differences in listeners' perception. It can't be subjective. It can't work on the theory of 'aesthetic subjectivism' that says that each person has his/her own sense of beauty. So, your lyrics, selection of *raga,* and *taal* (beats) should be aesthetically balanced. Legendary artist, Pandit Chhannulal Mishra said that the aesthetic of music includes lyricism, harmony, hypnotism, emotiveness and resonance. However, there has been a strong tendency in the aesthetic of music to emphasize musical structure as the most important element in the experience of music.

Once Pandit Govardhan Mishra said that the singer should give focus on *aamad* (indication to reach *SAMA*). It can be considered as the climax of embellishment because it gives the signal or anticipation of *sama. Sama* is the first beat of *taala.* It establishes a point of resolution or you can consider it as a pivot. It gives a musical release and in a way to reach the same is the goal of every singer and in between he shows his talent of improvisation for evoking emotions i.e., emoting *rasa* or to touch the unfold emotions of listeners.

Like aesthetic objectivism and aesthetic subjectivism, the other key pillar is "aesthetic relativism." It refers to how views on beauty are relative to differences in perception and consideration. They intrinsically have no absolute truth or validity. Thus, it denies any set standards of truth or morality and aesthetic judgment. According to relativism, there is no universal objective truth. One of the major categories of relativism is cultural relativism, the idea that a person's beliefs, values, ideas and practices should be understood based on that person's own culture. For example, in historical terms, the female form is depicted in Venus of Willendorf; and women in the painting of Rubens would today be regarded as overweight. On the other hand, the slim models on the covers of contemporary fashion magazines would no doubt be regarded in a negative light by our predecessors. In contemporary (cross-cultural) terms body modification among primitive people is sometimes regarded as grotesque by western society. There were certain musical maestros who were highly appreciated in their times for their skill and vocal ability but may not appeal much to the listeners now. This doesn't take away their credit from their ability. It is time, context, culture and sensibilities which matter in appreciation of art.

On the theme of openness to learning, Pandit Ajoy Chakrabarty says that the confinement of anything cannot last long. More than love, respect, rewards or money, everyone wants freedom. Poetry and music are the highest form of expression. And the highest form of freedom is freedom of expression. I find great joy in learning good things from others, even learning from youngsters is so energizing. It's a wonderful feeling. We found similar thinking in the case of Siddheshwari Devi ji. She was very progressive; always keen on learning new things but without losing touch with tradition. During her interaction, Dr. Shanti Hiranand said that she learns a lot from her disciple. Pandit Rajan Mishra said, "I keep listening to great artists' recordings and learn many good things from them." Other stalwarts also shared their views on openness to learning. Open individuals have been found to present a more positive aesthetic attitude and more interest in consuming art (Chamorro-Premuzic, Furnhum *and* Reimers, 2007, McManus & Furnhum, 2006).

Psychological aesthetics has primarily focused on one aspect of the aesthetic experience in the form of liking, pleasure and preference. Aesthetic association with personality, primarily openness/intellect, have focused almost exclusively on individual differences in liking different types of arts. There is an influence of openness and intellectual aspects on several different aesthetic emotions. Those higher in openness were particularly influenced by novelty and beauty in art works.

Extraversion is positively related to awareness of aesthetic objects (Alkan *et al.*, 2007). Agreeableness positively correlates with feelings of being touched by art (Silivia *and* Nusbaum, 2011) whole conscientiousness determined less interest in art in general (Chamorro-Premuzic et al., 2007, Mcmanus *and* Furnaham 2006). There have been some claims regarding an "artistic personality", whose openness and creativity leads to greater proclivity for aesthetic experiences (Chamorro-Premuzic et al., 2007). To appreciate the beauty of any art form like in the music (emotions, lyrics, selection of *ragas*, beat, way of presentation as well as artist appreciation) a person needs to have aesthetic quotient.

The reasons why an individual possesses specific stable aesthetic preferences are often studied by researchers (Furnham and Walker, 2001) but they have also started taking interest in the various abilities that are involved when evaluating art: Are we all equally "armed" to process aesthetic stimuli? Certain researchers have proposed a multi-content approach to this area, focusing on comprehensive assessment of what has been called the "Aesthetic Quotient" (AQ). It would include facets of aesthetic ability such as aesthetic balance, recognition, aesthetic exploration, art experience, sensitivity to complexity and aesthetic empathy. Rather than questioning the existence of AQ, various researchers have emphasized that, "T" (good taste) is to aesthetic ability what "g" is to mental ability. It has been understood that various sources of individual difference such as sensitivity to complexity, art knowledge, aesthetic empathy, attention, perceptual tendencies and exploration create a basis that enable individuals to process art. AQ has been defined as the global capacity to identify, explore, understand, seek stimulation and respond to the elements, composition and meaning of art and aesthetic objects. AQ has been considered as a useful scientific concept, notably in the prediction and explanation of creativity. Researchers suggest that AQ components are helpful in predicting various outcomes related to creativity- both the 'reception end' and 'productive end' of aesthetic stimuli.

As the discovery of g (general mental ability) indicates a factor that is useful to explain and understand scores pertaining to mental ability tests and also to predict various outcomes such as academic achievement; making similar point for AQ, we acknowledge that the idea that aesthetic judgment can be measured - better or worse, and consequently, individuals capable of making better judgment have better taste. It is rather a philosophical question.

Rules don't play any role in aesthetic judgment; hence it relies fundamentally on felt response to its object. It is not something that can be passed second hand on objects. It becomes necessary to define the target audience and almost handcraft the "experienceable properties" that may entice appropriate aesthetic response from the audience and delight them as well.

Artists believe that if the performers share the literature and the background on which the performance would be based, it helps the audience in relishing and appreciating the performance better and may help them in increasing their AQ. In order to go deeper, the performer should help in building the mood and communicating it through his music and also probably through sharing here and there, this enhances the interest in the performance and also helps the audience in relishing the subtle beauty of the art which is not skin deep.

Moreover, since the aim of art is to experience pleasure, the artist will try to reveal the hidden unities that may delight the mind. They may aim to penetrate the surface of common experiences and try to go deep underneath the mere obvious. Thus, both the performer and the audience along with him will go beyond the mere mechanism of imitation. The poet, for example, manifests latent emotional harmonies among the most widely subdued things.

The singer sometimes enters into the soul of humans, into the private and individual realm by their songs (music) uncovering the hidden connections among thoughts, feelings and impulses. Any great art work revives and re-adapts with time and space. Perhaps one of the measures of its success is the extent to which it makes the artist and its audience an inhabitant of that world, which would invite the artist and especially the audience to let breathe in its strange and special air.

Looking at the views of stalwarts on aesthetic of music or *thumri* it is clear that it is a combination of the aesthetic aspects of the constituents that give the whole its beauty. It is therefore not possible to separate out and examine these aesthetic factors individually.

CHAPTER 5

Understanding Emotions in *Rasa* and *Raga*

Music is an emotional experience, and that is what imprints itself on the soul. I think for me, any great art is art which communicates human emotion.

- Greg Lake

Understanding Emotion in *Rasa* and *Raga*

Raga and *rasa* are like cause and effect and have been a fascinating area of interest in both music and psychology. The term *raga* in the musical sense came to be used when it was discovered that a group of notes with a specific frequency roused a particular feeling. Added with the background of *shrutis,* the emotion or the effect of *raga* was clearly perceived and this marks an important landmark in the history of Indian music. The idea of *rasa* is one of the most fundamental concepts in Indian aesthetics. The drone, i.e. the meter through which the frequency relationships of notes are established, is of great importance since the interrelation of the notes of a *raga* determines its *rasa*. Music is rightly styled in the language of emotions. *Rasa-bhava* through music is an experience which has a psychological basis.

Emotions are considered to be one of the most fascinating features of the human mind and music as they add an extraordinary character of expression to it. Understanding the special integration between the two may take us closer to understanding the fundamental nature of both. No art stirs the emotions as deeply as music.

In order to study music and emotion, it is imperative to understand the psychological relationship between the two. It is the branch of music psychology which investigates numerous areas including the nature of emotional reaction to music, how characteristics of the listener determine which emotions are felt by him/her and which component of a musical composition or performance may elicit a certain kind of reaction. The field draws upon and has important implications for areas such as philosophy, musicology, music theory and aesthetic as well as the acts of musical compositions and performance.

"If scent has a hotline to memory, it seems music has a hotline to emotion."

– sync project.co

Music has the power to stimulate strong emotions within us, perhaps, to the extent that it is probably rare not to be emotionally impacted by music in one or the other way. The mechanism through which music evokes emotions is a rich field of research, yet there are several unanswered questions. Do we perceive emotional information in musical features? Why do we feel the urge to move when listening to music? By adding to the scientific understanding of the universal as well as the individual principles behind music-evoked emotions, we would better understand the effects that music can have on us.

Perhaps the primary reason for listening to music is its capacity for evoking and evolving our emotions. It has been reported that music is capable of evoking the full range of human emotions ranging from sad, nostalgic to happy, relaxed, calm and joyous. Correspondingly, neuro-imaging studies have shown that music can activate brain areas that are typically associated with felt emotions - the limbic, the amygdala and the hippocampus as well as the pathways that transmit dopamine (for pleasure associated with music listening). The relationship between music and the dopaminergic pathway could be a highly plausible reason behind the chills that many people report experiencing while listening to music. There are visible physiological reactions that people have reported like goosebumps and the common experience of "shiver down your spine" that accompany intense, peak emotional experiences.

Researchers have found that the amount of activation in the brain areas associated with reward and pleasure predicted how much money a person would be willing to spend on a new and unheard piece of music.

However, one doesn't always listen to music to be moved - sometimes people use music for other effects as well. For instance, many people listen to music to help them concentrate or do better in certain cognitively demanding tasks. In spite of this, it is believed that many of the cognitive benefits people experience from music itself range from goosebumps to just getting a simple task done. The way that music may 'strum' or 'pluck' your emotions perhaps are at the root of why it helps the way it does.

A very important question and an equally relevant research area is the exploration of how something that is nothing but just an organized pattern of sounds may bring us to tears. Scientific investigation of the possible mechanisms behind emotions evolved from music is a rich field of inquiry within psychology and the neuroscience of music. Researchers also speculate that music may convey emotional information by activating what is called the mirror neuron system (i.e. supporting the idea that emotions are contagious).

Emotional pain results in the release of prolactin - a hormone that generates feelings of gratification and relaxation. It is one thing to assert that sounds and visual perception can be passed through the amygdala to produce a non-cognitive appraisal and the corresponding physiological response and another thing to claim that beliefs can be processed in this same way. Before giving any emotional response, even reading fiction requires a basic conceptual and linguistic understanding of the reading material. There is substantial reason to think that the appraisals generated by works of literature may be rather different than those involved in, for example, a startle response.

There has been a mention of "jazzercise effect", It is believed that one experiences the physiological aspect of an emotion without or before making the effective assessment that is appropriate to it. Robhinson's account of emotion is based on extensive psychological and neurological studies of emotions like fear, where the stimulus for the emotion is a visual or auditory event such as a love, startle or a threatening shape and motion (fear). However, perhaps the greatest gift of music lies in its capacity to allow people to experience emotions without being buried under the burden of experiencing the life events that lead to them. We can experience even extreme emotions in a controlled manner in comfortable musical circumstances.

Emotions may alert us and grab our attention, protecting us from dangers, when we experience fear and should run away. They may also assure us, we feel joy when we are safe and nourished after a meal. Understanding and reacting to our emotions is how we function; perhaps no other sense has played a larger role in deriving emotional cues from our environment than sight. As far as listening to music and feeling emotions is concerned, the role of auditory systems becomes all the more important.

Studies using functional MRIs reveal that some regions of the brain involved in experiencing emotions are activated when shown aesthetically pleasing art. The emotions stimulated by art are not necessarily intentional or planned. They could be individual and culture specific. Philosopher William Lyons points out that a Japanese viewer of the white Turkeys depicted in Monet's *"Turkey at Montgeron"* may experience a sense of sadness or melancholy since white is associated with death in that culture.

Despite the very obvious differences between looking at Monet's woman with a parrot and listening to Elgar's cello concerts, both experiences provoke similar questions in the thoughtful aesthete: Why does the painting seem to express reverie and the music, nostalgia? How do we experience the reverie and nostalgia of such works of art? Why do we find these experiences rewarding in similar ways? Our awareness of emotion in art and our engagement with art's emotions in something that an aesthete may tell you makes a special contribution to their life. So, it is timely for a philosopher to strive to account for the nature and significance of the experience of art's emotion.

In psychology, the relationship between art and emotion has recently been subject of extensive study and the credit for it goes to the intervention of esteemed art historian Alexander Nemevor. Emotional or aesthetic responses are often regarded as the keystone to experiencing art and the creation of an emotional experience has been argued to be the basic purpose of artistic expression.

Robinson (2005) wrote about some of the most controversial topics in the philosophy of art, the role of emotion in music. There are three main topics addressed here—what it means to say that music "expresses emotion", the role of emotion in understanding and appreciating music and how music produces emotions in the listeners. In each case, Robinson takes on the dominant theories in the field and uses the differences between emotion in response to art and real life emotions that we experienced. Emotions, according to Robinson, focus our attention on "things in the environment significance to me or mine" and "it gets my body ready for appropriate action." The physiological change produced in an emotion serves the evolutionary function of directing our attention in appropriate ways such as reorienting one's body to get visual information about the stimulus, as Robinson argues happens in startle responses. Robinson claims that the same happens when reading literature.

Treatises on music in Sanskrit and vernacular written during the ancient, medieval and modern period exist, but very few of them have dealt with this subject at length. The subject of *rasa* in music has not received as much attention as *rasa* in literature and drama. When we talk about interaction between art and emotions, especially in Indian context, one of the major contributions was given by Bharat Muni, who was the first to write on this topic. He had written about theater of which music was a major and integral part at that time and continues to be so. *Natyashastra* or the science of theater is said to have been authored by Bharat muni sometime between 200 BC and 200 AD. *Natyshastra* devotes itself mainly to theatre, dance and music. But, it also touches on the related areas of cultural life of India. He had coined the concept of *Bhava, Vibhava, Anubhava and Rasa* in his studies.

In a composition, through the sphere of art music, the composer is primarily concerned with the portrayal of the *raga bhava* in all its rich and colorful aspects and not with the *rasa* aspect. However, when a composer writes a song belonging to the sphere of applied music, the position is different. The *sahitya* herein is an important factor and emphasizes a definite idea. The music which clothes the *sahitya* is a powerful contributory factor in determining its *rasa* and is in consonance with the spirit of the idea expressed. The tune is composed with a *rasa* conscience. Factors like pitch, intensity, timber, language, form, grace, rhythm are also major contributors in establishing the *rasa*. The emotional effect of *raga* is dependent upon the frequency of the notes that enter into its formation and also on its *vaadi, samvaadi* and *nyasa* (mainly used to end the *raga*) *swaras*. The *vaadi swaras* are the quintessential components giving life to the *raga*. Another way to express the *bhava* of a *raga* is through its *pakada*, which is a cluster of *swaras* that brings out the *raga bhava* or *raga's* essence or mood.

Bhava or to emote is the essence of literacy and performing art. *Bhava* refers to the 'becoming'. In other words, everything (objective or material) that can exist or comes into existence is *bhava*. Going by this simple understanding, the state of mind and even material conditions like birth and death or growth and decay are *bhava*. This understanding can be extended to artistic creativity. The feeling and thought process are the direct outcome of the state in real life and at the same time, attributes like place, time, action, movement, gesture, posture etc. can also be defined and described as *bhava*. The only difference that needs to be acknowledged is that in real life, 'becoming' is more due to direct implications of what we call the law of causation. This means that something that has happened leads to a particular *bhava* and with reference to artistic creativity, it is the artist who influences it using the sheer power of their imagination and creativity.

The artist does this by creating situations, incidents, characters and infusing attributes like feelings, thoughts, actions etc. It would be termed as the process of 'becoming' with reference to artistic creativity more as induced or caused and not as a production of material things. In this light, Bharat Muni's coining of the term *Nispatti* should be more interpreted as *Samaritti* which is basically the process of creating intellectual awareness of an emotional experience through the means of *Vibhava* and other factors in the minds of *Bhavaka* or the spectator. This only leads to the conclusion that whether it is a mental or material state, *bhava* means nothing but depiction of consciousness as rightly put by Bharat Muni *"Bhavayatiiti Bhava"* and in this context, relating *Bhava* with the expression artistic creativity is very much justified.

Till now we have discussed the relationship of art and emotion and the concepts of emotion given by Bharat Muni and other theorists. Now we will discuss the influence of emotions as described by our stalwarts.

Music without emotions is like a body without soul and the most prominent aspect of *thumri* is expression of emotions. It is an art that is completely based on emotions, its expression, presentation and the total package. Siddheshwari Devi had a quality of creating an atmosphere of intense pathos and anguish when she would sing *viraha*, extreme love when she would sing *vatsalya* and complete devotion, surrender and submission when she would sing *Bhakti*. This has been agreed over again and again by her audience, various music critics, stalwarts and musicologists.

While singing *Vatsalya*, once she created such an atmosphere when her audience actually could feel the anxiety of Mother Yashoda who was imploring Krishna to return home as evening had descended (*Sanjh bhai ghar aao nandlala)*. She could easily connect to the pain of Yashoda who was concerned for her young son. This could have been generated from her childhood experience wherein she had experienced the pain of a child who was separated from her parents and matured earlier than her age to care for everyone in the household. She was the sister, companion and guardian to Kamleshwari. Thus, she could very well relate to the other side also wherein she would be the mother waiting for her child earnestly to come back safe and sound. Interestingly, the impact of her rendition was such that one of the female listeners in the audience got up and apologized to Siddheshwari Devi for her apparent 'rudeness' as she wanted to leave the hall and go back home to check if her son was home or not.

The famous poet Jayashankar Prasad would often say that she would successfully hide her sorrows behind her laughter and her pain was reflected in her music. This pain that she portrayed was definitely a reflection of her life, her childhood separation, and her physical and emotional injuries. The early encounters with pain and hurt lived with her but she would always look for silver lining in the dark sky which definitely speaks of the strength of her character and personality as an individual.

Through Draupadi's pleas for Krishna (*Manmohan Murari, shyamsudh lo hamari*), she recreated the ecstasy of union and agony of separation (*viraha)*, fulfillment of spirit and yearning for love. Her lonely childhood perhaps found a companion in Krishna. She would tease and cajole Krishna through her *thumris* and *bhajans.* She herself would say, "I have been a *virahini* since my birth pleading to the Lord to accept and assimilate me into him."

Once, when I was sitting with my *Guru,* she started telling me how the experience of pain leaves an impact on an individual's life. While taking her own experience and example, she told me how she felt that her voice has gained more depth and sincerity after her son's death. She also recollected how her mother and *guru,* the *thumri* queen Maa Siddheshwari Devi would tell her, *"Chot naa lage to rooh ki ghiza nahi aati"* (Pain acts like food or nutrients for the soul). It was after the tragic incident of her son's death that my *guru,* Savita Devi could understand *Maa's* words completely.

It has been believed that pain extends beyond tissues and hurts feelings. It includes distress, existential angst and grief. There is a saying in Tibetan, "tragedy should be utilized as a source of strength." In the case of Begum Akhtar too, pain shaped her personality and had a huge impact on her music. As Dr. Shanti Hiranand (Begum Akhtar's disciple and biographer) recalls in her work *Ammi,* Begum Akhtar is one of the greatest examples of how personal tragedy could be the differentiating edge between a great performer and a truly exceptional one which Begum Sahiba was.

The early trauma of Begum Akhtar's life resulted in the singer being consumed by melancholy. She always felt a deep vacuum in her life. As soon as she started performing publicly, she fell in love with a certain Ali, a landlord from Gaya, who deceived her. She had admitted that he was the only man she had ever loved in her life. This would have had a lasting impact on the young singer's music whose *gayaki* was filled with depth and pain right from the beginning. She herself believed that this heartbreak had an indelible impact on her mind. This would have definitely helped her in bringing life to the great piece, *"ae mohobbat tere anjaam pe rona aaya."*

Once while teaching Shanti Ji, she was singing a *thumri "abke saawan ghar aaja"* and suddenly burst into tears and said, "You are too young to understand these things." This reflects how an artist engages with the melody in order to evoke the emotions. The experiences are reflected in the song that the singer sings. *Begum Sahiba* felt that being a young girl who was protected from the world, Shanti Ji would not be able to understand the plight of a woman who is yearning to see her beloved and wants him to come back home to her at least this monsoon season.

The death of Begum Akhtar's mother in 1950 took a toll on her emotional and physical health. Her husband Abbassi Sahab would recall that she would sit and weep endlessly. She was completely absorbed in pain and became hysterical. One of her physicians advised him to tell her to start singing again. Perhaps music would help her to come out of the grief or perhaps this would become a reason for her to connect with her pain and come in contact with her reality. Music possibly also served as a bond that connected Begum Akhtar with her mother. Abbassi Sahab allowed her to resume her music in a bid to bring her out of her terrible depression. She had renewed her contacts at the radio station and resumed her career again. The strength of experience also lies in the pain. It's a feeling that, when embraced, wakes us up. It is the reality of a person and connects one to their true self.

Pain was her inspiration. She would live a wily life of a tragic courtesan to evoke those feelings in her song. It perhaps helped her create heart-breaking music. It was like an inner dichotomy which she lived and endured. Shanti

Ji recalled, "Ammi would waver willingly on the edge of an anticipated heartbreak and wallow in imagined sorrow with such cruel intensity that it was frightening." While singing, her voice would crack at a particular point which otherwise was a flaw but in her case was considered an added emotive. It would further give depth to her music which was drenched in pathos.

Rita Ganguly, another student of Begum Sahiba states in her book that her *taaseer* (soulful sound) was the result of years of "loneliness, pain, suppression and silence." Akhtar was a master of what Brecht called the 'alienation effect'; she had the ability to sing the saddest song with the brightest smile (2008).

This doesn't mean that an artist only has to go through tragic incidents in their life to create good music. Vidushi Girija Devi, fondly called *Appaa Ji*, very aptly puts it that the variety of experiences in an artist's life makes them gentle, practical and reasonable. An artist can't run away from experiencing a variety of emotions and shunning the reality of life. They connect with their surroundings and reality makes them mature enough to understand things in daily life and then this also elevates their music. The ups and downs, variety of experiences and circumstances help an individual in honing their perspective which is a must for both a counselor to understand his client and an artist to portray a character on stage.

Pt. Chhannulal Mishra feels that every day is new and comes with its own sets of hurdles and challenges and thus the mood and frame of mind is never the same. Even though the grammar of music or the *raga* remains the same, each time it's a new rendition because of the different mindset.

One of the stalwarts recounts how as a young adult facing certain challenges in life, he was advised by his friends to take refuge in alcohol to numb certain senses of his mind which could provide him temporary but immediate relief. He further shared that he did indulge in it but was once called by his father who was also his *guru.* He asked him if he had started drinking and the stalwart, although very scared, admitted to the fact. Then the *Guru* told him that he could teach him various *ragas* and melodies that would have the same impact on an individual as alcohol and the impact would be long lasting, satisfactory and definitely without any side-effects. The *shisya* (stalwart) tried this and never again felt the need to resort back to alcohol again. This could be the medicinal and calming impact of music on an individual.

Bade Ghulam Ali Khan believed that music embraces every possible emotion. Music can create a rainbow of various moods and feelings. In a private concert, his portrayal of *shringara* was mesmerizing wherein he started with *Raga Yaman,* as he himself was in a cheerful and elated mood. He started with the words, *"Saajan gal baahin, aindi aindi dole, mori chunariya, saajan ki peeli pagariya, ulajh rahi kaise."* (with his arms around my neck I am showing off and as though I'm walking on the thin air. My multi-colored scarf and his yellow turban have got entangled.). Through the *raga,* he would create ever new romantic patterns as though he was building a magic castle with his *swaras* and *taans*. He himself said, *"my throat is like a paint brush and I paint on the waves of air with my voice. The swaras of the raga are my colors. It is like a painting created in the air, which is my canvas."*

He believed that during his *riyaaz,* he developed a remarkable ability to interpret effects of nocturnal 'sounds' and 'silence' into his singing. The changing colors of sky, sparkle of stars and golden rays from the moon all joined together to infuse a unique effect into his thoughts and emotions. His sensitive intellect could focus his thoughts into the *raga* that he sang.

Talking about how the emotion is induced and felt in a composition he said, *"when we 'create' a sur, we bring it out from the innermost depth of our being, by powerfully mixing our breath with sound. This requires a great deal of stamina and this is how the emotion also gets conveyed. This is kaar-karkhane-e-kudrath."*

Bade Ghulam Ali believed that music is a medium to communicate the innermost feelings through the *raga* and create a desired impact on the listeners in the process. He felt that music is not possible without emotions. In order to convey the emotion, one has to recognize and imbibe the purity and depth of the *swaras* and *shrutis*. He said, *"shuddh gayan se hi assar hota hai."* Music is an art of expression and can be put to use very well to understand and communicate emotion. It can become a screen to project inner longings and desires. When Khan Sahab's first wife Allah Jiwai died, he turned to music knowing it would be his only solace and savior in the hour of grief. He poured out his heart, soul and grief into the melody and the words came spontaneously as *viraha-shringara - "Yaad piya ki aaye, Yeh dukh saha na jaaye, Hai Ram."* Perhaps, even without being consciously aware of it, a *thumri* came into being. Another heart-piercing *thumri* that became famous and which also reflected the loss of his wife was: *"Aye na baalam, kaa karoon sajni. Rovat rovat kalnaaparat hai, yaad aavat ab unki batiyaan."*

Emotional self-awareness is an important factor in emotional intelligence and can be seen here very well. Ghulam Ali seemed to be a person who could perceive and understand his emotion and also manage it. His emotion became a threshold for him to create art. Thus, it promotes positive growth and well-being.

A *thumri* singer uses various *ragas* to depict various scenes and ongoing emotions. Khan Sahab would often use a bouquet of *ragas* to capture a scene and believed that the power of music is such that it all seems like a picture running in front of your eyes. His audience admits that he had a way to make them experience this. Another stalwart also reiterates the fact that *"thumri is like a bouquet of ragas, so a lot of times so many ragas are used to capture a particular scene and that becomes a sight to behold communicating all that is there in you."* Thus, music has the power to create any kind of imagery for its listeners and helps the artist in communicating their innermost feelings through the *raga, crafting* the desired impact on listeners and creating *rasa* in the process.

Music is impossible without emotions and to convey emotions, one has to recognize and absorb the purity and depth of both the *swaras* and *shrutis*. Understanding an emotion helps in delivering a particular composition and also feel the bliss created by that particular piece. Pt. Govardhan Mishra used to believe "in a composition of art music, the composer primarily is concerned with the portrayal of *raga-bhava* in all its rich and colorful aspects and not with just the *rasa* aspect. But when a composer writes songs belonging to the sphere of applied music, the position is different. *Sahitya* (literature) here is an important factor and emphasizes a definite idea. The music which imbibes the Sahitya is a powerful contributory factor in determining its *rasa*. Then the tune is composed with a *rasa* conscience. Factors like pitch, intensity, timber, form, rhythm, grace have a major role to play."

Carl Jung had said that speech is originally a system of emotional and intuitive sounds - sounds that express terror, fear, anger, love etc. Music as a combination of words and tune - *sahitya* and *sur* form the emotional symbolism of man's inner depth.

In *Abhinava Bharati*, the term *rasa* has been used in two different senses. At the first stage in the transcendental level, where the universalized object is realized by the universalized subject, *rasa* means the 'object of relish' (*rasayat eiti rasah*). Here, it is the basic mental stage that is relished, and hence it is *rasa*. On the second level, the basic mental stage sinks into the subconscious and there is the *ananda* aspect of the self-consisting of introversion and rest within itself. *Rasa* here means the act of relishing (*rasanamrasah*) (Deshpande, 1992) and that is the ultimate aim of the art and the artist.

Music is believed to be a great stress buster thus it can be concluded that it helps in promoting optimism and positive feelings. It helps in promoting mental and physical well-being for both the artist and the audience. The *swaras* used in *Hindustani* music are believed to have healing powers and thus encourage positive growth, change and well-being.

Both hope and optimism correlate positively and are predictive of physical and mental health. Reviews of research with adult singers have concluded that there are a range of health benefits of participating in a choir or any musical activity. These benefits include physical relaxation and release of physical tension; emotional release and reduction of feelings of stress; a sense of happiness, positive mood, joy, elation and feeling high; a sense of greater personal, emotional and physical well-being; an increased sense of arousal and energy; stimulation of cognitive capacities - attention, concentration, memory and learning; an increased sense of self-confidence and self-esteem; a sense of therapeutic benefit in relation to long-standing psychological and social problems (Clift *et al.*, 2008). Evidence has been provided that singing in harmony with others is particularly beneficial. It may help people cope with and recover from daily stresses as well as mental illnesses such as depression. It can help people in making them believe in themselves and relieve them of hopelessness. They can start setting meaningful goals for themselves and then develop ways to achieve them. Motivational and encouraging factors could be the lyrics of the song, applause and appreciation from others, sense of achievement in self, satisfaction of doing something, maybe just being with others and getting encouraged by them or the calming, healing and therapeutic impact of music being sung and heard.

We can use the emotional experiences of stalwarts for increasing the emotional adjustment in the upcoming generation. This might help them in coping with various situations in their lives.

Adolescence is a period when physical changes occur which have a huge impact on their psychological, emotional and social understanding. For instance, the children ask for independence in the process of decision-making with regard to their education, lifestyle, career and much more. The act seems irrelevant to both family, society, and other institutional groups. An adolescent, at this stage, looks for recognition and privacy. They prefer their friends over their parents and spend most of their time with their friends. Giving utmost importance to their physical appearance, at this stage, the new experiences provide them the opportunities to become more responsible individuals to benefit themselves and the society as a whole.

The indifferent behavior may have a negative impact, and would further build a bad impression in the minds of the parents. With an urge to maintain privacy in all their matters, they hide their abnormal behavior from their parents. This may lead to the development of an isolated behavior. Similarly, teachers and friends play an important role in outlining the personality of an adolescent. Teachers or their role models help them learn certain acceptable behaviors and habits. At times, the peer group induces the adolescents to experience risky behaviors and substance abuse. Smoking, drinking, teasing and even sexual experimentation is a common practice at this stage. These behaviors are reflected by them in the form of various emotions such as eagerness, anticipation, nervousness, and happiness. These emotions may create adjustment issues and may also impact their mental health adversely.

The term "adjustment" is literally used as an alternative expression for accommodation and adaptation. Specifically, the term represents the results of equilibrium, which may be affected by either of these processes (Monroe, 1990). It is also used to emphasize an individual's struggle to survive in his/her social and physical environment. In this regard several studies have been reported, especially in the domain of social, educational, health and emotional adjustment of school students of both sexes. Attempts have been made to relate adjustment with variables like intellect, achievement, age, sex, socio-economic status, needs, anxiety, and also security. Along with it, student's reaction to frustration has also been investigated. A few studies focused on the nature, causes, and extent of indiscipline among students. The relation between indiscipline and variables like achievement, participation in co-curricular activities such as music, drama, etc., have also been examined. A review of the studies carried out in the field of adjustment as reported in the three surveys of educational research edited by Buch (1991) reveals that no systematic attempt has yet been made to develop a tool for the assessment of adjustment problems of school students.

Oliva and Parra, (2001) investigated the influence of relationships with parents and peers on emotional adjustment in a sample of 221 boys and 292 girls. The results of this study have revealed that the peer attachment and parental support and affection promote emotional adjustment of both boys and girls, especially during middle adolescence. For older adolescents, peer relationships seem to be more important than parental support. Betsur Ningamma and Mahmoudi Armin (2010) studied whether self-esteem has any relation to adjustment among adolescents studying in class 9 in Mysuru, India. Two scales were administered on them - Bell's Adjustment Inventory (1968) (which measured adjustment of an individual in 4 areas - Home, health, social and emotional) and Self-esteem inventory developed by Coopersmith (1987), which measured self-esteem of an individual in 5 areas - general self, social self, home parents, lie scale and school academic.

The study revealed that home, parents and self-esteem had a seemingly positive influence over emotional adjustment of the students. The analysis revealed that higher self-esteem is better for adjustment. School, academic self-esteem also had a positive influence over the health adjustment of the students.

Achievement theorists have differentiated between two types of achievement goals that characterize a student's purpose for task engagement: performance goals, which focus on the presentation of the ability, and mastery of goals, which focus on the development of skills and abilities in an individual (Ames *and* Archer, 1988). Music as an art form, takes into account both the aspects very clearly. Due to music being a performing art, the presentation ability holds a lot of value, which is also linked with the skill set and techniques the individual learns throughout.

Later, a more elaborate 2 x 2 achievement goal model was suggested (Elliot, 1999) in which the mastery goal construct, as well as the performance goal construct, was branched in terms of approach and avoidance.

Thereby, the 2 x 2 achievement goal framework crosses the performance-mastery distinction with the approach - avoidance distinction (Elliot *and* Church, 1997). The performance-mastery distinction is interpreted as representing how competence is defined (according to a task-based or intrapersonal standard, respectively), and the approach-avoidance distinction is understood as representing how competence is seen as per the valences (according to positive possibilities or negative possibilities, respectively). This framework comprises four achievement goals: mastery-approach, performance approach, mastery avoidance, and performance avoidance.

A mastery goal refers to a striving to learn, understand, and improve skills based on an intrapersonal evaluative standard, while a performance goal is seen as an endeavor to outperform others and appear competent based on an interpersonal standard. Mastery-approach goals entail striving to do better than what one has done before or the way one has performed earlier, whereas mastery-avoidance goals require striving to avoid doing worse than one has done before (Van Yperen, 2006). These forms of regulation represent mastery goals because they focus on intrapersonal development; they represent approach and avoidance goals, respectively, because they focus on a potential positive vs. negative outcome. Many studies have revealed that a mastery goal orientation is associated with school adaptive pattern, such as having higher levels of self-esteem and self-efficacy (Middleton *and* Midgley, 1997) and persisting longer on difficult tasks (Elliott *and* Dweck, 1988) and greater educational adjustment (i.e., educational aspiration, frequent courses, homework frequency).

Performance goals are also related to the whys of students' learning. They are based on students' beliefs about what is significant in an achievement situation (Ames, 1992). Performance goals position the students to define and evaluate competence relative to others, to attribute outcomes to ability and to consider difficulty as interpretation of low ability. For example, a student may try to learn a foreign language and to display ability in that language.

This is best explained through a personal anecdote. My *guru* Vidushi Savita Devi would often tell me that practice is something through which one could spend the best time with someone they love or being loved the most, without much expectations or conditions. In due course of time, I realized that she was my best critic, never failed to find mistakes even from my best renditions and always made me feel the necessity to face unbiased criticism. She was this person who I could never satisfy with my singing and I wanted to remain like that because that would push me to strive for better. Whenever I would lose my focus or feel less motivated to practice, I loved to observe her and now remember her after her demise.

There is, however, some debate about whether these rather negative processes are associated only with avoidance or also with approach forms of ability goals and whether ability-approach goals are also associated with some of the positive outcomes (Harackiewicz *et al.*, 2002; Midgley, Kaplan, *and* Middleton, 2001). Regarding the consequences of engagement in learning, a greater educational adjustment has been found among students with high levels of engagement. For instance, students who report more positive emotions in class are more interested in school (Valleland *and* Bissonnette, 1992) and implicitly manifest more educational adjustment. Furthermore, high school dropouts have been found to be less persistent in learning activity (Valleland, Fortier, *and* Guay, 1997). However, the relationship between school adjustment and the different forms of engagement in learning has been less studied. As such we intend to study the relationship between emotional and behavioral engagement and educational adjustment operationalized by dropouts' intentions, absenteeism, homework frequency, and educational aspirations.

According to Daniel Goleman, emotional quotient (EQ) consists of self-awareness, self-regulation, motivation, empathy and social skills. Self-awareness is important as it ensures that our response to something is measured and appropriate, not flawed by the heat of the moment. Self-regulation is important to teach oneself calmness and when one is calm, other people around are reassured and motivated to take better and positive action. Motivation is getting a grip of 'why' you want something and requires self-reflection which is where high emotional intelligence has a role to play. Empathy is an important skill that helps us in taking another person's perspective and helps people around to be a part of your team and navigate difficult situations. Social skills are about the art of making an emotional connection with communication. Emotional intelligence in this case demonstrates that they respect the needs, fears, and hopes of other people around them.

Certain life skills help them to cope with their difficulties and develop an acceptable attitude within them. These life skills have to be nourished among adolescent school students in different ways and means such as discussion, role play which induces creativity among adolescent students. Teachers should promote group discussion among the school students to solve the problems being faced by adolescent students and enable them to draw suggestions for their personal improvement. This will, in a way, advance the problem-solving and the decision-making capacity of the adolescent school students. Adolescents need to analyze the real-life situations in the form of case studies which will help them to analyze the case studies in an objective manner. Further, this might work as a factor to enhance their critical thinking ability. In the larger scheme of the universe, each one of us has a musician inside us, with a unique tonal quality. What we may have in common, forges a mighty bond, that is, the desire to evolve and reach ultimate mastership in life through any medium.

Concluding this chapter with a beautiful example of high emotional intelligence of veteran thumri exponent and an outstanding Guru Padma Vibhushan Girija Devi. When she was asked at the age of 85 how doyen feels. It was a long journey almost of eight decades, you must have seen ups and downs related to finance, opportunities, family burden, and so on. Immediately she held my fore arms with tears. I can still feel the soft touch of her palm. She continued, your Nani Siddheshwari jiji could have given better reply. After nodding I deliberately gazed at the roof of the room and within seconds I found that she could manage her emotions very well and spoke in cheerful and firm way. Yes, I am very happy, with other stalwarts of thumri genre, I have also worked a lot for thumri, gave so many performances, taught so many disciples and in turn this genre, gave me immense honour, awards and respect, Good emotional balance is also a sign of confident personality. I am happy that you are interviewing me for your research work. I would like to convey my new sparks that these are learnable psychological traits. You can also be emotionally intelligent, emotionally balanced.

CHAPTER 6

Relevance of *Guru-Shishya Parampara* in Today's Times

"Thank you!! For enriching my life and widening my horizons. Without you, many aspects of my life would have been unexplored.

Relevance of *Guru-Shishya Parampara* in Today's Times

The *Guru-shishya parampara* is one of the unique features of Indian art traditions, especially in Indian Classical music. The *guru* is more than someone who teaches specific knowledge pertaining to a particular skill or art, and includes in its scope someone who is also a guide, counselor, a parental figure and someone who inculcates values and experimental knowledge as much as specific knowledge. The *guru* becomes an example or a model in life, an inspirational source, and the one who reveals the purpose and meaning of life.

India has traditionally given a position of prominence to *gurus*. They were revered, respected and also feared. The *guru* was like the sculptor who would give a shape and form to the life of a student. The parents too had complete faith in the teacher. All worked for the benefit and progress of the student and their education. The thirst of knowledge was encouraged. A *guru* is filled with a wealth of knowledge and experience about a particular subject. They are also expected to have spiritual wisdom.

Om shri Gurubhyo Namah (Salutation to the Guru).

The invocation to the *guru* is intended to be singular but it is projected not to be plural. It represents a *parampara* (tradition), an unbroken chain of *gurus*. It is believed that, while *Arthgati vidya* (money paid, money earned) is easy. *Shashtra vidya* (higher education) can be achieved only by the grace of *Ishwar* (God).

ॐसहनाववतु।
सहनौभुनफ्तु।
सहवीर्यंकरवावहै।
तेजस्विशि नावधीतमस्फु मा विद्विषाव है।
ॐ शान्ति: शान्ति: शान्ति: ॥

In the above hymn, both *guru* and *shishya* pray together for blessings from that, that which protects (*avtu*). *Shishya* has to pray for the *guru* and vice versa. *Ishwara* (God) must nourish the intellect (*bhunktu*) of both *guru* and *shishya.* Together they have to endeavor for knowledge, what they learn has to be as clear as sunshine, added with brilliance and clarity leading to the fulfillment of knowledge. The mantra *om shanti* is repeated three times to remove three types of obstacles. First, *adhidevika* - those hurdles which are not in our hands, second, *adhibhautika*- those obstacles which come from other people and lastly, *adhyatmika*- those which we create ourselves.

Pt. Rajan Mishra had once mentioned that good posture always plays an important role in singing. "After the *ganda-bandhan* ceremony, I generally ask my disciples to sit properly in *chin mudra or jnan mudra,* the best posture for singing. It improves your concentration as well as reading." Pt. Sajan Mishra continued, "in *chin mudra* where the index finger touches the thumb, the *Ahamkara* (ego) is surrendered at the feet of the *purusha* (creator of the universe) represented by the *guru* through his thumb. You are learning a traditional art and here you are supposed to be devoid of ego." The remaining three fingers (middle, ring and little finger) signify the stages of self-purification, enlightenment, and spiritual transformation respectively. The index finger represents the limited perspective of self and the thumb is the expanded perspective of self. When the two join, the limited self is connected to the spacious universal self.

During an interaction, Girija Devi commented on music and its links with yoga. She believed music to be a type of yoga itself. Breathing has a very important role in music, both for singing and meditation through music. Meditative breathing can lead the body towards wellness and the mind toward calmness. It is the single most important element in singing. In order to control your voice, you have to exhale exactly the amount of air you need for the sound you want. That breath needs to be as focused as a laser beam. How you exhale controls the quality of the sound, the volume, the pitch and the tone. How you inhale governs how you exhale. Thus, breathing has to be controlled and focused and there is a 'correct' way of breathing which is also encouraged by various branches of yoga - *pranayama and asanas*.

Pt. Govardhan Mishra said, "your voice is an instrument like any other. It takes time to learn to play it - time, patience and practice." Breathing directly influences the state of body and mind in a lot of ways which may or may not be apparent to us always. It is a process that is partly voluntary and partly involuntary. Music teaches us to control our breathing - a vital life function which is basically a voluntary doorway to the involuntary body, perhaps a conscious doorway to the subconscious mind.

Knowledge in ancient India was disseminated through

word of mouth. The *Vedas*, the *Upanishads*, and the other religious texts were spread for many generations by word of mouth. Only later were these ancient texts recorded to the written word. The ancient tradition of imparting knowledge orally is still practiced in India today. *Ayurveda*, one of the ancient systems of medicine, is still taught through traditional teaching methods. Ancient Indian legends, fables, and myths came vividly to life as children heard their grandparents recount them in various formats such as, drama, theater, dance, and classical music. However, it depended on the ability of the respective masters, the *guru*, the extent of expertise they hold in their garb on these arts, which would be subsequently be inherited by generations.

According to the ancient Indian conception, the *guru* is the representative of the Divine who is now veiled to the eyes of humanity. *Guru* leads the disciple from ignorance to enlightenment. It suggests the symbolic power of the *guru* – the honored preceptor at the heart of traditional learning in the Indian culture. Since the Vedic times, it was typical for a father, the first *guru* to pass the heritage to his progeny, thus propagating the old age knowledge through uninterrupted row or series of *parampara* (the tradition). The principal elements of this tradition are: the *guru* (teacher), the *shishya* (student), and the *shlokas* (principle).

This *parampara* also symbolizes the succession of teachers and disciples in traditional Indian cultures and religions. It is the tradition of spiritual relationship and mentoring where teachings are transmitted from a *guru* 'teacher' to a *shishya* 'disciple'. Such knowledge, whether it is vedic, agemic, architectural, musical, or spiritual, passes on through development of the relationship between the *guru* and *shishya*. It is believed that this relationship is based on the originality of the *guru* and respect, irrespective of the age or creed. Commitment, devotion, and obedience of the disciple is required for a smooth transfer of knowledge - subtle or specialized. The disciple eventually masters the knowledge that the *guru* passes on to him.

The importance of the bond between *guru* and *shishya* cannot be overstated, particularly with respect to spiritual education, where knowledge is descended through *guru* to *shishya* through silence, or a purely mental form of telepathy (perhaps due to the role of the *medulla oblongata*).

Some of the best examples of *guru-shishya* relationships could be found in the Indian epic, The *Mahabharata,* a saga that questions our sense of right and wrong at every turn. The obvious *guru-shishya* relationship in Mahabharata is that between Arjuna (the *shishya*) and Krishna (the *guru*) but we find the extol of the relationship between Arjuna and his childhood *guru,* Dronacharya, to be far more interesting. Arjuna and his four brothers (along with many cousins) lived and studied in Dronacharya's *gurukul.* Quickly, Arjuna who was an inherently gifted archer, became Dronacharya's favorite disciple and the *guru* went so far as to promise Arjuna that he would make him the greatest warrior of his time. In this context, it is vital to note that the story of Mahabharata takes place at a time when verbal promises were considered binding by all parties and upheld, almost without fail.

In music too, a very special relationship exists between a teacher and student. It is traditionally believed that music cannot be learnt truly without such a system. Some people also believe such a meeting between two seekers of music is pre-destined. Historians and artists maintain that this tradition has kept the institution of Indian music alive due to which there has been a continuity which can be observed in the development of the music. Traditions bring in a balance, perseverance, and persistence in India music. A lot of importance has been given to the system of *Parampara*. It is a well-known truth that without keeping *Parampara* of music in mind, we cannot ever imagine learning Hindustani classical music. However, it doesn't mean that there is no scope for new experiments and inventions. In fact, innovations had always been a part of Indian traditional music. But all these were always inside the boundaries of ancient traditional music.

Within this integrated *Parampara*, students begin their studies under the guidance of a *guru*, only after submitting themselves to an elaborate initiation ceremony. This includes typing a girdle around the waist or wrist of *shishya*, symbolic of a protective umbilical cord. This ceremony is called the *'gandabandhan'* ceremony. The *guru* has a sacred obligation to pass on their knowledge. *Gurus* protect their knowledge and ensure that the most valued material in their repertories are revealed to only the most dedicated and worthiest of the students.

In the mythic past, music *gurus* accepted their pupils into their homes like family members providing room to their students to reside, and the opportunity to teach their tradition, thus keeping the old system of music alive. Those musicians who followed the traditions, continued their practice of the *gurukul* even today. However, changing socio-economic conditions of India, especially in the post-Independence era, have greatly diminished this aspect of musical tradition.

In her book, *'Begum Akhtar, the story of my* Ammi', Dr. Shanti Hiranand, said that my *guru* Begum Akhtar was putting her best to teach me *ghazal, thumri* etc., but she never cared about a *Gandha-Bandhan* ceremony. She recalled, "Once it so happened that Neelam Bai, a singer from Bombay, was visiting *Ammi*. When she saw us learning from her, she took up the issue of *shagirdi* with *Ammi*. Addressing her with familiarity, she said, 'What is this Akhtari?'. If you are teaching them, they should be bound to you. Otherwise what is the use of taking such pain in teaching them? At that time Mrs. Anjali Banerjee, the famous *Ghazal* singer was also learning from her. *Ammi* tied *ganda* to both of us to solemnize our relationship as *Guru-Shishya*. So, it was our privilege to be Begum Sahiba's first *Ganda-Bandh shagirda."*

The sacred ritual ensured that the *guru* and the *shishyas* were bound to each other. It is akin to signing a bond. Both the student and teacher have an equal responsibility to nurture the relationship. Besides, during those days one did not have the freedom to flit from one teacher to another as might be the case these days. The ritual had an extremely positive effect on a student, as it provided them with a clear focus. To avoid the situation of shifting from one *guru* to another, there is a saying that *"Guru banao jaanke, Paani piyo chhan ke"*. It means that before accepting a person as your *guru* you should have complete detail about their knowledge and nature. Similarly, the *guru* should also know about the disciple well. Siddheshwari Devi used to say that people gave me respect for my singing but I know that it was all credited to the support and vast knowledge of my *Guru* Pt. Siyaji Maharaj, was a storehouse of different kinds of *bandish*. She remembered him as an exceptionally good composer himself, a master artist and master craftsman of rhythm. But at the same time, Siddheshwari Ji was a keen, honest and hardworking student. Her *guru* treated her like his own child and took care of her nourishment too as he believed that it was important to build and maintain strong lungs which are essential to continue classical singing. When SiyaJi died, Siddheshwari Ji lent a shoulder to his bier like a son would. True to her *Guru*'s expectations, Shiddheshwari ji took care of her *Gurumaa* (her *Guru*'s wife) till her last breath.

Following the *Parampara, Guru Purnima* has great importance and is the medium for celebrating the bond between *guru* and *shishya*. This festival is celebrated on the day of the full moon of the month of *Aasad* (June–July). It is a festival during which one pays homage and respect to their *guru* or teacher. Traditionally in India, when a child reached an appropriate age, he would move out of his parent's home, to commence his studies in a *gurukul*. Here, he along with a number of other students, would live under the supervision of a *guru*. In addition to receiving an education, the *shishya* would also participate in the day to day chores of *gurukul*. There were no monetary costs attached to attend the *gurukul*, but at the end of their stay, they offered a '*gurudakshina*', a gift of thanks which could either be monetary or a task that the *guru* requests the *shishya* to perform. In effect, the *gurukul* was an extended family which gave birth to the *guru shishya parampara*, one of the most sacred of relationships in Indian culture.

There were four types of *gurus*: *Acharya, Pravakta, Shrotriya*, and *Adhyapak*. There were two types of *shishya*: one who paid fees to the *guru*, or the *Acharya Bhaga* and the other who learnt by performing domestic chores in the *guru*'s house, known as *Dharma Shishya*. For instance, Siddheshwari Devi and Bade Ghulam Ali Khan were *dharma shishyas* who chose to learn from their *gurus* by serving them and learning in their company. This relation is based on complete 'submission to the *guru*'. When a *shishya* 'submits' to their *guru*, they welcome the free flow of the energy of their *guru* in the form of knowledge. The intent of the *guru* cannot be doubted, as it is always and only accounted for the betterment, well-being and growth of the disciple. Unconditional trust on the *guru* doesn't mean that if the *shishya* leaves everything to the *guru*, they will receive the knowledge. The *shishya* has to repay the divine knowledge through his or her hard work. Prabhati Mukher ji believes that the sacred bond between the *guru* and the *shishya* is built over trust and if the *shishya* keeps doubting him then there is no learning.

The *guru* knows what a student is lacking and also finds out the possible ways that would teach him. Thus, as a student should have faith in the *guru*'s words and follow them with devotion.

In music, a beautiful example of a *shishya*'s undoubted faith and unconditioned submission to his *guru* exists. Saint Surdasa was a legendary poet and a devotional or bhajan singer (and a staunch devotee of Lord Krishna). His *guru* instilled patience in Surdasa and managed his anger which was hampering his knowledg-seeking pursuits. Surdasa was an eager student who wanted to learn about spirituality through music. He met a *guru* who accepted him as his disciple. The *guru* found that Surdasa was limiting his quality by being perturbed and angry, thus preventing him from learning. The *guru* decided to shrug Surdasa of his loud-mouthed ways and anger. He asked Surdasa to chant God's name while performing all his activities for a period of one month and come back. Surdasa followed the *guru's* instructions religiously, and the day after one month, he went to meet his *guru*. On his way to his *guru*'s ashram, a sweeper on the street carelessly spilled dirt on his clothes; Surdasa was enraged and scolded the sweeper. He went home, changed his clothes and then met his *guru*.

To his utter surprise, the *guru* told Surdasa that he was not yet ready to learn and he had to chant and do his chores for another month. Surdasa returned sadly and continued to chant God's name for another month along with his routine chores. After a month, he eagerly went to his *guru*'s ashram and the same thing happened again. Surdasa became angry and blamed the sweeper again for his carelessness and mis-doings. After bathing, he met his *guru* who asked Surdasa to chant god's name for another month. One month passed, and the same incident happened when Surdasa was on his way to meet his *guru*. However, this time Surdasa addressed him softly saying "Thank you, you are my master. You have helped me to overcome my anger." The sweeper felt bad for his actions. After this, Surdasa approached his *guru*'s hermitage, who was waiting for him in front of the hermitage and welcomed him. *Guru* told Surdasa that he is ready to teach him. He could finally understand the process he went through. Here we find that Surdasa had followed the instructions of his *guru* without any doubt or questions which is considered to be the key in Indian tradition.

The existing *Guru-Shishya Parampara* in the world of Indian music consists of three aspects: *Gayan* (Vocal Music), *Vaadan* (Instrumental Music) and *Nritya* (Dance), have meandered through different forms and phases, which later took the form of *Gharanas.*

The *Gharana* system is of great importance in the field of music. The system is found in all the above three aspects of music. It is mandatory even today that a student of music has to learn from his *guru*. It is mandatory even today that a student of music learn from his *guru*. The reason behind this is the essence of the relationship. Apart from the basic taaleem, the *guru* imparts his/her students with the special skills, techniques and style of his gharana which the student carries forward. These specialties are grasped by the *shishya* in a close-knit environment and these learnings are carried by the *shishya* not just in the form of music but becomes a part of his lifestyle. The reason behind this is the essence of the relationship. Apart from the basic taleem, the *guru* impacts his lifestyle.

According to Pandit Ajoy Chakrabarty, "a *gharana* is hereditary in ethos and the basis of this heredity is expected to be held in a higher regard than bonds of the bloodline". *Gharaanedaar taleem (training)* expresses itself through the passing on of *bandishs* and *taans* as well as the manner of singing them. The *gharana's* distinctive ways of rendering *swara*-patterns and nuances as slides, glides, twists and turns, deflections and oscillations are also passed on. Deviations are generally not encouraged. He further continued, "I made an offering of just Rs. 250, a *kurta* and some sweets. That was the best that we could manage. A *saadhak* (worshiper) of the swara like his *guru*, Ustad Munawar Ali Khan accepted it with graciousness. He tied the *gandha* and took me under his wings. He was now my *Ustad* (teacher) and I was now his *shagird* (disciple)" (Pt. Ajoy Chakarabarti, as quoted from Shyam Banerji's book).

Over the years, ancient knowledge has deserted us, which indeed is an enormous loss. However, still there are many, who want to reincarnate this and involve themselves in the meta-psychosis of the *parampara*. It is for this reason; many intellectuals play an important role to bring forth the utility of *parampara*.

To relive the same, a very serious endeavor was made by Indian Tobacco Company - Sangeet Research Academy (ITC-SRA, Kolkata). They created an environment, which was quite similar to *Gurukul Paddhyati* or the *Gurukul* System. In this system, the student lives in juxtaposition with the *guru*, who in turn, takes care of the student. In contemporary times *gurukuls* such as the Siddheshwari Devi Academy of Indian Music, *Viraam* (Pt. Rajan-Sajan Misra), *Vrindavan* (Pt. Hari Prasad Chaurasia), *Shrutinandan* (Pt. Ajoy Chakrvarty) are some of the most prominent institutions based on the ideals of *guru-shishya parampara.*

The traditional way of teaching is very spontaneous and the *gurus* don't adhere to a prescribed format or syllabus. In fact, it is based on the mood, interest and capabilities of both the *guru* and the *shishya.* Girija Devi believed that the nature of the relationship between the *guru and shishya* defines the process of learning and comes at the spur of the moment. She said, " *if disciples of two gurus sing and even if they are from one gharana there will be differences in the singing style and even improvisations.*"

While describing the sacred *guru-shishya* relationship, Rita Ganguly said that her relationship with her *gurus* has been more than that of a parent-child relationship. She felt as if her soul was connected with her *amma* (Siddheshwari Devi) and *ammi* (Begum Akhtar). She recalled how Siddheshwari Devi would attend her performances very often to encourage her and would give her constructive feedback to improve further.

Most artists believe that a very important role of a *guru* is to keep the interest for the art alive in students and let their naivety be intact. Naivety doesn't mean immaturity when it comes to the rules and skills but the child-like innocence and curiosity which makes the renditions honest, pure and heartfelt. Prabhati Mukherjee has emphasized how the *guru* is supposed to keep artificiality away and thus also keep the learning material interesting.

The legends believe that living with the *guru* and learning from them on a daily basis by observing them daily helped their craft a lot. It was not just about learning the skill but also learning a lifestyle. Pt. Kameshwar Pathak during his interview said that, "this relation is not a meeting of *Guru and Shishya* of one lifetime. You carry forward this relation from previous births. Either *the guru* will approach you or you will approach the *guru,* but the meeting is already destined.

You can take birth in *Guru's* family or you will come in his/her contact as a disciple. Now I am playing the role of a *Guru* and I observe my disciples very closely and if I find that he doesn't possess a genuine talent for music, I advise him to quit the field and sincerely pursue something else. I never want anyone to waste his/her time. I believe it is the moral and social-responsibility of a *guru.* I would request all the *gurus* to give such type of advice to their disciples."

Self-motivation of the *guru* himself emerged as a prominent aspect in the data collected for this book. Artists believe that it is important to determine how optimistic, positive and hopeful the *guru* is about the art as it would reflect in his personality and body language. Pt. Chhannulal Mishra mentioned that "as a *guru* is the role model, anything he does becomes a benchmark for the students. Therefore, he himself has to be motivated. If he is not convinced about something, how will he convince others?"

Apart from the *guru*'s own personality and grounding, his success would also determine his level of interest and motivation. His enthusiasm, involvement in the field would determine his level of motivation which would impact the disciples both directly and indirectly. Discussing this further, Prabhati Mukherjee said that, "*guru* has to inspire his disciples to live and even materialize their dreams, even if the situations are adverse, he shouldn't leave hope." Further, Pt. Govardhan Mishra said that, "an artist has to be optimistic; this is what instills confidence in him and it would make him conscientious and persevering."

A study of more than 300 British university students found that those who are high in conscientiousness were more organized, self-disciplined and achievement oriented in terms of planning for future goals (Corner & Abraham, 2001). Moreover, they are physically healthier and optimistic in nature (Booth-Kewley and Vickens, 1994; Friedman et al, 1993, Marshal et al, 1994).

Another view that came forward was the role of the *guru* in making the *shishya* self-reliant and not his own shadow. It is important to understand that a *guru's* reflection might be seen in the disciple while singing or even in other aspects but that should not take away the individual flavor of the *shishya* - his individuality. Mrs. Rita Ganguly believes that, "*guru-shishya* is like a parent child relationship and like that only *guru* has to teach the *shishya* to become an independent artist and face the fraternity." She said that this is one of the most divine and sovereign relationships. This relationship is beyond any blood relation as this is a deep relationship of knowledge; values of respect, surrender and absolute belief in the *Guru*. In our music, *Gurumukhi Vidya* is the only way to acquire knowledge. She said that, "All my *Gurus* loved me a lot. My *Guru* Begum Akhtar introduced me on stage by often announcing that today's main artist is Mrs. Rita Ganguly and she will be accompanied by Begum Akhtar on harmonium, Munne Khan on tabla and Hazi Ghulam Sabir on *sarangi*." She further said that Amma (Siddheshwari Devi) never missed any of my concerts especially if she was present in the city.

Pt. Govardhan Mishra once said that *guru-shihsya/ bhagwaan-bhakt,* relationship is such wherein one takes care of the other. He narrated a short story which goes like this, "once a *bhakt* (devotee) was following his *bhagwaan* (God) and another man nearby was observing them. After a short while, the *bhakt* disappeared and this spectator curiously went and asked God about the devotee. God then replied that as he had picked up his speed and pace (while walking), the devotee was unable to keep up with him thus, and he had embraced the devotee and picked him up before moving forward." Similarly, I recall, once when I was in the midst of learning a *thumri* in *Raga Bhairavi (Shyaam ko dhoondan jaaun)*, I could follow my *guru* comfortably in the beginning. As we proceeded towards the *antara,* it became difficult for me to keep pace with her stylistic improvisations. She sensed this and smiled. After a while, I realized that I was also singing with her suddenly and matching her pace. Pt. Govardhan Mishra's story reminded me of this incident where I felt as if my *guru* picked me up in her lap so that I could be with her throughout the journey of this *thumri.*

Pt. Rajan-Sajan Misra recalled one of their interactions with their *guru* and shared, "when you sing, play a musical instrument or dance, it releases some specific type of waves which creates harmony in the surroundings. This harmony creates a positive aura in cosmic energy and such type of music is healing as music is the ultimate form of yoga." Thus, they emphasized that *gurus* go beyond ordinary text and syllabus.

The crux of this relationship is submission of *shishya* to a *guru*. Submission to the *guru* leads the *shishya* towards self-empowerment. When we leave ourselves completely to the *guru* or mentor, we are welcoming his knowledge through and around ourselves. The *guru* who has vast knowledge of the subject knows how to come over the most arduous of the things. This *parampara* takes its time and due to this reason, the *shishyas* attain refinement. They inherited a certain style and gained efficiency in performing the tasks with complete authority on their art form.

At the same time this *Parampara* also had a few demerits. The student never gets to glance at the genres because they relied on the knowledge descended only through their *guru*. There is no time period allotted for the course. The *shishya depended* on the *guru* totally. Today it is not possible for both the *shishya* and *guru* to have harmony on such a basis due to the rapidly changing socio-economic scenario. Whatever may be the socio-economic scenario, the *guru* should know the interest, aptitude and passion of the *shishya* and the *guru* should instill hope and optimism in the *shishya* during their training. While carefully choosing, blending and harmonizing of all the possibilities on the keyboard- *harmonium* of life, we make the disciple master composers who would go on to produce the most beautiful and creative melody called inner peace.

If you want to acquire authentic knowledge of Indian classical music and semi-classical music, especially *thumri* and its branches, the legacy of *guru-shishya parampara* can be substituted by none. This *parampara* helps us in transforming our learning and education of years into ever developing our learning and education of years into ever developing knowledge is precisely why we need more *gurukul* like ITCSRA. Although the legends are carrying forward the tradition, the government also needs to take initiative in promoting it.

A critical discussion on this "Tradition"

Myself being disciple of one of the stalwarts, it's my personal take away that the teaching is interdisciplinary in nature. Through theoretical and practical knowledge of music, one also learns about language, rituals, self-management, especially traits for adapting in a given environment, way of communication dressing, and self-actualization. The teachers in the tradition are egalitarian who provide equal opportunity for such holistic education, thus, students from all backgrounds are taught.

The *Gurukul* setting (*Guru-shishya parampara*) is more humane and personal, encouraging abstract thinking, allowing creativity and at the same time also allows for cognitive-behavioral and experiential learning. The *Guru* also plays the role of a counselor. They closely observe the beginners and try to help them. As a student of clinical psychology, I am using these psychological jargons but the *Guru* does it as a part of training. I found that we can help the new and old both category of disciples by using various techniques from CBT and experiential therapy to deal with their day-to-day issues and problems they may encounter while learning. The *Guru* can even hire some professional counselors for this purpose to the academies or *Gurukuls*. As the *gurus* are adept in maintaining and nurturing interpersonal relationships, they become much closer to their disciples (even closer than the parents) which helps them in knowing their *shishyas* better and thus helping them when they are struggling in life. Disciples share almost every problem with their *Guru* who never reveals it to others as they consider it to be unethical valuing the bond and confidentiality of the relationship very high. Here I would like to add that after knowing the problems of students the *Guru* can take help of professionals to take care of their emotions associated with learning difficulties, performances, success, disappointments, responsibility and self- esteem. Under the guidance of a trained counselor the student can begin to release and explore negative feelings, shame in performing before others, causes of nervousness, emotional imbalance. They release and get- rid of their repressed negative emotions from the past and start experiencing positive feeling such as a love, forgiveness and calm in the present, changing their perception of reality, which a must for learning any art or we can say any subject. The focus is on the student as a whole and not just the music training aspect.

Sometimes *Guru* shares stories from *Itihaasa* (History), from their own experience and about the predecessors, sometimes about other great artists of the field. This is socio-emotional learning, value-education, non-formal learning and life & subject coaching at its best. A *Guru* is someone who removes our spiritual ignorance. Such a *Guru* is highly revered, exalted at par with God. *Guru Poornima* is celebrated to pay tribute to his greatness. I have already recounted it earlier in different chapters.

The learning process is dialogic and scientific. The manner in which knowledge is imparted is back and forth dialogic exchange between a *Guru* and a *shishya*. The *shishya* models the *Guru* closely, yet there is scope for questions and individual growth in the teaching-learning process. There are questions- answers sessions in *Gurukul*.

When you approach a *Guru* to study any art, especially in the field of music (Vocal, instrumental & dance), you are immediately transported to the *kula* of the *Guru*, i.e. the guild of the *Guru*, you have a new family now, all the *Guru*'s students are your *Guru bhais* and *bahens*, it is inclusive, diverse and equitable. You are not required to convert your religion or completely change your belief system, it does not matter who you are, all the students of every denomination are treated at par with one another. It is akin to a socialist system where everyone does their share of work. I am speaking from a lived experience perspective; I am a part of my *Gurukul* since last 14-15 years and in close proximity to those who were there.

Some people oppose the system and say that it was all "Brahminical" in nature and that one must not forget how difficult it was to get educated especially for women and non-brahmin males until Jyotirao Phule and Savitribai Phule came into the picture fighting for their rights. They often cite a story to solidify their stance. In history of India, we have seen that when "Eklavaya" a young brilliant Nishada Prince (Nishada is a tribe of hunters) went to the *Gurukul* of *Guru* Dronacharya the greatest teacher of art of archery and the science of warfare to get trained as an archer, after knowing Eklavaya's caste and community, *Guru* Drona refused to teach him. The anecdote mentions that he said, Eklavya, if you are a Nishada hunter, then you are a *Shudra,* the lowest caste in the kingdom. I am a Brahmin, the highest of castes. All my students are Kshatriyas the, warrior caste. I cannot teach a *Shudra* boy. Eklavya was surprised, he left the *Gurukul* and went back to the forest. Then he built an idol of *Guru* Dronacharya with mud and placed it in a secluded corner and practiced throughout the day. After years of practicing he became a skilled archer even surpassing the best archer in the Kingdom-Arjuna. This might have been true in those times but now-a-days situation has changed and *Guru* and *Shishya* both come from all *jatis, kula, varna* and all are working together for the growth of art and individual. This is a wonderful civilizational unbroken system of teacher and student exchange that is more than five thousand years old.

Historian K.M. Shrimati in an article on knowledge transmission in ancient India contrasts this with the Shamanic traditions (reforming to the heterodox traditions of Budddhists and Jainas; as opposed to the orthodox brahmanas), where social inclusion through dissemination of knowledge was given primacy. This, the Buddha understanding of nirvana was intrinsically tied to removing the veil of ignorance – *avidya/avijja.*

T.M. Krishna raises the issue of a specialized form of knowledge, that of music and performance, which celebrates the *Guru-Shishya* relationship, and how it has been recast in modern times. Despite their recasting, he points out, it has retained so many of its regressive, exclusionary and discriminatory elements. Even more disturbing is the excess that are permitted to the teacher vis-a-vis the student in such a system. In the context of sexual harassment and rape allegations in one such *Gurukul,* the internalization of those elements is pointed out by him, where there is a resounding silence on the part of many eminent performers and teachers, where students fearing reprisals tend to hold their peace. Although this situation may persist in certain so-called *gurukuls,* one need not lose faith in the system; it's the flaw of the individual teacher that needs to be reprimanded rather than questioning the sanctity of the system. Having said that, some rituals or norms that impede the growth of the system shall be deliberated upon by the scholars and amendments should be made in that.

Modern societies celebrate the pursuit of knowledge and claim to provide equal opportunities for all to gain this knowledge. They also institutionalize certain practices and attitude through what Gramsci has called the ideological apparatuses, our educational institutions being among them, what for Nehru were the new temples of learning. And as Foucault has argued, discipline and punishment are at the core of these institutions, for it is only then that the ideal citizen is born and matured, who will go on to strengthen the nation-state. So while boys and girls, men and women have apparently equal access to those educational institutions, ultimately these are in a way preparing for their future roles within society and the nation at large.

Let's pay attention to a few more anecdotes to understand the tradition and issues with it. During my interactions, one disciple shared how a *Guru* used every opportunity to 'prove' that they were in the wrong, either in their performance on stage or in class discussion leaving them extremely worried, which affected their emotional well-being. And in some cases, there was no option but to transfer to another institution. But most *Guru*'s are committed who have been supportive, going out of their way to counsel their disciples and helping them overcome their learning difficulties.

While criticism and disagreement is very important in

any academic debate, lack of grace in accepting dissent or disagreement is problematic. At times rejection teaches us a lot. The legendary historian of Modern India, Bipin Chandra personified this for generations of students. Introducing a scholar on one occasion, he said, this is one of the most brilliant intellectuals I have known, who I had the good fortune to have. He contradicted me, disagreed with me and provided alternate views on issues, and while I may not have always responded positively, they certainly have impelled me to reflect on my own purpose as a teacher.

At present time, when a certain degree of institutional responsibility has been acknowledged at least in the motive educational system (even today, training in professional music or dance is seen as at the most an extracurricular activity), the importance of sensitivity to caste, class, gender, religious identities and the social discriminations faced by people because of these becomes imperative.

In the present time it is not possible to continue the system of *Gurukul* (where disciple lives with *Guru* for years like a family member) but NGOs, Government and even traditional *Guru*s with their capable *Shishya*s should put their best efforts to nurture the artistic talent of children. In every case instead of considering music as a profession this art should be encouraged as an entertainment, de-stressing, inspiring and even as a treatment tool of so many health problems. Music needs to be learnt without the pressure of a career. That's when it will have the depth and true music will slowly unfold. And after letting music seeping in so many years, a genuine talent will start thinking and rendering new improvisation without altering the *swaroop* (originality) of the song. In every talented singer's career, there have been slow times or dull moments. You must have patience not only with yourself, but with others that you work with. It's the key to keep healthy and focused while you are waiting for your career to unfold in its true sense. For this, our country needs more institutions like "*Gandharva-Vidyalaya*".

The *Guru-Shishya* system is very effective as it recognizes that learning is not possible without equal contribution from the teacher and students. Peers are given importance but only to further one's own grades via good projects but not to learn from as for giving oneself sometimes to allow the subject to seep in, that is where we all lack patience and trust. We are in a mad rush to make name, fame, money, not really as much in a hurry to actually know anything. It is important to remember that 'knowing' something takes time. This is where the *Guru-Shishya* tradition excels, it lets you just be.

If you want to acquire authentic knowledge of Indian classical music and semi-classical music, especially *thumri* and its branches, the legacy of *Guru-shishya parampara* cannot be substituted by anyone. This *parampara* helps us in transforming our learning and education into ever developing knowledge. In this tradition the disciple should show his intrest, hardwork and wisdom to get best from his guru. This is precisely why we need more *Gurukul* like ITC-SRA. Although the legends are carrying forward the tradition, the government also needs to take initiative in promoting it.

The Creative Legends of Thumri

Queen of Thumri Siddheshwari Devi with her daughter Vidushi Savita Devi

Doyen Begum Akhtar with her disciple Vidushi Rita Ganguly

Thumri Maestro- Vidushi Prabha Atre

Girija Devi – the creative genius of Thumri

Thumri doyen Vidushi Shobha Gurtu ji

Pandit Ajoy Chakrabarty with his father Pandit Ajit Chakrabarty both the legends in a creative mood.

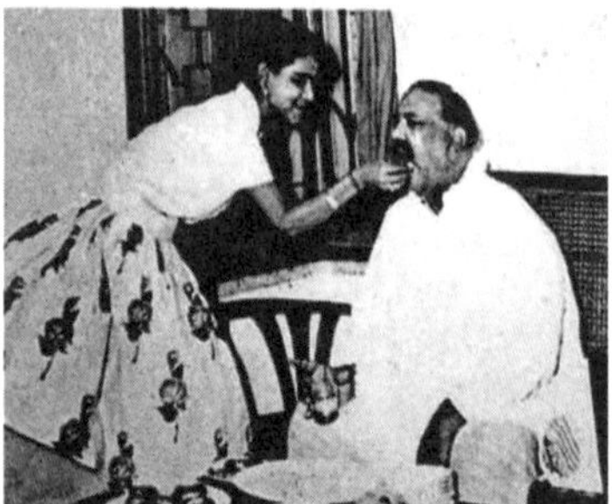

Good mood enhances creativity. Ustad Bade Ghulam Ali Khan with her disciple Prabhati Mukherjee

CHAPTER 7

The Idea of Being Innovative

If you want to be creative in any field,
you have to observe. The deepest possible
observation will bring enormous vision.

– Sadhguru

The Idea of Being Innovative

The Eastern view of creativity considers music as an expression of personal truth and self-growth (Lubart, 1999). It focuses on discovery and emphasizes harmony and balance. Indian classical music has two fundamental elements, Ragas and Taalas. The Ragas form the fabric of a melodic structure, while the taal measures the time cycle. The Raga gives artists a palette to build the melody form of sounds, the taal provides them with a 'creative framework' for rhythmic improvisation using time. Here comes the role of 'aesthetic balance', because it is the unity and beautiful balance between raga and taal. Even if they are in conflict (Larant-Bhirant) with one-another, they need or supplement each other. Moreover, since the aim of the art is to afford pleasure in life, the artist tries to reveal the hidden unities that delight the mind. He will aim to penetrate beneath the surface of experience observed by common perception to its more obscure logic underneath. Here he becomes "creative." He will go beyond what the mere mechanism of initiation had required. For example, the singers sometimes enter into the soul of man, into his private and individual selfhood by his songs and uncover the hidden connections among thoughts, feelings and impulses. Here he shows the ability of thinking beyond the main stream and receiving new experience.

Indian-thought views creativity as a process of understanding and enlightenment, not just as a product of mass entertainment or some academic pursuit. Thus, the social environment also plays a very important role in identifying development. When people engage in communication they internalize certain social scripts through their day-to-day interactions and they require a situation to externalize the concept in the mind. According to Csikszentmihalyi (1996, 1999) the process of creativity is an interaction between a creative individual who has become immersed in a field with his talents, personality traits, motivation and his social environment. To be creative, an idea has to be adapted to its social environment and then transmitted through time. According to Boden (1998), creativity is a feature of human intelligence grounded in his individual capacities such as association of ideas, perception, analogical thinking, reflecting on self-criticism. However, motivation and emotions are also closely linked to social and cultural contexts. If creativity has been construed as a socio-cultural behavior (Bhawuk, 2003), then it is important to understand the contextual situatedness of creativity both as a process and as a product.

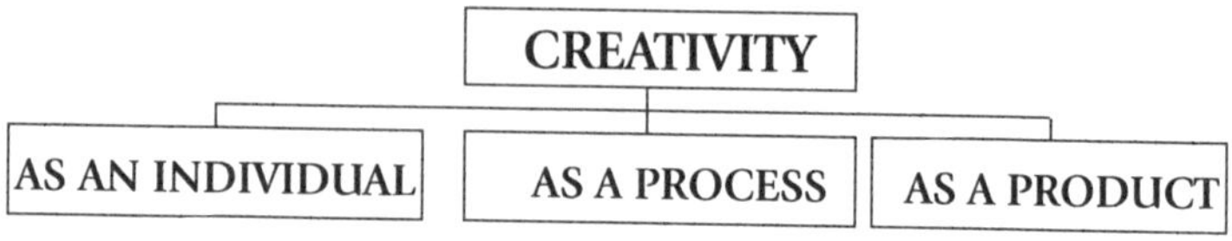

Figure 1: Explaining Creativity

As an Individual: Creative individuals present certain fundamental thoughts, expressions, actions and behaviors. For instance, they ask uncomfortable questions, they are more tolerant of unclarity, they are determined and self-reliant, their self-comprehensiveness is higher and they indulge in debate to resolve a dispute or question and recommend various options etc.

Creativity as a process: From the lived to the unlived being, this was another core category generated from the data reflecting the intricacies of the creative processes with less emphasis on the product part of creativity. Now we will read some important conditions of creative process and views of stalwarts towards these processes.

Openness to experience being: Openness to experience is the degree to which a person is willing to consider new ideas and prospects. It runs along a continuum: on one end are people who have the idea of doing something new; they are ready to receive and accept a variety of experiences and expressions; on the other are those who like to stay with familiar ideas and tried and tested activities. "Openness to experience is one of the big five factors of personality and is fundamental to creativity. It predicts creativity in a wide range of domains of analysis" (Fei'st and Barron, 2003).

Pt. Govardhan Mishra felt that, "instead of tampering majorly with the older compositions it is better to listen to a variety of them and then come up with a new one to which people of this generation can relate to." He further said that his exposure to varied music has resulted in him composing *thumris* in various dialects and languages. Thus, listening to a variety of people and being sensitive to all kinds of life experiences helps an artist in inculcating an active imagination. It makes them aesthetically sensitive and would also allow them to be attentive to their inner feelings.

In the similar fervor, Rita Ganguly emphasized that for an artist, learning more than one art or being open to more than one forms is important as it creates space to think, relate and enrich the expression and experience, thus, adding quality to the art and the artist.

According to a study done with 150 university students, knowing about their musical preferences, openness to experience was found to be consistent with the view that it is the association with a willingness to be open to a wide range of rich and novel experiences. Its aesthetical facet attempts to measure the importance of music, art and poetry to the individual (Rawlings and Ciancarelli, 1997) and, the degree to which he has developed "a wider knowledge and appreciation to that of the average individual" (Costa and McCrae, 1992: 17).

According to Girja Devi, music is all about putting the state of mind in front of her and others through her music. For this, it also becomes important to understand one's own state of mind. Sometimes when there is a lot of chaos and no clarity of mind, music might help in understanding it and calming it. The tragic life experience of his wife's death compelled Ustad Bade Ghulam Ali Khan to pour out his heart and its grief in the melody he created, "Yaad piya ki aaye, ye dukh sahaa na jaaye hai raam" (Gilani, 2003), wherein he was lamenting on the demise of his wife and coping with the unbearable pain it caused him. Thus, music becomes a way of self-awareness, self-expression, and also self-expansion. It has been clearly established that music is critical in facilitating self-expression in the songwriter. The transformative power of music influences self-expression, as the artist is driven to create a song that fulfills his own needs (Baker, 2013).

Life presented difficult times for Bade Ghulam Ali Khan as the left side of his body got paralyzed and he could not even produce a single sound. However, he overcame all these impediments to once again come into "his own world." People who had heard him singing earlier then said, "earlier the Ustaad's singing was the sound of the waterfall striking against the mountain-side and rushing forward with great force to mingle with the ocean. Now, it resembled the vast ocean whose might and depth was unfathomable." Thus, life's struggles and life's experiences impact our personality and in turn the music that the artist creates. His paralysis made him more contemplative and somber, which got reflected in his music. Music and narratives share similar goals: expression of thoughts, feelings, emotions and meanings. Mishler (1999) suggested that the artist "performs" his identity through the narratives in which they "express" and display who they are and who they would like to be.

Siddeshwari Devi was poisoned by her rivals due to which she could not sing for one complete year. It was her determination and will to be open to the experiences happening to her and her body helped her in coming out of it and resume her career. The artist uses music to reinforce or explore a sense of self, whether or not he wishes to share it with others (Baker, 2013). This also makes the process of song-writing and composing therapeutic.

Permeability of self with the other: Pt. Kameshwar Pathak talked about an interaction between the audience and the performer, which reaches a climax when both are lost in each other and only the 'music piece' shines as one. A unified creation expressing the inner feelings of both the audience and the artist.

According to the stalwarts, riyaz and performance are two completely different aspects of the art; although they complement each other, they are vastly different in nature. Ms. Prabhati Mukherjee said that, "Riyaz is for self-growth and expansion." Adding to this SavitaJi said that, "It is important to hone the skill and talent but performance is mainly for the audience, it is to showcase that honed skill." According to Indian art, the responsibility of taking the audience to a state of bliss lies with the artist. The calm, reposeful state of rasa is essentially good as not only does it release the personality (both of the audience and the performer) from daily tensions but it enables the individual to realize their intrinsic nature. It is considered a liberating experience for both, as in its final moment the inner essence of the individual is completely identified with the essence of art-work (Pandit, 1977).

"Because music is about communicating the innermost feelings and longings, through the raga an attempt is made to create a desired impact on the listener", said Girja Devi. It is considered important to charm and entice the audience by some of the participants in this book by combining the purity of expression with clarity of voice: "Shudha mudra, shudha vaani" (Bade Ghulam Ali Khan). Therefore, music making is not a process which is the musician's responsibility alone: the artist and the audience interact to create something which holds value for them. It is believed that as we engage in it, we jointly experience events and behaviors as having meanings that are shared and yet are intensely personal (Cross, 2014). Music is a mode of social interaction because of the formed social connection between the artists and listeners. A performer is able to communicate to audiences large and small, while receiving both verbal and non-verbal feedback (Schnare et al., 2011).

Being in the moment: Bade Ghulam Ali Khan had just finished a song during a performance and was preparing for another one when a cat suddenly jumped into the center of the gathering and shuffled away. This movement caught the maestro's eye and he lost no time in remarking, this is how it went. He then went on to produce an impromptu taan which in respect in the manner of its run, appeared a very close parallel to the way the cat had rushed in and out of the gathering (Gilani, 2003).

According to Indian tradition, while learning, conscious effort is placed on mastering the patterns during the daily course of riyaz which comes as a genuine and ready response to the aesthetic impulse of the moment that comes to the vocalist because he is ready to accept everything happening around and then act on it in his unique way.

The focus of expressive arts is not on a specific technique or the quality of the product itself. It is on the power and process of symbolic expression of the arts for healing, and integration. Engaging in music as a spiritual practice means honoring the process of meaning-making and of cultivating a relationship to mystery (Paintner, 2007).

For Siddheshwari Devi, creativity was about expression of self and being true or honest to oneself. To create something, talent (God-gifted), training and practice are all important, but the most important thing seems to be "being in the moment" (living in the moment). Bade Ghulam Ali Khan used to say, "realizing it and then acting on that impulse without bothering much about the consequences is important." Authentic temporality is authentic resoluteness in the present. Present is not "now"; it is a "moment of vision" and what is present at hand (Heidegger, translated by Macquarrie and Robinson, 1962).

Transcending beyond: tradition and structure as the catalyst: Indian classical music provides a beautiful blend of standing by the tradition and improving within it. Since it is believed that every raga is born anew every time it is sung, it gives the artist liberty to carve the character of the raga in her own style, based on the contours provided (Hess, 2009).

Girija Devi adds to it by saying that keeping the traditional compositions is important but definitely while putting one's own imprint on it. The improvisation comes from the experience of the artist and her way of understanding the musical piece. The creativity of *thumri* lies in the "emotional content" that it presents. One can sing a particular word in a variety of ways depending on their mood, playing and swinging with the rhythm. The artist tries to deliver various bhavas (emotions) using one particular word with different phrases and that is their creative intellect. This array of phrases evokes a variety of emotions using various techniques to improvise. It seems that emotions require a cognitive appraisal and, thus, singing depends on how people subjectively experience their environment which is strongly correlated to the emotions. The artist builds a story, her own story around the age-old narrative, communicating it in her own way. This has a lot to do with the artist's personality, her state of mind, her perspective of various aspects, experiences and also her perception of life. Malloch (1999) asserts that communicative musicality lies beneath all human communication and that the element of pulse, quality, and narrative are the "tools by which emotion is conveyed and companionship formed."

Pt. Ajoy Chakrabarty opined that creativity lies in the engagement of the disciple with the art of traditional riyaz is a must to reach a stage wherein one can be creative." Along with this, he believed that guru's guidance and a liberal mindset are important factors in the creativity of the disciple. He further said that a creative person can see the different components of the whole and take them apart to put together a different whole. At the same time, he or she can see the oneness that can be created from that which is lying around in bits and pieces. A creative person can see that which others cannot.

Pt. Chhannulal Mishra believed that it was important to preserve the past, "preserve what was learnt but the artist's rendition of it and his response to the moment while singing (when at Riyaz or while performing) is where the act or idea of creativity lies." The structure of Indian music offers or provides it a beauty which is very helpful in transcendence. As the phrases are rigorously practiced they help the artist in the journey from the known to the unknown. As believed in Indian thought:

Asato ma sadgamaya
Tamaso ma jyotirgamaya
Mrityormaamritamgamaya
(*From ignorance lead me to truth*
From darkness lead me to light
From death lead me to immortality)
(Except of excerpt from Brihdarnayaka Upnishad)

Creativity as a product: it has flow, originality, diversity and amplification.

Dimensions related to creativity:

- The relationship between creativity and intelligence: Bine said "understanding a problem, making arguments, right decisions are necessary actions of intelligence." From this definition, it is clear that intelligence is a general power. It helps a person learn new things and by the action of learning it can be expressed. Although several experiments have proven that it is not necessary for highly intelligent children to be creative, certain researchers have discussed that intellectual capacity has an important role to play in artistic creativity.

- The relationship between creativity and curiosity: Murphy said in 1958, "curiosity is the tendency to search for any direct novelty or receiving any subject." Curiosity is a basis of fundamental tendency and knowledge. It is true that curiosity is the cause of high levels of creativity. Children create their curiosity by asking questions like "what and how." Their parents and teachers should give proper solutions.
- Relationship between creativity and concentration: Concentration can be explained in general terms staying engrossed in a task and having the ability to maintain it without any preoccupations. It is the ability to focus attention on the task and not be affected or disturbed by any internal or external distractions.
- Creativity and aptitude: It is an emotional action. It is our driving force, which impels our attention towards desirable tasks by diverting it from other things. It is that inspiring power which motivates us towards any person, thing or action.
- The relationship between creativity and motivation-motivation and creativity have positive correlation because motivated people may become exemplary creatives. They need encouragement, awards and penalties, developing a sense of healthy competition, appreciation of self etc.
- The relationship between creativity and maturity: Maturity could be a secondary developmental factor and would be required before learning processes. The development of physical and mental aptitude is called maturity. It is a continuous process of development and it exercises a crucial impact on creativity i.e. a more creative child is supposed to have more mature thoughts.
- The relationship between creativity and language: Language is the means through which people can share their thoughts. As electricity can't run without wire, in the same way thoughts and emotions also require language. It is a

powerful way of expressing feelings and thoughts. Without language it is impossible to exchange creative thoughts. Sincerity and simplicity can be seen in thoughts and feelings. Thoughts and feelings play a vital role in creating something new and language provides it with expression and meaning.

Thinking and Creativity: thinking is the basis of creativity. Thinking capacity and quality of a student determines their creativity. Pt. Rajan-Sajan Mishra believe that music and creativity go hand in hand and it is not possible without thinking. "One should think about different ragas, talas, your own swaras and their combination." When something different from the norms is carved, it is considered as divergent and may be creative as well. This way of working in a *'new manner'* where usual algorithms, steps and formulas are not followed is the basis of creative thinking.

The process of creativity begins with the primary processes of an immature brain. It is the effect of ego and the unconscious processes. Secondary processes begin with the mature brain. This involves the role of the conscious level, logical and systematic thinking. Pt. Ravi Shankar would often say that something that would make us think hard, a challenge, and the urge to overcome it leads to a creative process.

Along with divergent thinking and evolution, convergent thinking is the third aspect of creative power. Through thinking people can do work with fewer resources. It simply means that the person must have the power to interpret a situation.

Creativity uses both, the right brain's divergent thinking (imagination and expanding thinking to generate novel ideas) as well as the left brain's consequent thinking (narrowing down to the best choice). The Mozart effect from the 90's was the first study to link classical music to increased spatial cognition.

At Garage Group (a research group at Cincinnati), researchers enabled non-linear thinking such as mind-wandering and Associative thinking to move beyond the limited thinking capacity that we possess. It focuses on widening the experiential repertoire and not focusing on something specific to help us get into flow. As described by them, mind wandering is like putting your car into self-driving mode and the resulting creativity happens when we let our mind think freely without any conscious control. During this period of auto-pilot driving the imagination and flexibility networks are activated and working together. The term Mozart-effect was first coined by Alfred A. Tomatis, who used Mozart effect to cure disorders. Mozart effect showed two results:

- A set of research results indicate that listening to Mozart's music may induce a short-term improvement on the performance of a certain kind of mental task known as "spatial-temporal reasoning."
- Popularized version of the hypothesis which suggests that "listening to Mozart makes you smarter," or that early childhood exposure to classical music has a beneficial effect on mental development.

This finding supports Savita Devi's statement that "I want that every person should be exposed to music in his/her childhood for good mental development."

Guilford first proposed the concept of "divergent thinking" in the 1950, when he noticed that creative people tend to exhibit this type of thinking more than others. He thus associated divergent thinking with creativity, appointing it several characteristics such as: (1) Fluency: the ability to produce great number of ideas or problem solution in a short period of time; (2) Originality: the ability to produce new, original ideas; (3) Flexibility: the ability to simultaneously propose a variety of approaches to a specific problem; (4) Elaboration: the ability to try, systematize and organized the details of an idea in advance and carry it out; (5) The ability to go beyond the difficult situation: Those who possess such quality, features of creativity can be reflected in them; (6) The ability to reinterpret the problem: Such persons are endowed with creative power; (7) The ability to establish coordination of unique and relevant ideas; and (8) The ability to bring change in other's views: Those who are able to bring about fundamental and reasonable change in views, beliefs or concepts of others by thinking, reasoning and proofs are called to be creative.

Thinking is the basis of creativity, but it must be divergent. It is the development of abilities related to creative thinking that differs from other abilities. In all kinds of people different types of creativity as well as varying grades of thinking can be found. It is important to note that creative thinking suddenly appears like lightning but doesn't suddenly emerge. Of course it's not a planned activity but everything is already there in your store-house. According to Prabhati MukharJi, when we use our stored phrases during our concerts without any prior preparation we should call it "*upaj*" (creativity). It's creative because we had never planned to use it in our concert and it increases the level of your presentation. It gives a feeling of that "Aha! experience". Creativity might be present in the child at the time of their birth but its enhancement and expression depends on the psychosocial factors. It is related to various aspects of life. It is not necessary to have a particular subject for creativity, instead it is reflected in the day-to-day activities of mankind.

By taking the support of and impacting other aspects of a disciple's life, the guru can enhance their creativity. Encouragement of the family, educational tours for cultural exchange, creative dialogue and seminars, creative writing, providing time for thinking, meditation, and daydreaming can be some such areas and activities of life. The Guru provides opportunities for growth and performance by creating a harmonious environment which gives the disciple a platform to express, hone and re-express himself and thus be creative.

Human beings are creatures of creative use and are seen to display their abilities from their childhood. Creativity can be understood on a variety of levels – cognitively, spiritually, intellectually, socially, economically and from the humanitarian perspective. Students are likely to develop their creative capabilities if they have access to rich learning opportunities and an environment that nurtures and supports their creative development. They may develop their creative power from their surroundings. There are many stages of creating anything new which are connected with each other. Dr. Shanti Hiranand said that in Hindustani Sangeet, a composition comes into "being" spontaneously when the raga, bol, taan, laya and sur meet in unison. It is a confluence of melody, words, note and rhythm. She further continued that there is no equivalent in western music for "sur" and therefore no apt word for it in English, as it means a combination of different sounds

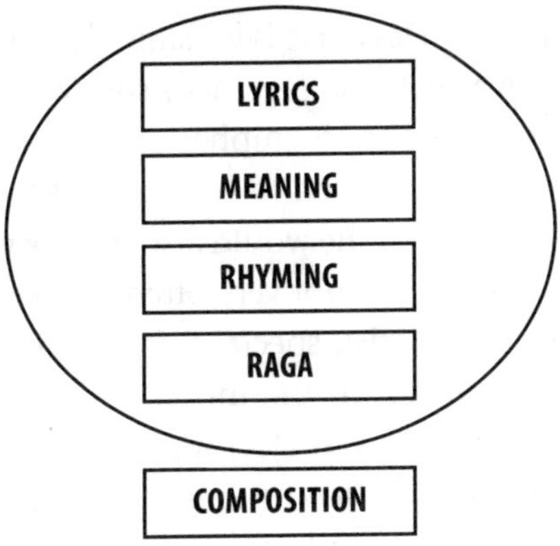

Fig 2: Understanding Learner's Perspective on Creative Music Making: Creating Musical pieces and compositions

or shrutis, which create their own impact. In order to be creative, the following four processes are important: imagination, observation, understanding and creation.

In this figure, researcher Dr. Durgesh K. Upadhyay (2014) has explained the process of creativity graphically. The first four stages from lyrics to raga selection reflect the stages of exploration and preparation, providing a fertile ground for creativity to manifest. At this stage after repetition of composed notes, suddenly a new, genuine and appropriate tune may emerge. During the last two stages, composition and feedback, a creative composition takes its final shape which has gone through several modifications, synthesizes and verifications. The conscious process of music making broadly follows the stages as propounded by Wallas (1926) in which he explained that the individual defines the problem and gathers the information in order to solve it.

While emphasizing the lyrics, it is important to highlight that the artists' choice and personal inclination also drives their creation or the piece he/she is improvising. For instance, while improvising, some artists like to choose nouns to elaborate upon, whereas some select verbs. For instance, when Siddheshwari Devi used to sing *thumri* "Jao Wahi Tum Shyam Jaha Sari Raina Jage ho"; she would select the word shyam to improvise to emphasize the 'pukaar' aspect (calling someone, which used to be a special feature of her performances). However, she would also use the verb form to improvise and expand but not very often. It exemplifies the aesthetic sense of the artist, special features of the gharana, and would also depend on the mood and mind frame of the artist. Since Siddheshwari Devi was an ardent devotee of Lord Krishna, she would often try to invoke Shyam by adding 'a' vowel in between the word 'Jao' and expanding on it, like Ja aa aa aa aa aao. Thus, one of the interpretations could be, Krishna wherever you had spent the night or had gone I have nothing to do with it, but, once you have come here to your devotee Radha (Here singer is perhaps representing goddess Radha), she requests you to stay with her with total devotion.

Begum Akhtar was a pure aesthetic. She was a real creative genius. She used to compose her ghazals on her own. She knew how to do justice with the lyrics. She used to create bhav pradhan songs, one that appeals to the emotions. There was a very high degree of fidelity in her art form. Her husband, Mr. Abbassi, had added class to her knowledge of Urdu poetry. In these days it was a matter of honour among poets to get the stamp of Begum Sahiba's on their poems. Poets like Shamim, Shakeel and others would vie with each other to get their verses composed and sung by her.

Natural process of Music Making: A common pattern could be observed through the responses of the participants and a 'creative product' emerges naturally through these stimulating factors (lyrics, Raga, Mood etc). All have shared that the process in which music emerges from some unknown sources which may not be conveyed explicitly. For natural creation, most of the stalwarts shared this belief that one must be talented, it's not just the training. Savita Ji disclosed that "I always keep a paper and a notebook, wherever some new bandish or dhun comes to my mind, I note it down, otherwise it will disappear. And this something new that happens makes me feel a step closer to my inner being."

Creativity has the duel qualities of being universal and individualistic at the same time. Creativity techniques are methods that encourage original thoughts and divergent thinking. Some methods may require group of two or more people while other methods can be accomplished alone. Once Dr. Shanti Hiranand during her interaction said that some time I create something new with my accompanists- the tabla player, the harmonium player, sarangi player and also with some of my senior disciples and sometimes all alone. In this chapter we found that different stalwarts have different views towards creativity. Creativity is as subjective as each creative individual.

According to Girija ji creativity cannot be learnt. It is aleatoric. Aleatory means "pertaining to luck". Randomly it comes. So, it is based on principle of randomness. Randomness is a lack of order, purpose, cause or predictability. Dr. Shanti Hiranand generally believed in brain storming with group while creating something new. Brain storming is a method by which a person or group attempts to find a solution for a specific problem by amassing all the ideas spontaneously by its members or alone. In music when an artist creates some new composition on demand of organisers of concert or create something with the audience in mind either alone or with the help of his/ her group is called brain storming method. As per Pandit Rajan - Sajan Mishra ji sometimes creativity comes by luck but generally "it is a learnt behaviour". It empowers people by adding strength to their natural abilities which improves team work, individual capacity and productivity. Pandit Goverdhan Mishra used to say that when you start thinking to create something new your thinking about reasoning is not immediately obvious and about ideas that may not be obtainable by using traditional step-by-step logic. Vertical thinking follows logical and traditional way but when you seek the solution of a problem through unorthodox methods or elements which would normally be ignored by logical thinking, it is called lateral thinking.

So, we can conclude that creativity is a talent as well as a learnt skill. During group brainstorming we should focus on maximum quantity of ideas, criticism should be put "on hold", unusual ideas should be welcomed because sometimes new ways of thinking provide better solution and lastly good ideas can be combined to form a single very good idea.

CHAPTER 8

... but Who Enters the Flow

Flow is the process of achieving happiness through control over one's inner life. The optimal state of inner experience is order in consciousness. This happens when we focus our attention (psychic energy) on realistic goals and when our skills match the challenges we face.

– Mihaly Csikszentmihalyi

... but Who Enters the Flow

Flow is the mental state of being completely present and fully immersed in a task. It is a strong contributor to creativity. When in flow, the creator and the universe become one, outside distractions recede from consciousness, once mind is fully open and attuned to the act of creation. There is very little self-awareness or critical self-judgment; just intrinsic joy for the task. Since flow is so essential to creativity and well-being across many slices of life from sports to music to physics to religion to spirituality – it's important that we learn more about the characteristics associated with *flow* so that we may all learn how to tap into this precious mental resource. The concept of flow was developed by Csikzentmihalyi (1990, 1999, 1998).

But who enters the flow? What are these lucky folks look like? Recent research shows that people differ from each other in the frequency and intensity of their flow experiences. These differences are not just found in Western cultures. In a study conducted on Japanese students, those who reported experiencing flow more often in their daily lives engaged in more daily activities and were more likely to have higher levels of self-esteem, *jujitsukan* (a sense of fulfillment), life-satisfaction, better coping strategies and lower anxiety.

Research has shown that those high in neuroticism tend to have less motivation to become involved in activities and experience a great sense of futility in engaging fully in life. The researcher in the above study offered some possible mechanism that could account for the association. One possibility is that the negative emotions that come with high neuroticism interfere with the state of joy that occurs when a person is in flow state. Another possibility is that the fluctuation in emotion that comes with neuroticism can also affect both the cognitive and emotional aspects of flow, causing a disruption in flow. A third possibility is that neuroticism impacts flow indirectly, through the life choices of those high in neuroticism make on a moment-to-moment basis. As I mentioned earlier, those high on neuroticism tend to have less motivation to become involved in activities and experience a greater sense of futility in emerging fully in life. For instance, an artist opined, *"When I make a new composition, initially I do enjoy but eventually I feel that it amounts to nothing. Neither to popularity nor to money. This is the reason why I am unable to create a master-piece even though I am aware of my capabilities."*

An association between flow and conscientiousness has also been found. Those who are more dutiful and preserving also tend to report higher levels of flow in their daily lives. This association is probably due to the fact that conscientiousness is positively related to other variables that are also associated with flow, such as social problem solving, life satisfaction, subjective happiness, positive affect, and intrinsic motivation. Conscientious individuals are also more likely to spend the time practicing to master challenging tasks, conditions which make flow more likely. "It seems likely that high conscientiousness involves emotional and motivational mechanisms that make an individual engaged in flow-promoting activities. Girija Devi said, "Once I sit for rigorous *riyaz,* hours and hours pass but at the end of the *riyaz* ,I found myself elated and satisfied. During *riyaz* I felt connected to God and I ended up shedding tears during *riyaz.*"

Intelligence would be related to flow due to its ability to control attention. But, flow maybe a state of effortless attention that relies on different mechanisms from those involved in attention during mental efforts. Being prone to Flow is associated with personality rather than intelligence.

Flow is an experience of enjoyment, concentration, and low self-awareness that occurs during active task performance. It is a self-reflective state that may also alter time perception of an individual. Pt. Kameshwar Pathak said, "When I create compositions I neither feel hungry nor thirsty. When I end up making a beautiful composition it gives me immense joy. For hours and hours I sing that composition with my disciples. Differing taste of music of various people is not a source of concern for me while composing. There is this incredible sense of joy which is inexpressible."

Hence, flow is highly enjoyable, i.e. performance is accompanied by positive effect.

According to Pt. Govardhan Mishra, flow denotes the holistic sensation when we act with total involvement. It is the state in which action follows upon action according to an internal logic which seems to need no conscious intervention on our part. We experience it as a unified action flowing from one moment to the next, in which we feel in control of our action and in which there is a little difference between self and environment or between stimulus and response. He talked about total involvement in the activity when nothing else mattered while doing it. He shared that "once I was trying to compose a song in *Raga Malkauns* but I was not fully satisfied by the composition. I kept working on it for 7 to 8 hours and became extremely emotional while creating it. I was all alone there and unable to remember how and when I slept there. But, in my sleep I dreamt that I am trying to swim and cross a river but I am unable to do so. After a few moments I felt that someone is holding my hand and taking me across the river. I kept following the person without any fear. After sometime I got up from my sleep, must be around 4:00 a.m. in the morning and I again started composing, but this time I found that without any other thought my fingers were playing *Raga Bhairavi* and a very beautiful composition came out. I will call it a flow experience. It was a very enjoyable moment of my life and I was so involved in this activity that nothing else mattered while doing it."

In my interactions with Vidushi Savita Devi, I observed her bodily movement and facial expressions, which reflected an intense expression of emotions. During her rehearsal many times she would enter flow because she would be free from being judged. But, in her performance she hardly entered the flow like any other artists.

Flow can be understood in three phases: 1. Finding Flow 2. Experiencing flow, and 3. The impact of flow experience on the performer's life. After an experience of flow, Dr. Shanti Hiranand said, "I have found my happiness that comes from within. If you always play music with your heart, you could find your own happiness that you create by yourself. So, basically it all starts from within." Pt. Kameshwar Pathak shared that he started learning Hindustani classical music when he was 6 years old. His guru told him to work very hard and join many music *baithak* with other performers and every time he was supposed to be outstanding. He felt that challenge was more demanding than his skills. It became difficult for him to connect with the soul of the compositions and experience something akin to flow even during his *riyaz*, because to experience flow the challenge should be balanced with the skills. Moreover, his goal to win the competition was an exotelic experience, and flow is all about an autotelic experience and intrinsic motivation.

Once during a conversation Ms. Prabhati Mukherjee said that flow is about positive emotion, so one should use their cognitive process first and then emotional process to enter the flow. Your personality and disposition to use your cognition (thinking, knowing, remembering, judging and problem solving in gaining knowledge of music) also require you to process the experience merging action, awareness and loss of self-consciousness.

Every artist could find his/her own experience of flow. Environmental support and life events are significant factors in helping someone to find flow. Personality disposition to cognition needs different process to experience flow which is positive emotion and also find suitable activities which involves cognition process before emotion process. The teaching method and environmental support is a significant factor to help someone to find the flow experience; teaching method to play music by heart and environmental support to help someone doing activity by intrinsic motivation or autotelic experience.

Once Girija Ji said, "When I had started learning music, I used to be alert while singing but after some years of training I started feeling really comfortable and enjoying *thumri.*" Sometimes she would feel as if she started losing her self-consciousness and experiencing intrinsic motivation to just go on. This would perhaps be called experiencing intense flow. She continued, "Sometimes, I experience as if I were on a different plane altogether... where there is just me and my music during my performance. The kind of music to be performed and the audience is something that I have always kept in mind initially because I want to communicate something to audience through music."

At the age of 87, she said "I always try to perform well in every performance, so it becomes a challenging skill to balance for her. She said "I always sing *thumri* by heart. I am not aware that I have sung for three-four hours. It always happens when I rehearse with my team." She further said, "When I have life problems and I have to rehearse or perform, I just forget my problems. I only feel for me and my music and not about other things."

This made her sing with a sense of control. She would feel good enough to perform with no worries. Her flow experience facilitated the peak performances so that she could improvise better in her every performance. It would be the moment when she could be more productive and creative. She herself narrated that she couldn't repeat the improvisation after performance. It would just happen spontaneously for her. Positive emotion from her performance made her feel more connected to the audience. Pt. Chhannulal Mishra said, "When I compose something new, there is no external effort as such; it's basically my feelings and something that is inside me that comes out through this practiced skill that I have. I forget myself, time and my surrounding. I look for a quite place to concentrate while composing music. Then it feels like automatically my mind is getting accompanied by the team of my musicians." This is perhaps finding flow in creativity. He added, "I feel so satisfied and happy when I make music to be a story for listeners; music made from what I am seeing, thinking and feeling."

When I asked Savita Ji about flow, she said, "Not often, but sometimes I enter flow while singing." She shared an incident of 29th March 1996, which she believed to be miraculous and something that defied any logic. "Those days I was working very hard on new compositions for my cassette named *'Baramasa.'* Like any other day, that day also I woke up early in the morning around 5:30 a.m. and settled down with my harmonium. I put on the cassette recorder and started singing *"Bhor hi Madhupur jaaye re udho."* While setting the composition in *Raga Lalit,* I was fully immersed in my music. I had no self-awareness as such. After setting the composition, I rewound the tape and heard it again. To my utter astonishment I felt that there was another voice singing along with me. It was followed by a distinct breathing sound. As the tape played on, a deep-throated voice could be heard from it, which was clearly audible. I went numb and I played the tape again and again till there was no doubt left in my mind that the other voice on the tape belonged to my mother, who had died many years ago before this incident. A sense of great joy and exhilaration swept over me. I ran up to wake up my son, who also heard the tape and confirmed that the other voice really did belong to my mother and she sang the *aalaap* when it was required to fill the gap. I have preserved that cassette carefully. I strongly believe that my *maa* came to bless me that morning."

Pt. Rajan-Sajan Mishra also said, "Generally, ego comes with success in human beings and in order to keep it with us, artists select songs which would captivate the audiences but they can never enter flow at such moments as the emphasis is on pleasing the audience."

In their opinion, flow is "like a gap that is filled by some heavenly power – God and the only way to enter it is through surrender. We sing for God and he joins us in our singing through flow by snatching our consciousness for some moments".

They further elaborated that an artist becomes egoless when he/she feels that they are just a medium through which their gurus are expressing themselves.

Sometimes the presentation and performance of the artists is such that the audience also experience the timelessness and abundant joy, thus entering flow. One of the music lovers recalled that once when Akhtari Bai was singing a *hori* in *Raga Peelu,* it started raining suddenly. She swiftly shifted to a *kajri* in *Raga Peelu.* The audience was also singing with her and shifted to *kajri.* After a while when it stopped raining, Begum Sahiba addressed the audience and brought their attention to it. The audience was so mesmerized and enthralled that they hardly recognized the shift until Begum Sahiba pointed it out herself. And then, she again came back to her *hori* very smoothly, showcasing her prowess and creativity. The gradual shift was the creation of the moment and was the result of her surrender to the performance and her total involvement. This would be nothing less than a flow experience.

Flow experiences in a wide range of activities from playing chess playing to climbing mountains (Csikszetmihalyi, 1998). While there appear to be considerable differences between individuals with regard to the conditions and tasks that are conducive to flow, the state itself is described in remarkably similar terms regardless of socio-economic states, age, culture and ethnicity (Asakawa, 2004, 2009, Bassi and Fave, 2004, Csikszetmihalyi and Csikszetmihalyi, 1988, Moneta, 2004).

There is large individual difference that exists in frequency and intensity of flow experiences (Asakawa 2009, Csikszetmihalyi and Schneider, 2000, Moneta 2004). These differences are likely to depend both on individual traits and on situational variables. Flow proneness is positively related to self-esteem, self-concept and perceived ability (Adlai-Gail, 1994, Asakawa, 2009; Jackson, Thomas, Marsh and Smelthurst, 2001). Negative relations have been reported between flow experience and anxiety (Asakawa, 2009, Jackson *et al;* 1998).

The greatest part of our happiness depends on our dispositions, not on our circumstances. Siddeshwari Devi believed that satisfaction and contentment in life are two most important ingredients to lead a 'rich' life. It helps the individual in finding meaning and happiness in everything around them. According to her such people are capable of experiencing bliss provided by life and universe. Research also suggests that people experiencing high flow is significantly related to life satisfaction. According to Abraham Maslow (1970) "Joy and Peak Experiences", happiness accompanies growth towards self-actualization. According to this view, happiness is both a result and an accelerator of growth.

In relation to satisfaction with self, the result showed:

- Significant relationship between flow and satisfaction of self.
- Age is significantly related to flow experience in the total pool. Thus, the intensity of flow increases with age.
- Education is significantly related to flow experience.

CONDITIONS OF FLOW

First, the goal should be clear for the activity. Secondly, experiencing a balance between the challenge of the task and the skills of the individual. Thirdly, receiving immediate feedback concerning the performance of the individual in the activity. Finally, the task shouldn't be judged by anyone while entering the flow.

Flow has been investigated in terms of its influence on psychological well-being and findings intricate relationships with several other variables. It is characterized by complete absorption in what one does, a resulting loss in one's sense of space and time and instilling hope and optimism for future.

CHAPTER 9

Seeing Sliver Lining in Dark Cloud

Hope is such an energy by which any dark part of life can be illuminated.

- Avinash Mestry

Seeing Sliver Lining in Dark Cloud

Till now, various predispositions necessary for an artist have been discussed but another important one in this bouquet is hope and optimism. In the absence of these two traits a person can't get a hold on himself during his trial or bad days. Life is a journey which combines both smooth and tough times and optimism is very important to continue this journey. Pandit Rajan-Sajan Mishra were extremely optimistic during their interaction, their key advice was to have faith and believe in yourself and your abilities. They said, "with a boundless vision, determination, motivation and dedication towards your guru and your musical riyaaz, anything is achievable. We should always be hopeful because there is a light despite all of the darkness. We have seen so many ups and downs in our lives."

Rita Ganguly, as I have already recounted, is a highly educated and multi-talented artist full of hope and optimism. She came across as a supportive and motivating living legend who tries her best to instill hope in upcoming artists. She helps them in getting opportunities to showcase their talents. Several established artists feel grateful to her for her contribution in their career and the push she gave them when they were struggling. She is a true senior and guide, a powerhouse of hope and optimism.

Hope has been defined as the goal-directed thinking in which people perceive that they can produce routes to desired goals (considered as pathways thinking) and the requisite motivation to use those routes (called as agency thinking). Thus, hope is understood as the sum of two components (i) the ability to plan pathways to desired goals despite obstacles and (ii) motivation to use those pathways. Siddheshwari Devi had undying optimism, and the ability to perceive hope in the most hopeless of situations. She saw something positive even in the most depressing times. Life had never been easy for her. She had struggled hard for all that she achieved, and she knew that for her this struggle would be unending. Experience had taught her that it was important to detect a silver lining under each cloud, and then polish it until it lit up the cloud, like a halo. The expulsion from her aunt, Rajeshwari Devi's house threw her out of the shelter. This brought hunger and insecurity but it also brought freedom from the hard work of daily chores. Now Siddheshwari had a lot of time for her taleem with her guru. She progressed quickly. However, the pressure to sing and earn money was an absolute necessity for her livelihood. She started giving performances in weddings and religious festivals to earn money. She was very optimistic. She continued her learning. Her first big public performance was in 1925 at Ranka in Sarguja (Madhya Pradesh) at the young age of seventeen. She sang khyal *thumri*, dadra, bhajan. The great Kesarbai was also there. By the grace of God, the number of her performances grew larger each day and her voice travelled far and wide.In any situation where a valued goal is pursued, the hopeful goal-directed behavior will be determined by the interaction of the degree to which the outcome or goal is valued, interaction of thoughts about possible pathways to the goals and related expectations about how effective these will be in achieving the outcome or goal and interaction of the thought about personal motivation and effective one will be in following paths to goals. Pt. Ajoy Chakravarty believed that faith in guru, God, one's skill, and optimistic attitude are the key to success and overcoming all kinds of struggles. He emphasized the importance of riyaaz that one puts in, in order to achieve his/her goal.

All three of these factors depend upon thoughts brought to the situation based on past experience and development in two areas: (i) thoughts about pathways to goals based on developmental lessons concerning correlations and causality, and (ii) thoughts about motivation based on developmental lessons about the self. Here, many artists believe that in developing this sort of motivation, the guru has a major role to play as they not only help the individual with the craft but also helps with daily living, teach a way of life and encourage personal betterment. Our very charming and happy-go-lucky stalwart Vidushi Prabhati Mukherjee says that hope and optimism are two most beautiful colours and a powerful source of motivation in human life. I have attained my professional training under Ustad Bade Ghulam Ali Khan Sahib and Begum Akhtar Sahiba, the two towering personalities of Indian classical music. Apart from music training, they always made me psychologically prepared for life's struggles. Khan Sahib always used to tell me that the lives of artists are full of struggles better to be proposed for. She said, "I have heard so many struggle full and sad stories of my AmmiJi, Begum Akhter's life. I have also faced so many tough times in my life but the streams of hope from rivers of

Punjab (Bade Ghulam Ali Khan) and rivers of Uttar Pradesh (Begum Akhtar) always flow in my life. So have faith in your Gurus, your parents and other elders' blessings in your life. They will raise hope and optimism in every junction of your life. My blessings to all the budding artists to have courage, hope and optimism in life, you all will definitely achieve your goals through good guidance and hard-work."

Snyder (2000) suggests that hope develops in a clearly defined way over the course of infancy, childhood and adolescence. By the first year of life, object constancy and cause and effect schemes allow infants to have anticipatory thoughts about pathways to goals. During the preschool period from 3-6 years, the rapid development of language, preoperational intuitive thinking, interest in story-telling, and predictable routines, allows for the further growth of hopeful pathway planning in the face of barriers and obstacles. In middle childhood and preadolescence there is a rapid growth in logical rather than intuitive thinking skills, memory skills, reading skills and advanced social perspective taking skills. These allow for increasingly sophisticated hopeful planning and pursuing pathways towards valued goals and doing so within a social context mindful of the wishes of their parents, siblings and teachers. Children who develop a hopeful disposition typically have parents who serve as hopeful role models and who guide them in developing and executing plans to circumvent barriers to valued goals. These children generally have a secure attachment to their parents who provide them with a warm family environment in which conflict is managed in a predictable and fair way. When Shanti Ji was asked about her personal view on hope she said that, "in the field of art at this stage of life I carve each student very honestly with full optimism because they are the future hope of the nation in the field of Indian music. My Ammi (Begum Akhtar) has passed her sanskar (ordination) to me." She used to say that every earthen pot has an inherent capacity to contain untold treasures. That is the Guru's duty to teach each student to the best of his or her capacity and let the student sore. "Some of the students take the knowledge given by me as a blessing in present time too, although commercialization has entered this field too. My Guru even told me that those teachers who hide things from their students were doing a disservice to the Guru-shishya relationship and also fiddling with the future of upcoming artists."

Adolescence and youngsters develop abstract reasoning skills. These skills facilitate the management of complex issues including autonomy from parents, forming exclusive intimate relationships and developing career plans. These challenges provide opportunities for hopeful planning and hopeful pursuit of plans despite setbacks and barriers. During his interaction Pandit Govardhan Mishra said that, "once my child came to me and asked papa when will I get a break in this field? Since my childhood I have been learning this art from you. I try to contact so many cultural institutions but no one calls me back. I am helping my friends with music. Then I replied to him that you will definitely get a very good chance. You start saving money and go to the recording studio, start sending your resume with your recorded piece. And for this start doing rigorous riyaaz. If you desire to receive you must first give. He said I don't have that money. I advised him to take tuitions. It will improve your level of understanding of the subject too. Then from the very next day he started contacting people for tuition. He got one student. He was happy and more opportunities followed. The optimism in his voice was significant. I was also very happy. After some months of tuition and personal riyaaz, he collected money for recording and did it successfully. After 6 months he got a break. Now he was hopeful to get more but he continued his tuition classes. He was quite popular among students."

Some but not all children who are neglected, abused, bereaved or who are exposed to ongoing inter-parental conflict associated with separation or divorce may fail to develop a hopeful disposition. Children who grow up in a particularly stressed environment are more likely to become resilient and hopeful under certain circumstances (Mahoney, 1991). First, these children become aware that their parents have difficulties and so categorize their parent's inadequate parenting as a parental shortcoming rather than a personal shortcoming. Second, these children have other adults who can routinely meet their needs for care, control and intellectual stimulation. Third, these children identify and refine a special talent or gift early in their lives which gives them access to new supportive social networks. Fourth, they have a high motivation to develop their talents marked by persistence and tenacity. Finally, they address adversity as a challenge or opportunity for development rather than an obstacle.

Hopeful adults have distinctive profiles (Snyder, 2000). Adults, who have high levels of hope have experienced as many setbacks as others in their lives, but have developed beliefs that they can adapt to challenges and cope with adversity. They maintain an ongoing positive internal dialogue including statements such as 'I can do it', 'I will not give up', etc. They focus on success rather than failure. This may be because they creatively generate alternative routes to achieve their goals when they encounter barriers or flexibly select other more achievable goals. When people with low hope encounter surrounding table barriers their emotions follow a relatively predictable sequence from rage to despair to apathy. When faced with problems in adult life, people with high levels of hope tend to break large vague problems into small clearly defined and manageable problems. Before becoming a professional vocalist, Pt. Kameshwar Pathak was working as an executive in a firm in Kolkata. He had an understanding of music with a rich and melodious voice but didn't think of pursuing it professionally. Once Gyan Prakash Ghosh Ji heard his singing at a party, he told him to quit his job. Pathak Ji left his job and went back to his home state Bihar and got involved in riyaaz. It was his hope and optimism which initiated the process for him. Pt. Kameshwar Pathak also shared about his financial struggles, especially after leaving his job to pursue music and give his time and effort to daily and rigorous riyaaz. But, he would also say, "I always had a ray of hope in my mind that I will definitely succeed one day and believed that the goddess of hope will surely fulfill my wish." He further added how his optimistic attitude helped him in striving further and continuing his riyaaz, despite all the circumstantial difficulties.

Another important term worth discussing here is optimism. At one extreme, optimism has been conceptualized as a broad personality trait characterized by general optimistic expectations (Scheier and Carver, 1985) while at the other it has construed as an explanatory style (Seligman, 1998), that is, researchers have made a distinction between dispositional optimism and optimistic explanatory style in which the causes of negative events are attributed to external, transient, specific factors rather than internal, stable, global factors. After the sad demise of her husband the *thumri* queen of her era Padma Vibhushan Girija Ji had stopped singing. She said that, "my husband was my strength, my source of hope and optimism in the field of music, as well as my life." But after some time, other artists, her relatives and other friends advised her to start singing again. She was offered the seat of Guru from Poorab Ang in ITC- SRA, Kolkata, a Gurukul of present time and a beautiful example of guru-shishya parampara. She migrated to Kolkata as she was not willing to sing in Banaras. She started singing and teaching music to her disciples. She said that, "when I started singing, I could feel the presence of my husband as if he was still inspiring me to sing. In every disciple I could see the lamp of hope, who are not only going to light up the gayaki of Poorab Ang but also keep the tradition alive and growing day-by-day. I must appreciate the ambience of ITC-SRA, which again raised hope and optimism in me." So hope is stronger than any setbacks. Hope and optimism tells us that our potential is limitless. Girija Ji earned immense respect as a guru and as an artist and had been conferred one of the highest civilian awards Padma Vibhushan.

Dispositional optimism is a belief that more good things than bad will happen in the future. Scherer and Colleagues argue that optimistic people, in the face of difficulties, continue to pursue their valued goals and regulate themselves and their personal states using effective coping strategies so that they are likely to achieve their goals. After spending 5-6 years of marital life with her husband Tabla maestro Pandit Kishan Maharaj, Vidushi Savita led a separated life and reared her two sons alone. When her elder son was 18 years old and younger son was 16 years old both the brothers met with a car accident. It was a head on collision and the elder son lost his life on the spot and the younger one was rushed to the intensive care unit. Savita Ji on one hand had to manage the last rites of her elder son all alone and on the other hand she had to take care of her younger son who was in I.C.U. and circling death. At this moment when I am writing about this incident, I am getting goosebumps because I am writing about my own Guru's sons, my extended family. Fortunately, the younger son won the battle but Savita Ji slipped into a deep depression after this incident. Artists are generally of a self-beating nature. She said that after some months of my son's sad demise, I saw him in my dream. He was saying to me "Maa stop remembering me. Whenever you remember me I have to come to you and it hurts me. Can't you see my forehead, it's bleeding. I was coming to meet you through a boat and I got injured. So please stop remembering me." Savita Ji wept like anything. Then she gradually started diverting her mind and stopped remembering her son frequently as per his demand, a very tough time for a mother. As time passed she felt a ray of hope in her. One day her late mother the legend Vidushi Siddheshwari Ji came in her dream and told her to get up, be strong and restart singing. "You are the only hope and source of inspiration for your younger son. You have the responsibility to carry forward the family lineage." Then she again started teaching her disciples and performing on the stage. So parenthood instilled a sense of purpose, motivation, hope and optimism in life. And her optimism made her a signature vocalist of Banaras Gharana. Optimism is the faith that led to achievement. Apart from her own achievements, her son is also a big achiever. He is a top executive in a leading multinational company. Hats off to her!

Dispositional intervention is associated with good health and a positive response to medical interventions for conditions such as heart disease and cancer. This impact of dispositional optimism on recovery from medical proceedings is mediated by effective coping strategies as redefinition or reframing. Persists, in contrast, use avoidant coping strategies or disengage from coping with problems. Ustad Bade Gulam Ali Khan Sahib had always been an extremely generous person. In 1961, when he fell ill all the savings were spent on his treatment. When a performing artist is bedridden, he cannot earn in any other way and has to depend on his savings and the support of his family and friends. At the time of his illness, the film industry rose to occasion. A big concert was organized to raise funds for his medical treatment. Bade Ghulam Ali Khan Sahib was not even allowed to move, let alone roar like a lion in a small cage. His left side was totally paralyzed and he could barely speak. For the past fifty years, it had been his daily routine to do his riyaz first thing in the morning, but now when he tried to sing, no sound emerged from his throat! This was a great tragedy and the height of misfortune for a mighty vocalist like him, but his spirit was undaunted and even while in the hospital, he would try to sing. It was risky for him to strain his heart. His reply was, "I don't want to live if I cannot sing." His family believed that some enemy had cast an evil spell on Khan Sahib by doing some black magic to destroy his career. Within two weeks, he was allowed to go home from the hospital and gradually his health improved. He was such an optimistic man he started his riyaz. His home was once again resounded with the mighty torrents of Bade Ghulam Ali Khan Sahib's powerful voice. He said that I have done strenuous riyaz three times in my life. The first when I was a child and being trained by my Guru and uncle Kaale Khan Sahib, second after my Guru's death. I practiced on my own-18 to 20 hours a day, and the third and most difficult riyaz was bringing my voice into action after my paralytic attack. This time his voice resembled the vast ocean whose might and depth was unfathomable. If he could evoke the mood of solemnity and high seriousness, he could also bring about the feeling of light heartedness and joy, of good cheer, and well-being. So, optimism is a happiness magnet.

Once while Begum Akhtar was at a concert in Bombay, she suddenly decided to go to Mecca for the Haj. The Haj authorities in Bombay tried to dissuade her as it was against the tenets of Islam to go to perform Haj in such an unplanned way. She did not care about anything, just said I have a personal equation with God. "I am optimistic he will take care of everything." She just collected her programme fees and bought a ticket and flew off. Nothing could deter her.

Now when she reached Madina, she had no money in her pocket. What could she possibly do? The Roza at Madina, the jaali that covers the prophet Mohammad's resting place, is a very sacred spot. She began to recite the holy Naat there. People collected and soon enough everyone realized who she was. Immediately the local Radio Station approached her to come and record the Naat on radio. She did so and received a payment for it. And thus, she could complete the rest of her journey; a personality full of confidence, optimism and faith in her beliefs and value system. She used to say, "they (disciples) have to carry this lineage for the next generation. I believe that if I stay positive, good things and good people will automatically come to me."

The development of optimism is determined by parental mental health, role models offered by parents and society and also the degree to which they encourage and reward various deeds. Individuals with an optimistic explanation are less likely to develop physical ill-health, depression or suicidality when presented with major stressful events. In adulthood optimisms are associated with better academic achievement, sports performance, occupational adjustment and family life and response to bereavement and loss.

CHAPTER 10

Behavior Says It All

The prime responsibility of a leader is to help people to be successful.

Behavior Says It All

SINGERS TEND TO BE PREDOMINANTLY ARTISTIC INDIVIDUALS, THAT is, they are creative and original and work well in a setting that allows for self-expression. They also tend to be enterprising, which means that they are usually quite natural leaders who are good at influencing others.

Confidence may not bring success but gives power to face any challenge in life. Most confident people that I know of today were shy, socially anxious and desperate in their teens and early 20s. However, they decided to bring a change and build the habits and behavior of confident individuals hence this trait is not essentially an inherent trait.

Most stalwarts I met were very confident and knowledgeable people, very keen to transform the society through their music. They were also very cautious towards health and hygiene. They had strong body languages and were relaxed in their environment. Once Girija Ji said that whatever may be the circumstances, the show must go on successfully. It is the prime responsibility of the main artist. He or she has to behave like a good leader who has self-control as well as control over their team members. She added that it's her message for upcoming artists that they should be prepared to adapt themselves in any adverse situation. To quote her exact words, she said, "Whenever you face an adverse time you should not run around anxiously. Slow down yourself and take a deep breath. You will instantly feel more confident, and then move with ease and intention to your destination."

Dr. Shanti Hiranand said this during an interaction, "If you want to be an artist you have to behave like a confident leader." She suggested that young artists should speak less and listen to others more and give their suggestions only when they have something important to contribute. Further, she said that one shouldn't waste words and time on unimportant matters.

Confident people don't care about the opinions of others and this is reflected by the facts. Generally, they speak their truth. Pandit Chhannulal Mishra shared his experience and said, "I am from a poor family background. Sometimes I had to spend my time on one *chapati* and chutney (sauce). I was born in Haripur, Bihar. My father used to send five rupees and it would cater to the needs of 10-12 people. That time we used to buy 12 kg of rice worth 1 rupee. I am in my early 80's. We have worked very hard in our lives. One thing was there; I never waited for permission from anyone, if I believed my move was right." Pandit Govardhan Mishra too said, "I have always chartered my own path without asking anyone." Dr. Shanti Hiranand writes in her book, *The Story of my Ammi*, "To a large extent, I feel even my husband could not develop into a more meaningful bond because my first priority was always my love to Ammi." She is so confident that she did not care about the opinions of others and spoke the truth.

These are the qualities of a confident leader. Pandit Rajan-Sajan Mishra Ji spoke without any hesitation about their 'struggling phase' when they shifted to Delhi. They used to commute by bus. Even Savita Ji used to commute by bus from her college to home. Pandit Ajoy Chakrabarty said this in his interview, "We were financially weak during our young age. I have worked very hard in my life." We very well know that all the stalwarts are *Padma Bhushan* awardees, amongst other recognitions. Thus, success comes at a great cost. Confident people speak their truths whenever and wherever possible, this is reflected in their interactions as well.

Pandit Govardhan Mishra, who was my *Shastra Guru,* used to say, "Many a times, I laugh at my own mistakes and shortcomings. When someone laughs at me, I try to blow it off and turn it into a joke." This is a sign of a confident person because he knows that no one is flawless and without any shortcomings.

Sometimes I used to tell him that I do not know the many nuances of music, then his reply was, "So what! I know you very well, you possess so many good traits, which others don't. You have good knowledge in other subjects." A good Guru always tries to inspire you. In this way, we make a balance of knowledge in society, you are the only one who has to live with yourself, your knowledge and your decisions hence, lead a relaxed life.

Stalwarts usually treat others with respect. All of them are great Gurus (teachers in *Guru- Shishya Parampara*) and a Guru has to play the role of knowledgeable and confident leader or guide. They are always keen to learn new things despite being highly knowledgeable people in their field. Even though they refuse to accept immature ideas from other people, they are kind to others and never humiliate people to make themselves look better in any dimension. My Gurus, Vidushi Savita Ji or Pandit Govardhan Mishra or even my Guru Pandit Mohinder Sareen Sahib always gave me freedom to express myself. They used to lift me up. They listened to my songs or ideas very carefully and always said, "that you are right but I have a suggestion which you can add to evoke emotions in lyrics and make it more meaningful." They always invested their intelligence in my ideas to improve its quality.

I found one common feature among all the stalwarts: that they complement others and flatter their new acquaintances. They know that the only way to get ahead in life is to help other people and they are masters at shifting the spotlight from themselves to others. They always take care of their team members, students and other people who are related to their fields. My view is that in the field of art one must know to make others feel special and before speaking anything one should let one's words pass through three tests: Is it true? Is it necessary? Is it kind?

A good artist has to have very good character, which is based on their personality. They should be empathetic and forgiving. They should challenge themselves to be a better person. They should be committed to their art and faithful to everyone, especially to their Guru, parents, colleagues and family. A guide should be loyal even to his disciples; a guru should stay true to their words and themselves as people with integrity are highly respected. According to Mr. Kameshwar Pathak, one can't go very high in one's career without having high moral values and for this they should be loyal to their parents, life partners and be a role model for their children and disciples. They should be passionate towards their work with motivated people who want to create an extraordinary life filled with good choices. Kameshwar Pathak once said, "Meenakshi Ji, I would like to tell you one thing, when I start teaching a student and I find that there are no possibilities for him in the field of music, then I clearly advise him or her that if you are learning this art for de-stressing yourself or just as a hobby then it's OK but you should not treat this subject as your future career; go read something else. We should always give right advice to newcomers. After all, it's our moral responsibility. I am a mentor; I have to serve others. If I won't show the right path to my disciples, it will be a sin against God."

Actually, all the stalwarts are human beings first and they know that having high character and skills are most important which would benefit them in becoming successful and remaining at their seats. They have unanimously agreed upon self-control as an important behavior to lead a respectful life.

Singing with emotion connects you with your audience in a very real way. They have let the audience enter into their world and through their voice they give the audience a glimpse into their heart and soul. A great singer relives the emotion and feeling, not only in his singing but with his entire body. If it is a sad song for instance, think about how you feel when you are feeling sad? And secrete it physically through your facial expression, with an icky feeling in your chest as well as emotionally and produce that feeling though the song. Find a comfortable place, take a moment to recreate an emotion and use the vowels like Hai (हाय), Oh (ओह), Oof (उफ) etc.

The singer is not merely planning his *swaras* accurately in the scale but is putting himself into the act of singing, a vital part of it is how the music appears to him. It is important from the view-point of phenomenological aesthetics, because when a musician seems to be singing with his throat alone, however manifested by its grammatical correctness, the *rasika* will not be able to establish connection with it, and the singing will only offer a surface-level satisfaction. That's why a live recital by Ameer Khan or Kumar Gandharva could appear much more convincing and spellbinding than their recorded music. Likewise, in the field of *thumri*, performances of Ustad Bade Ghulam Ali Khan, Begum Akhtar, Girija Devi, Pandit Chhannulal Mishra and many more are much appreciated. The fact that they are lost, contemplating their music, serves as directly, if not as discursively, to deepen the power of their music as *abhinaya*.

The special quality of Siddheshwari Devi's music came from her deep spiritualism. When she sang, she seemed to be singing not merely for her immediate audience but for some higher being. This mystic quality of her singing is what made her different from the other musical exponents of her time. While singing, her whole being appeared to be immersed in the melody as though she had transcended to a higher world of her own. While discussing her philosophy of music and its grand mystique, she often used to say, 'Music is love-- the greatest prayer. It is both the easiest and the most difficult endeavor of human life. Prayer means meditation, and music is the meditation of love.'

In this world of illusion or *maya*, Siddheshwari Devi's anchor in life remained her profound faith in the existence of God. She believed with deep intensity that her life and destiny were shaped by an unseen force much beyond her comprehension. Yet it was within her reach because she approached it with a chaste and uncorrupted heart and mind.

In Girija Devi's singing the amorous remonstrations of Radha got infused with the spiritual. This added a much more exquisite colors than the usual red, yellow and pink *gulaal* to the Holi she described in her songs. Girija Devi often said that she felt closest to her God when she was lost in music. As one of the audiences said, she had a special love for *thumris* - and she had a storehouse, a *bandhar*, full of them. Her rendering of *"Ras ke bhare tore nain"* and *"Maa, kari badariya barse"* are unforgettable.

Many female artists discussed gender discrimination

in this field. Supporting the prevailing stereotype and assigned gender roles, it has been believed that one gender is intrinsically superior to another. Sexism can affect anyone but primarily affects women and girls and that has been the case in this field as well. Girija Ji mentioned that "tentatively less than 5 percent of producers are women, less than 10 percent females are on the decision making seats in cultural organizations." Except governmental organizations where fees of the artists are fixed as per a given criteria, the non-governmental organization makes payments willfully. Sometimes female artists are even better than male artists, but are paid less. But now many women have started refusing less payments in a plea for equal respect. One of the female stalwarts said, that young female artists at times also face sexual harassment and objectification. She considered this to be a major challenge for the profession.

ShantiJi said that, "I am happy that now females are learning all the instruments like tabla, sarangi, harmonium and they are making their own groups. Young artists should come forward and raise their voice against any kind of abuse or harassment happening with them. These efforts will improve the image and also create a fear free environment for female artists". Savita Ji said that not only in music but in all the fields girls should come forward, do hard work and try to grab the decision making posts. When the resources will be female-dominated only then gender based harassment will come to an end, not only in the field of music but in all the sectors of society.

Prabhati Ji said that to improve the environment for more opportunities for women, seeing more female representations and leadership, providing more support and recognition will help in tackling sexual harassment and objectification. Siddheshwari Devi used to say that we can solve this problem of society by not only empowering our female segment but by sowing seeds of moral value, discipline and respect for each other at a very young age. She was definitely a visionary.

Success is learning that losing a few battles can help you win a war. Successful people choose their battles wisely. When you know which battles will ultimately help you achieve your goals, you will be successful. When you feel like giving up, remind yourself what you are fighting for. Your "why" should be very strong.

In the following section, I would like to mention the views of stalwarts on success.

As Pandit Ajoy Chakrabarty said that success is a gift that we give to ourselves with the hard work that we put into developing the potential that we have. No one can push anyone into becoming successful, because success is an inward journey that one has to eventually undertake on the strength of one's own merits and commitments. He says about highly successful people like Vijay Kichlu and Ustad Zakir Hussain that people like them are giants not just on the scale of contribution to music but also on the scale of human goodness and humility. On the 1990 Europe tour, he sang in Florence, in Italy. He remembers the visit for two reasons: one, because there was no stage and second because Ustad Zakir Hussain, world superstar by all measures accompanied him on *tabla* and Vijay Kichlu Sahib on *tanpura*. "I had also enjoyed accompanying Zakir bhai on tanpura and harmonium".

Shanti Ji's view on success was: *"I can't define success in one sentence, it consists of many things. One could argue that the definition depends on the individual and that one size does not fit all. But I must say it can be achieved when you try your best in all aspects of everything you do, even if that does not lead to big results. If you have done your best, you should feel proud of your efforts."*

Savita Ji said this about success, "Be realistic when setting goals; if you know where you are heading that is success in itself, even if you don't ultimately arrive at the planned destination."

As per Prabhati Ji, if you are able to tell yourself that you can achieve the goals in your plan, you are doing great. It is the belief that "you can and you will definitely succeed" that she emphasized.

As per Kameshwar Pathak Ji, success is the fact that you have achieved what you want; doing well and becoming famous, rich or whatever your goals were. In the field of music, you have to do very hard work to achieve that. However, sometimes your success can harm your relationships.

According to Rajan-Sajan Mishra Ji, success is your guide for personal and professional development through inspiration, motivation and training. It requires exceptionally good training and rigorous *riyaaz.* "Every disciple comes to me with the expectations of name, fame and money. Up to a certain extent it is justified but the road to success needs a focused traveler with motivation, hope and inspiration provided by his or her Guru (guide) and his hard work."

Pandit Govardhan Mishra Ji used to say that no doubt success is your eventual goal but it brings ego and arrogance with it which is very harmful for the growth of established artists as well as upcoming artists.

Interpersonal relationship is an association between two or more people that may range from fleeting to enduring. The concept of interpersonal relationship involves social association, connections or affiliation between two or more people. It can be between friends, colleagues, family members etc. They are built on mutual respect, trust and loyalty and they can provide us with support, care and even love.

Pandit Rajan-Sajan Mishra said that an artist should be very good at maintaining interpersonal relationships. They must respect others. It is important for an individual to be honest and transparent and must stand by their friends in times of need.

Shanti Hiranand said, "We artists should avoid criticism and pulling legs. There can be professional rivalry but we should avoid such petty behavior since our interests and goals are similar, so we feel a strong bond with each-other. Sometimes we meet for tea or dinner and talk about some topic related to our field and enjoy the conversation."

Girija Ji said, "In my case, interpersonal relations play a very important role. I can't stay alone. Maintaining good interpersonal relationships is important for your overall physical and emotional happiness. It gives you a sense of purpose in life. Relationships have a positive impact on your personal and professional life. You should have the knack to build up relationships for making them enduring; you should frequently meet them. And remember one thing that meetings should not be for work or goal all the time, we must meet one another just as an informal get together."

According to Prabhati Ji, in our relationships, we should avoid the point of contention. It is important to listen to others point of view with full interest. If you have some issues with your colleagues, family members or everyone be sure to tell them. Hopefully they will reciprocate with respect and honesty. You should maintain a positive attitude.

Savita Ji said that one should be open to constructive criticism and feedback without letting the emotions take over. For maintaining good interpersonal relations, you should be very good at communication. This requires in-person discussions about your feelings, even at your workplace. Good leadership and effective communication play a pivotal role in building the ecosystem of strong interpersonal relationships and this profession requires hours of teamwork. Thus, it is very important to maintain a conflict free environment.

In the art world 'being social' is a must. Change in an

individual occurs because of contact with other people. People are influenced by the presence, opinions or behavior of others. We learn from other people, which is useful in understanding the norm, it is also important to affiliate with other people. Similarly, need for achievement and need power are other social motives than an individual strives for. Our stalwarts have also shed light on such issues.

According to Kameshwar Pathak, "in the art world being social is something you can't afford to avoid. Potential audiences need to hear from you to explain your art (background and meaning of lyrics before you start performing) and what makes it worth paying attention to." The more connections you make; the more opportunities you will learn about. This means more concerts will come your way. This is undoubtedly the best way to explain your art story. That's why it is essential to be social as a part of your profession. You can build relationships with others by attending concerts of different artists and you should also join the local artist community. Apart from your own concert, you should also support other artists and if you are an introverted person, perhaps initially you can take support of your close friend for interacting with new people. Show a genuine interest in their work. You never know what new connection you might make for your own profession. So, without socialization you won't get opportunities.

Since personal and social relations had a high priority in the scheme of things planned by Siddheshwari Devi, her house in Delhi too came to be known for its hospitality. Everyone could be sure of a warm welcome. It soon became a place where one could enjoy long drawn *addas*, conversations and free flowing discussions on music, dance, food, or anything that caught one's fancy. Accompanied by an unending supply of sweets, tea or sherbets, the *adda*s are still remembered by many who went there regularly or occasionally. She loved cooking and feeding people; almost every other day there was a feast cooked in the house. She herself was very fond of eating good and rich food. Sitting on a string cot with her box of betel leaves, she would flash her large sunny smile when greeting her visitors and would converse with them on many subjects.

Begum Akhtar was very particular in socializing. Once she was advising one of her friends that "Bibi, we should be very careful during our meeting. We should never try to equate ourselves with others. Always be in your boundary." Begum Sahiba had very good relations with almost all great artists as well as people of high society. She was so social that she used to have permanent bookings in hotels of Mumbai, Delhi and other big cities to visit the people of those places whenever she felt like. In Delhi she always preferred Nirula's Hotel and partied late into the night with her friends there. Poets would be there with their new works; musicians would stand in attendance for the 'Queen of Melody' from Lucknow. Her room was a beehive of activity from morning to night. Poets like Shakeel and Shamim would vie with each other to get their verses sung by her.

Bade Ghulam Ali Khan Sahab's home was also a meeting place for artists and musicians. He was very friendly and social and this nature helped him in establishing himself in Mumbai after his arrival there in 1940 from Punjab. Ganga Bai was a fine singer from Kumaon based in Mumbai, she was a popular singer, Ghulam Ali had heard from his guru, Kaale Khan Sahib about Ganga Bai and her helping nature. He met her in Bhindi Bazaar. Ganga Bai felt protective towards him in the same way as an elder sister would. Khan Sahib used to say that it was because of Ganga Bai's friendship and encouragement that he was able to establish himself in Mumbai. Genuine artists live in a world of their own and they can readily understand the emotional, financial problems of their sisters and brothers in the profession. He always helped other artists. He had a sunny and cheerful nature, because a genuine artist is truly content. He was always pleased to see visitors, greeted them warmly and immediately became interested and involved in their personal lives. It is believed that the Ustad of his caliber are supposed to be highly snobbish but he was very down to earth and innocent person. He served people by all means, financially, by sharing his knowledge and helped others in whatever way he could do.

Pandit Rajan Mishra said that there are so many ways to socialize online these days. One should use these opportunities to evolve. One could also join an artist association. He said that, "The more involved you are the more people you will meet. So make use of everything, attend events, volunteer in your colleagues' concerts, and take active part in events organized by your own Guru's academy." Pandit Sajan Mishra emphasized that "all your socializing doesn't have to be strictly with the artist's community. It is just equally important to get out, meet your friends with different interests." This also has an important role to play in the expansion of an artist and getting to hear all kinds of viewpoints.

According to Savita Devi, attending music workshops are a very useful gateway to make important connections for an upcoming artist, to add so many new things to your knowledge, workshops are important for beginners to professionals, so it is a great place to meet other artists, while learning a new skill. You can organize your own workshop. If you are nervous about teaching, get all your questions answered by your own guru or any guide on how to teach at your first artist workshop. Nowadays professionals are also available to guide you. But always try to put your best efforts to be excellent in "communication."

Communication as a key trait

Communication plays a very important role in music and art teaching and other teaching fields. The ability to communicate strongly in the mental, emotional and behavioral areas plays an important role in providing students with knowledge and skills. Empathy, empowerment and an understanding approach will always be the factors that increase success in collective and individual studies. Successful communication will provide positive contributions to the freedom and self-confidence of students in showing their abilities. Establishing a good connection and making co-operation with the parents and establishing the right communication with other colleagues and administrators will also increase professional success. It is seen that the communication skills of the disciples in music are the same in terms of mental, emotional and behavioral aspects irrespective of their genders.

Through time immemorial, art has survived even if the dynasties have vanished and villages have become cities. Rulers have established themselves and are remembered because of what their dynasty left behind through their paintings, murals and also their architecture; trying to tell for the ages and generations to come, of the legacy of their rule. Art was an important pivot in this. Thus, even today the choice of art as communication continues.

Being social creatures, humans have always been creative in letting out their emotions. And art gives an immense possibility to those who opt it as a medium. It gives the freedom to reign one's imagination and articulate or profess what one feels. Art just doesn't communicate emotions but also the time and the era that went by or might come, the sense of place, the customs and practices of the places and so much more that maybe words might fall short off. Art has also been considered to be therapeutic, and many psychologist have considered 'Art Therapy' as one of the ways to heal and help people who suffer from mental illness like depression, schizophrenia etc; the gesture of hands, the coordination of movement used in making the art, and the colors together become creative in nature, during the process of creation. The intriguing use of textures, colors and materials and their interesting manipulation to bring out one's inner thoughts and emotions help the person to overcome the inhibitions that they might hold in expressing through other mediums. (Knepler, 1953).

Effective communication is a key skill to becoming a good leader. It is not what you say but how you say it. It is more than just exchanging information. It is about understanding the intentions behind the information and being able to clearly convey a message that makes the other person feel heard and understood (Humes, 2008).

Effective Communication Skills

1. *Active Listening:* Listening is the most fundamental component of interpersonal communication skills. As the name suggests, it is about listening actively and concentrating on what is being said instead of passively listening to the speaker. Below are a few active listening techniques:

- *Reiterating and Summarizing*—This will help the person in understanding how you perceived the conversation and signals that you are confirming what was being said.
- *Demonstrating Engagement*— Using verbal affirmations during the conversation such as "Sure", "I see", "I understand" are very helpful and encourage the speaker to continue with the conversation. Your body language can also aid in showing interest in the conversation like nodding, smiling etc. (The art of communicating effectively, James Humes).

- *Waiting to disclose your opinion* — While we all have opinions we want to give or say during a conversation, hold off on disclosing your opinion until you have heard and understood the entire context of the conversation. Avoid interrupting or trying to redirect the conversation to your concerns. A good leader knows when to be quiet and listen.

2. **Being Empathetic and Compassionate**— Empathize with the other person on what they are communicating. Try not to be judgmental or have any preconceived beliefs or ideas.
3. **Body Language/Non-Verbal Communication**— Nonverbal communication includes body movement, gestures, eye contact, posture, voice tone and facial expressions. Actions explain more about how you are feeling than words, ex: the way you are listening, or looking or even reacting to the person.
4. **Providing Feedback**— Providing succinct and timely feedback is key. Be appreciative and deliver more positive than negative feedback. Giving positive feedback shows that you care about them and puts them at ease, so they are more likely to receive constructive feedback well.
5. **Being Present**— Being present in a conversation means that you are paying attention to what the other person is saying or talking. Therefore, playing with you mobile phone or electronic devices, responding to emails or text messages, looking away and not making an eye contact, facial expressions that seem disinterested are a few indicators of showing disinterest in a conversation even when it's done unintentionally
6. **Customize your communication style for every role.** People have different learning styles. Some like a lot of detail and prefer to go through every step in the process and some like to figure things out on their own. It is all about tailoring your communication to match the preference of the

learning style of that individual.

7. **Ask before you speak**— Understand the perspective of the conversation before you put your statement/solution through. Ask specific questions and open-ended questions to seek clarification — During the conversation or at the end of it. This will help eliminate any misinterpretation or assumptions.

Thus, we can see how the stalwarts have not only emphasized on learning the skill and techniques of the art but have also shared that overall development of an individual, their moral and values, their personality, communication style, affiliation with others etc, have an important role to play in becoming an artist.

CHAPTER 11

The Way Forward

A blank canvas has unlimited possibilities.

– Stephanie Perkins

The Way Forward

After interviewing the stalwarts and engaging in discussions with them, there was a need to share these ideas with the young brigade, the next generation and future of Indian classic music. With that, I have also made an attempt to understand their concerns regarding the field and address them accordingly. Therefore, young students were approached for discussion, amateurs were interviewed and a workshop was also conducted with them to address their issues and concerns.

Although today's generation seem very passionate and positive about music, there were several hurdles and insecurities that they seem to be surrounded with. They are insecure when it comes to taking up music as a career due to the lack of support from society, family and the apprehension about not being accepted by the field.

In a week-long workshop held at one of the reputed colleges of Delhi University, I attempted to expose the teenagers and young adults who were passionate about music to the traditional art and some semi-classical forms like *kajri* and *thumri*. During the process, it was realized that some of them were really enthusiastic about pursuing music as a career but had a few apprehensions about it. To further explore the apprehensions and anxieties, two focus group discussions were also conducted with a few Delhi University students studying music. Some of the issues raised by the upcoming generation are given in figure 3.

CONCERNS OF YOUNG ARTISTS

WEAK PARENTAL SUPPORT

FINANCIAL INSECURITY

MUSIC: SOCIAL TABOO ESPECIALLY FOR GIRLS

HIGH FINANCIAL INVESTMENT INITIALLY

ESTABLISHING IN THE FIELD REQUIRES PATIENCE

DIFFICULT TO FIND GUIDE

Fig 3: Concerns of the young students understood and addressed in Focus group discussion and workshop

One of the biggest hurdles that were pointed out by the young enthusiasts was family disapproval in pursuing a performing art - music as a career. Parents usually don't support their children in endeavors like music the way they do in academics and other professional courses. They believe that chances of success in such a career are not that bright and thus in order to prevent their children from frustrations and failures later in life they try disengaging their children from it at an earlier stage only. One student who echoed the sentiment of many others said, "ultimately all of us have to settle down in life and earn for a living, so we are bothered by the fact that what will be our standing in the society after this. Nobody wants to regret later by thinking ``why am I not like others and my other friends who are settled, secure and earning well." They were encouraged by making them understand that at every stage of life they can't expect parental support. Even many of the stalwarts have faced financial hardships but they survived and proved themselves. They could do some part time jobs, if the parents are not providing financial support. Another aspect that I shared with them was that one should never leave regular education as it provides one with a wider range of experiences and understanding. Along with this, it can also be looked at as an alternative/back up option which may provide one with the additional security against total failure.

They believed that such a profession could never provide the required financial stability. Everyone felt that the field is full of struggles and politics and thus there are only a few who would acquire a respectable and successful position in the field. Taking examples from his own life and financial struggles, Pt. Ajoy Chakrabarty shared that these life situations and financial struggles are only a way to make an individual more patient, confident, hardworking and focused and one must not shy away from difficulties in life.

Another major issue in front of the parents was the social taboo associated with music. With changing times, society is building some kind of tolerance with arts like music but still it has a long way to go, especially when a girl states her desire to be a singer and a classical singer on top of that. Parents are worried for their girl child's safety and still feel that such a profession might not be safe for them. Then, there were some other genuine concerns like the fact that as initial investment in the field is high, many parents and children who were not of affluent background refrain from taking a plunge. Also, such an art requires a great deal of patience even on the part of the parents because at least initially (in the struggling days) the field doesn't guarantee any kind of financial stability.

Apart from this, the stalwarts of the field believe that the art requires immense patience and trust in the guru which is lacking in the present generation. They believe that the present generation doesn't want to toil hard and want success easily. The present generation feels that, "there are many struggles that a person would face as he has to prove himself at every stage" and this could be a major reason for them to abandon the thought of pursuing a career in the field. The stalwarts feel that perhaps the present generation is not composed of go-getters and thus would even doubt the passion of the young lads who blame the parents and field for not continuing in the field. They need to understand that difficult times could be endured better if they would retain the conviction that their existence holds a purpose and a cause to pursue along with a goal to achieve in life.

In today's times, *'guru-shishya parampara'* has also undergone a few changes, such as the practice of *shishyas* living with their gurus is no longer prevalent but that doesn't diminish the role of gurus in any way. Finding a knowledgeable guru is of paramount importance. A lot of the newcomers to the world of Indian Classical Music (including the students interviewed by the author) want to learn from the well-established artists. It is important to understand that to be a 'guru', one need not be an accomplished or rather a popular artist. There lies a difference between teaching and performing. A guru has to come to the level of the disciple to teach. The well-established artists may or may not have the resources in terms of time to start with the basics for a student. Therefore, these artists could later on help in grooming those who have learnt the basics and help in their advanced training. One should not restrict or limit themselves by only wanting to learn from well-established performers. The key is to find a knowledgeable guru who can effectively teach both the theoretical and practical aspects of the art in a systematic manner. Moreover, the disciple should be receptive to whatever the guru teaches; the disciple should be able to follow. Something which is extremely important in this whole process is: guru *bhakti* (surrender of the *shishya* to the guru) and *chetna* (awareness on their part) which ultimately paves the way for *jnana* (knowledge). The capability of a guru is not to be judged by name and fame, rather by their skill-set. In this regard, Savita Devi would often say, "*Paani Piyo Chaan ke, Guru banaao Jaan ke* (One should be cautious and careful while choosing a guru). I added another dimension to it while sharing advice with the students, that once the guru is chosen, it is imperative to have immense faith in them as there is no going back after that. It's only through complete dedication and surrender that one can learn in its truest sense. It's like building a multistorey house wherein the foundations of the house are of paramount importance to build a sturdy structure on it. Some students have rich voices with a faster learning capability. They just require a motivating environment and good guidance. The youngsters were made familiar with some good music academies, to start learning from a teacher who has good theoretical and practical knowledge of music. If they were not satisfied as a student, they could change the guide. But, they were also told that in any field of art it is necessary to surrender oneself to a guru who is a symbol of the divine. Surrender would mean dissolving one's ego and one's importance of self because it divides faith and confidence in guru. In our country, music is learned through imitation. Unless and until we have faith in our guru we won't imitate them willingly. It should also be noted that this is a time taking process. Thus, confidence in a guru is a must for a long term bond. Here it would be important to note one of the aspects that Pt. Ajoy Chakravarty believed and shared with the students. He completely agreed about the quality of surrender but also said that every individual is unique and comes with his/her own personality make up. Thus, the artist should devote himself/herself truly and completely to the guru, believe in him, learn the skill, learn the way of life but should also remember that "you are an individual and a different personality in your own way and thus should avoid copying your guru."

One of the participants, despite learning in a rich musical environment (in a University set up) felt confused in both theoretical and practical aspects and especially the disparity she could see between the two. Through our discussions, she realized that she should also start learning on a one-on-one basis wherein she could clarify all her doubts and would be groomed as per her potential. After, she started learning individually; she herself felt the difference and felt extremely satisfied. A musician should not let go of one aspect (theory) for another (practical). Stalwarts also suggest that students and young artists should attend various seminars, webinars, workshops and discussions as much as possible as this would give them an opportunity to interact with other artists and learn from the process. They should also engage in reading literature (books, newspapers, magazines, journals etc.) for a good historical and contextual grasp of a particular composition or time period. Further, they should also engage in reading biographies and autobiographies, as these may inspire them further. Students can also learn from the journeys of these great maestros.

Every pupil cannot be fortunate to be the son or daughter of the Guru. Biological children of renowned gurus might be privileged to some extent in terms of learning the performance aspect but they also need to carve their niche to rise further in the field. A performing artist is not just a singer on stage but has various social responsibilities as well. They need to be well aware of their surroundings and what's going on in the society and to know all this you need not be the biological child of a renowned personality. In fact, being the biological child of a renowned artist can also be a challenge in certain regards, for instance, they are often compared with their parents' towering figure rather than pupils or artists of their own age and experience. This is a major challenge for them.

The majority of us lead quiet, unheralded lives as we pass through this world. There will most likely be no ticker tape parades for us, no monument created in our honor. However, nothing should deter us from following our hearts and passions because in the end only that will lead to positive growth. It would definitely lead us to be able to leave something for the future generations. Thus, on the basis of feedback that we got from the young talents in the workshop, we would like to put forward a few suggestions for parents, students and the stalwarts.

The students need to keep faith in themselves and their gurus. They need to be patient and be ready to work hard for success. The need to understand that incentives would not always be available and there would be times when the incentive would not be material in nature is imperative. Thus, they need to keep themselves motivated with their passion for the art. Furthermore, upcoming artists need to be honest with their commitments and would be ready to sacrifice a bit initially. A successful entry in any profession is not a bed of roses so is the case with music and they would have to prove themselves on each and every step.

However, this should encourage them to move forward and not become a deterrent or lose faith in the field. They need to understand that every wound would shape them and every scar would help them in building their throne. They need to have patience in adverse situations. A lot of young artists talked about being nervous to get back to the stage especially after committing a mistake in previous performances. It would be important to remember here that committing mistakes is a part of the learning process and even the stalwarts have learnt this way. One should not fear making mistakes as they can prove pivotal in further knowledge expansion and enhancement. One should also consider taking guidance from a career counselor from time to time who could help them in understanding their interest, passion, and may suggest the way forward in the field. They may also help them in striking a balance between their personal and professional spaces.

Parents need to understand that if the child is motivated and passionate enough, he should be given a fair chance of following his desire. Of course, they should be vigilant towards safety and prosperity but without making it a hindrance for them in pursuing their dreams. Parents should look up to performing arts as a stable career option and not a fleeting one.

Since learning music requires devotion towards the art and Guru for a long duration, the optimistic approach of the individual is of utmost importance. Stalwarts also need to promote young talent and upcoming artists. They need to instill hope and optimism in them, so, even if they fail in a performance they should be motivated to prepare for the next performance. This would serve as a gesture which would make them hopeful for a bright career. In any situation where a valuable goal such as music is pursued, the hopeful goal–directed behavior will be determined by the interaction of the degree to which the outcome or goal is valued. Success will be determined by the interaction of thoughts about possible pathways to the goals and related expectations about how effective these will be in achieving the outcome or goal and interaction of the thought about personal motivation and effective one will be in following paths to goals (Snyder, 2000). Thus, hope would be an outcome of how much interest the artist takes in the art, the steps they take in the direction to realize the goal (learning the skill, performing etc.), and how effective these strategies would turn out to be. Another element important here would be their capability to overcome the tricky situations or problems that they may encounter. The author felt that the art and the guru definitely provide room for errors, because as humans and as budding artists we would all commit errors. If not a blatant error, there is a possibility of doing something in the performance that wouldn't click with the audience. Instead of stopping oneself to perform or experiment, the key would be to learn from it and not repeat such things further. Basically, it is important to analyze the moments of performance, discuss it with the guru and learn something from it. One is bound to make mistakes but should not repeat the same mistake again.

As a performing artform, the success of an artist depends upon how he has been received by the audience. But, the established artists need to give them a chance and platform to portray their skills and in the process hone their talent. Thus, we can say that the purpose of life is to discover your gifts and parents and society play a major role in discovering and then embracing it.

In music, creativity means composing something new and beautiful which can be used by others in the future. It should follow the rules of music including correct rhythmic pattern, notes, language and express proper sentiment (sad, happy, eroticism, devotion etc.). Some of them said that they compose new songs but due to a lack of confidence and shame do not share. They were told that they should share their compositions and creativity with their teachers. They can polish it and can further make them usable. This could give them confidence and work as an incentive.

Some of the students said that sometimes they prefer listening to music according to their mood and at that particular point in time they didn't prefer any sort of disturbance and interference. In fact, some of them shared a desire to create a world of their own (mental space), where they could live in isolation and witness their emotions. It is important to note here that these students were those who had experienced flow in one form or another. They enjoyed such moments as this motivated them to continue further. One of the participants shared that "whenever I create something…even if it is a phrase, it's a different feeling altogether and can't be repeated again because it came at that very moment. Even if I try I can't repeat it again." She was told that even stalwarts experience such moments of involvement and unity. She became delighted and felt that she was on the right path.

The use of musical powers for healing has always been emphasized. One of the participants shared her experience about how her epileptic seizures found their solution in music. "Till the time I am singing, I am fine. I had stopped practicing and going for music classes in 10th standard and that was the time when my seizures made a comeback. After I started practicing again, this problem didn't occur. It has been almost 8 years now." During the discussion another participant told her about meditation on 'OM'.

Based on the discussions with the stalwarts and the author's own experiences, the young generation was also given a few guidelines and suggestions which could help them in establishing their career in the field and also enjoying the art to the fullest which would be discussed in the remaining chapter.

Aesthetic value was highlighted by many stalwarts. Pt. Ravi Shankar believed that audiences expect a certain grace and finesse from their artists. Thus, an artist's language, communication skills, dressing style, stage presentation are all significant and should be attended to carefully. This also paves a way for the artists to connect with their audience which is further enhanced and helped by the artists' facial expressions, state of mind, and style of presentation. I also believe that dressing and *bhava* are intimately related. It sets the stage for the performance that would be followed. This is not to say that it is of ultimate importance or the only thing that would matter, but definitely is an important contributory factor for an artist's success as it also adds to the personality of the artist.

Authority over language is considered an important element for a musician, as it facilitates song-writing; helps in bringing out the meaning of any composition. In order to express any composition or its melody, understanding it thoroughly and getting engaged with it deeply is important--this requires command over the given language. It was also shared that language helps in improvisation. For instance, in a *thumri, "ankhyian rasili tori shyam"*, while improvising if the artist realizes that in order to adjust it on the meter (rhythmic cycle) he/she needs to cut down certain words, using a synonym would be helpful. Thus, using *naina* instead of *ankhiyan* can be useful, tactful and may even enhance the composition. However, for doing such quips effectively, knowing these synonyms is necessary. Govardhan Mishra would always encourage his disciples to read as much as possible. He believed that literature serves as a major source of inspiration for a successful artist. It opens up various avenues to think, visualize, compose, and express.

The composer and singer should be aware of his/her target audience, the one for whom performance is being done. The information about the audience is important as it could help in choosing lyrics and the style with which one should sing, choosing a theme as per the audience is also of great importance.

Knowledge about the notation system is very necessary to pen down the song on paper to make the composition clear and utilizable by helping the musicians for recording. It is also helpful when improvisations are done with a piece. This also builds an understanding of the principles that a particular composition follows. Selection of *taal* (rhythmic pattern), its tempo is also important as the mood of the composition may change with *taal* change. For instance, an energetic impact that can be created with *'drut ektaal'* can never match the composure and steadiness of *'vilambit ektaal'*.

Indian music is completely based on time theory. It gives knowledge about selection of ragas in any particular season over the year or it might help to choose the raga for any particular time period of a day. Singing a group of *swaras* or composition at that time is pleasing to the ears and may give the desired impact as well. For instance, with the young sun gradually maturing, the sets of *Raga Asavari, Jaunpuri, Gandhari* etc. sound appropriate.

Developing a voice culture is important for any artist. It is very helpful in voice production and presentation of various styles of singing. It involves perfect pitch ear training, breath control, stamina, along with daily riyaz (practice) and vocal power, which work as the building blocks for any artist. In order to build stamina and vocal power various stalwarts suggest various kinds of food habits. For instance, Bade Ghulam Ali Khan would focus on the importance of desi ghee (home-made butter). Others have emphasized a balanced and nutritious diet, lots of tea, turmeric milk and ample amounts of lukewarm water. Even the style of voice production is different in different genres of music. In Hindustani music, a strong and free chest tone is used for most of the pitches and an appropriate mix of chest and head tones is used to sing the higher pitches.

Expanding the chest voice is important for a Hindustani musician because the human voice changes qualities at different pitches. The chest voice is the one that comes most naturally when speaking or singing within your most comfortable pitch range. Different people have different vocal ranges for their natural voice. Some can sing lower pitches naturally while others are most comfortable with higher pitches. Savita Devi would say that, everyone's range can be expanded to a certain extent with voice training. After locating the natural voice, one can choose the keynote that locates his/her octave comfortably in the middle of that range and then sticking to the keynote for further training is a good idea.

Girija Devi would often say that, "Hindustani vocalists need a vocal range spanning about two octaves, and half way up the higher octave." To get the higher pitches correct, one has to learn the techniques of mixing the chest and head tones smoothly. According to Pt. Govardhan Mishra, best way to do so is by imitation of vocalization techniques. Most good vocalists have had the fortune of learning with a teacher whose style they could observe and imitate over many years. Teachers share certain vocal exercises that would help in opening up the voices in the upper octaves.

Another important aspect highlighted by Savita Devi was singing in *aakaar*. She shared how a song usually contains both vowels and consonants. "Consonants play a role in stabilizing the voice and helping in transition from one note to another. But take the consonant out and suddenly the story might change." Thus, the challenge is to train the voice to sing each note with precision and clarity even without the consonants. An artist must learn to sing in all the possible vowels (*a, e, i, o, u*) as well as the nasal consonants 'n' and 'm', because the voice behaves differently with different vowels. Some notes are harder to hit with certain vowels. An important reason to learn to sing in *aakaar* is the fact that when one sings rapid note pattern a *taan*, a pure vowel sound is all there is time for. Also, *aakaar* allows the artist to focus on and freely explore the melody while improvising.

In a nutshell, features like correct pronunciation, diction, knowledge of *swaras* and *shrutis*, knowledge of the ragas, expression of emotion, creativity, improvisation, effortlessness and focused singing, awareness of time and audience and confidence are very important components for an artist to flourish and establish.

Along with this, Pt. Govardhan Mishra would often use a phrase, *"Sharir ka khyaal karo, bhot zaroori hai"* (It is very important to take care of your body). He shared various such aspects with the author. He emphasized on doing basic physical exercises to keep the mind and body active and in good shape. The author would want to elaborate it further and believes that practicing warm-ups on a regular basis is important for a singer. One of the benefits of regular practice is the music memory that comes from putting your vocal chords through the same pattern and movements repeatedly. The vocal cords can absorb and respond to muscle memory. Thus, it is all about keeping the muscles trained. Another important point is drinking plenty of water. This has been focused upon by almost all the musicians. The reason being that there are direct correlations between the amounts of water one drinks and how well the vocal instrument is maintained. Singing is a product of mucous membranes of the body and these function best when they are adequately hydrated. Not smoking and being quiet for longer hours are also some good practices to build vocal stamina.

Vidushi Savita Devi, once recalled an incident that one of her gurus Pt. Ravi Shankar had shared with her. Before one of his performances, Pt. Ravi Shankar was feeling slightly unwell and thus decided not to perform. However, one of his so-called competitors challenged him to perform. He agreed to do so but was not carrying his medicines which could at least temporarily relieve him of his ailment. In conclusion, he couldn't perform well on that particular day but it taught him a life-long lesson of carrying his medicines, water and basic essentials with him, especially before the performances.

Preparation before the performance and those few hours before the actual performance are important moments for an artist. For budding artists, these moments can be really confusing and even scary initially. Pt. Govardhan Mishra shared that it's best to tame down certain emotions right before the performance. The excitement for its success should be there but should not turn into exuberance as it may disturb the natural calm of the mind. Basically, he believed that one should also be attentive and cautious, along with the excitement of the performance. He advised young artists to keep themselves away from any sort of negativity or pessimism, at least right before the performance. He believed even to perform something that has a *dukhi bhava* (element of sadness in it), one needs a balanced state of mind. This is to ensure that the artists know what they are doing. Entering flow or a trans in the midst of a performance, getting reminded of a certain thing in the midst of a performance is different from inducing that state beforehand. Preparing oneself psychologically for a performance is the biggest challenge and artists should pay a lot of attention to it.

Girija Devi pointed out another important facet which is essential for an artist throughout their lives but its foundations are laid in the early years itself. She believed that apart from the skill that has to be learned and finally performed, the personality and character of the artist also has got a role to play. This has been emphasized by many other artists as well. Most of them shared the importance of self-discipline, responsibility and being honest and fair. Shanti Hiranand discussed the relevance of being compassionate and humane for an artist. "Awareness of one's life situations, surroundings etc. is also of paramount importance" said Pt. Ajoy Chakrabarty. Apart from this, it is believed that it is importantforabuddingartisttobehighonself-respectandself-esteem, this doesn't mean that he has to be egoistic.

Determining the singing path requires a reality check. It is important for everyone to do an honest assessment of their singing skills to begin with. An honest guru is another authority who can give a person a reality check of the fact if they should tread this path. Other than this, listening to a variety of genres and artists also has a very unique role to play in the making of an artist or a 'good' artist for that matter. Certain types of music may inspire some artists during their creation process, or they become a realization tool making the artist aware of their genuine interest and passions.

The inner soul of the human being should be fed with what he feels good about, enjoys and is passionate about it. A person who has a high level of satisfaction with their life owing to opportunities, contentment and achievement in life and who experiences a greater positive effect and little less negative effect, would be deemed to have a high level of subjective well-being. Thus, positive growth and well-being is ultimately what anyone would want to achieve. Subjective well-being would be defined as 'a person's cognitive and affective evaluations of his/her life' (Diener, Lucas and Oshi, 2002). The cognitive element refers to what one thinks about their life satisfaction as a whole and in specific areas such as work and relationships. The effective component refers to emotions, moods and feelings and also their management. Data gathered using 31st survey of the Australian unity also emphasized the important role of engaging with music in the company of others with regard to subjective well-being, highlighting an interpersonal feature of music. Thus, describing how music is involved in emotional regulation (Weinberg and Joseph, 2016).

Another research found that certain aspects of flow are related to measures of subjective well-being. Clear goals, challenge-skill balance, concentration on the task and autotelic experience are important predictors of positive effect. It was concluded that experiencing flow is more related to emotional than cognitive aspects of subjective well-being (Fritz, 2007). The capacity of the humans to draw happiness from aesthetic objects and even material goods would depend primarily on the satisfaction - emotional or psychological, they would get from it. And, among them, the need for understanding, love and expression would be imperative. Music helps in catering to these needs.

Music is a discipline and a mistress of order and good manners,
she makes the people milder and gentler,
more moral and more reasonable.

- Martin Luther

CHAPTER 12

What A Man Can Be, He Must Be

A musician must make music; an artist must paint, a poet must write, if he is to be ultimately at peace with himself.

– Abraham Maslow

What A Man Can Be, He Must Be

THIS BOOK WOULD BE INCOMPLETE WITHOUT TOUCHING UPON the topic of self-hood, as self is considered a central ingredient in human personality. The discussion on self hoodbrings the reader full circle to the making of an artist and becoming a stalwart. All of us start our lives as *shishyas* in one or the other form and remain so throughout our lives. During this time we keep taking on other roles such as that of a guru in certain cases. All of this has an impact on how our self gets created and that defines us as a person along with defining our art or any other pursuit that we are involved in. I believe, throughout this book various aspects have been discussed, from the point of view of an author, reader, etc. all of us have undergone some or the other change through enhancing our worldview and that would have an impact on our self-hood.T hus, it becomes imperative to discuss this topic here.

If we pause to think about our own self, we become aware of a set of feelings and attitudes and a certain sense of who we are. This entity is known as the "self". Our self can be defined in two ways: the first is self-concept or self-image, and the second way is self as a process. The individual's perception of himself or herself - of the body, abilities, personality and traits is self-concept; self-process is the executive functions by means of which an individual thinks, remembers, perceives, manages, plans and copes with daily life. Consistency of behaviors and continuity of identity are two of the chief properties of the self-concept. There are several components of self-concept: Physical, Academic, Social and Transpersonal.

The physical aspect of self-concept relates to that which is concrete, what we look like, our sex, height, weight etc. what kind of clothes we wear, what kind of car we drive, what kind of homes we live in; and so forth. Our academic self-concept relates to how well we do in school or how well we learn. There are two levels; a general academic self-concept of how good we are overall and set of specific content-related self-concepts that describes how good we are in math, science, language, art, social sciences etc. The social self-concept describes how we relate ourselves to other people and the transpersonal self-concept describes how we relate to the super natural or unknown. Music helps in unfolding all these aspects of self. It helps in shaping the social self-concept by helping us in getting to know other people, take their perspective, and empathize with them. It also helps us in creating our own spaces in lives of others through the music we create or perform. Music also plays an important role in relating ourselves or unraveling the Divine forces, getting in touch with them and in turn getting in touch with our own personal nature and selves. It's an art that enhances and contributes to an individual's physical and mental health.

The self-concept composed of relatively permanent self-assessment, such as personality attributes, knowledge of one skill and abilities, one's occupation hobbies and awareness of one's physical attributes. For example, the statement, I am lazy is a self-assessment that contributes to the self-concept. In contrast, I am tired would not normally be considered part of someone's self-concept, since being tired is a temporary state. Never the less, a person's self-concept may change with time, possibly going through turbulent periods of identity crisis and reassessment along with the various life experiences.

There are other terms too related to self, such as self-actualization (satisfying higher needs), self-attribution (influencing certain qualities in ourselves), self-disclosure (the process through which one person lets himself/ herself be known by another) and self-fulfilling prophecy (behaving according to one's own exceptions in such a way that this behavior influences a situation and brings about what is expected). It's a truly dynamic concept because it covers both the "inner" and "outer" selves.

One of the greatest aspects of self is that it is constantly changing. As you grow, you change. Think back to when you were five years old. Are you the same person now? Perhaps in some ways you are; maybe you have the same hobbies or interests that have followed you through life. However, you probably can't consider yourself entirely the same. The reason is as you grow, so does your sense of self.

Music has long been considered as the soundtrack to our everyday lives. The translation of experience into expression has been called the poetics of experience. Human experience is also an aesthetic affair intimating sometimes in subtle and gentle ways and in an urgent and upfront manner at other times (Colapietro, 2010). Over the years artists have come to believe that in the moment of performance, the artist probably tries to represent everything, every part of their experience from birth to that of moment. Musicians and artists bear witness to the world as they find it. Music truly represents and communicates their realities (Peterson, 2006).

When people's life experiences begin to emerge, they focus on the inner life and to the belief that fulfillment might be enhanced by developing a deeper understanding of the inner self, music and poetry (the lyrics) could be one of the medium. This stage may coincide with their faith in their religion, God and their values till the time the experiences start merging for them or they change their lens and perspective to view things.

Pt. Gowardhan Mishra would often say that every day is new and comes up with its own challenges. My mood and frame of mind plays an important role in what I sing. The grammar doesn't change, rules remain the same; yet it is different. This difference is nothing but an expression of 'within' in the music. In the Indian tradition it is believed that the more deeply the self is absorbed in its being and the more conscious it becomes of its worth, the more complete is the pleasure afforded to it.

Vidushi Girija Devi had said that if the composition the artists sing has a connection with their personal lives, it adds to the sentiment one is trying to portray. She believed that a lot of times they take up mood congruent *ragas* or *bandish,* it might be a conscious choice but is also an unconscious process for certain participants.

Thus, it would not be an exaggeration to say that our music takes a lot from our life experiences and our life experiences may also play a role in defining the kind of music we compose. So, music is the product of individual's interaction with his/her self.

Carl Rogers (1947) described the self as a social product, developing out of inter personal relationship and striving for consistency. Rogers believed that there is a basic human need for positive attitude regarding both from others and from one self. He also believed that every person has a tendency towards self-actualization and development so long as this is permitted and encouraged by an inviting environment (Purkey and Schmidt, 1987). Self-concept is not innate, but is developed or constructed by the individual through interaction with environment and reflecting on that interaction. The dynamic aspect of self-concept is important because it indicates that it can be modified or changed. He believed that three contributing components to the development of sense of self: self-image, self-esteem and ideal self. The person's self-image includes personality traits and physical descriptions. Self-esteem is how you view and value yourself. Do you believe in yourself and love who you are? About this concept we read in detail in the last section of this chapter. An ideal self is the self, the person would like to be. When perceived self does not match the ideal self, this may be disturbing.

The discussion on self and music together also becomes imperative because, as per the Indian tradition, knowledge and enjoyment are not contradictory in nature but synonymous as they both talk about the highest act of transcendence which secures absolute freedom (*moksha*) from phenomenal ends. Vidushi Girija Devi mentioned during our interaction that music and this profession gave her everything that she could ever ask for or desire. At this stage of her life she wished for achieving *moksha* through music as she firmly believed that such an art could be a great medium to relieve someone from the cycle of death and re-birth.

The more deeply the self is absorbed in its being and the more conscious it becomes of its own true worth the more complete is the delight afforded to it. Absolute truth (*sat*), pure consciousness (*chit*) and bliss (*ananda*) are the three aspects of the same reality to which all existence tends (S. Radhakrishnan, 1958) and art could serve as a medium to achieve or realize it.

As Deshpande (1973) writes, Indian music is prone to be meditative and contemplative. It seeks to express the mysterious movement of man's sub-conscious; it tries to get at the very bottom of the sub-conscious. As the performance intensifies, the performer gradually assumes a more extroverted manner: the eyes open, engaging the fellow performers and even the audience thoroughly, hand gesture become larger and more frequent, and the performer may even talk to his fellow performers and the audience. It is a journey from internal to external and from subconscious to the interpersonal.

Self has been considered to be an organized cognitive structure comprised of a set of attitudes of a person, belief, values, and variety of habits, abilities, outlooks, ideas and feelings of a person.

In this chapter we will discuss social self and spiritual self-developed during the journey of music.

The Social Self: The social self is a multifaceted analysis of the self-concept based on the social nature of self. The emphasis is on self-esteemed along with self-centrality, self-complexity, social interest, identification, power marginality, openness and majority identification. So the focal point of this chapter will be Abraham Maslow's self-actualization theory. In his view we all have, higher level growth needs but that those higher needs only essence a dominant role in our lives after our more primitive needs (physiological needs, safety needs, needs for love and belongingness; and self-esteem needs). He emphasized that man has a higher and transcendent nature. To understand this transcendent nature, he believe that we should study transcendent people like businessmen, artists, sports person, creative housewives. Maslow (1967) found that this group of "optimal" people shared some distinguishing characteristic. They were open to experience with full concentration and total absorption. They were in tune with their inner beings, they were spontaneous with a fresh aspiration of people and events. They devoted total efforts to their goals at least as good as they could be. They were dedicated, fully and creatively to some cause outside themselves. They related to few others on a deep emotional plane.

So in nutshell we can say that his theory is about the ability to become the best version of oneself. Of course, we all hold different desires. Self-actualization, in his "need-hierarchy theory" is the highest level of psychological development, where personal potential is fully realized after basic bodily and ego needs have been fulfilled. In "Motivation and Personality (1954), Abraham Maslow states, "what a man can be, he must be: self-actualization needs are included "Personal and Creative self-growth, which are achieved through fulfillment of our full potential. Maslow studied on exemplary people on individual considered to have realized their full potential in their particular area of expertise or focus. They must have the capability to think and act spontaneously, these individuals tend to act and think within the accepted social norm and according to the expectations of others. They often display the need for personal freedom and privacy to test their both mental and physical strength and wellness. Self-actualized people must have experienced significance, fulfillment and spirituality i.e. Peak Experience.

Social interaction fosters further self-development. New born shows a particular interest in human faces, and begin to smile and engage their care givers in social interaction within their few first weeks of life. These exchanges become regulated and co-ordinated proving important information about the self in relation to others. Imitation may provide the earliest information about the self in relation to others Meltzoff and Moore (1977) studied facial imitation in infants who were 12-21 days old and infant and an adult were brought together, and the adult made various faces (e.g. stuck his tongue out, pursed his lips together) while the infant watched. The infant facial behavior was recorded and observers unaware of the adult's facial expression coded the infant expression. The result showed that infants imitated the adults' facial expressions. Likewise in music, in *Guru-Shishya parampara* a disciple imitates the facial gestures, sitting gestures, body language and how to connect with the audience. Thus, the disciple also learns how to conduct himself or herself which grooms him/her as an artist and also as a person that in return has a huge impact on the performance of the artist. During her interview Girija ji said that *"Guru-shishya" parampara* of music is one of the best ways of self-development. This *parampara* is not about only music, when disciple live with a Guru, they absorb a culture, a way of life. The Guru strives to transfer all his/her knowledge to the *shishya* and the student receives it like a blessings. To a true Guru, a *shishya* is his progeny. This *parampara* is akin to a family line. Here our self-concept develops. We interact with others. In addition to family members Guru and close friends (*Guru bahans* and *Guru bhais*) other people like audience, skilled accompanist also contribute to a disciple's self-identity. As per Rita Ganguly, a person gets a chance to listen to others also rather than talking about oneself. She believes this helps in evolving an individual's personality and developing a self-concept gradually. As children grow, parents, teachers and others react to their behavior, sometimes we approve their behavior and at other times we reprimand them. The child adds worth to his/her behavior through this action of the parents and the society. It also adds to an understanding of how much he/she likes, accepts, and values himself/herself.

From a social and personality psychology perspective, the interconnections between the individual and the social environment manifest themselves in life transitions, concerns and objectives which have received several labels such as personal strivings (Emmons, 1986), personal projects (Little 1983), life tastes (Cantor, Markus, Niedenltel & Nurius, 1988) etc.

The greatest challenge in life would be ones that they inadvertently created for themselves you will face various disappointments, problems and even tragedies in life, many of which you will have little or no power to control. But the primary cause of your unhappiness will be you (Mark. R. Leary). Others have also suggested that people are often their own worst enemies. As a social psychologist with the interest in self and identity, Leary came to the conclusion that the natural human tendencies to be egocentric, egotistical and otherwise egotistic play a central role in our problems at both the personal and societal levels. But, an art could be a medium to overcome this. For instance, we have described about the challenges Savita Devi had to face in her life throughout the book. Despite so many turbulences in her life she always came across as a friendly person, with a smile on her face. She seemed to have a considerable amount of stability in both her public and private life .She used to say that we should not hate our bitter experiences because they have helped us in shaping our personality. She further said that the self-concept is a collection of our beliefs. It tends to be more malleable when we are younger and still going through the self-discovery. As we grow older our concept of "who we are" becomes more detailed and well organized i.e. natured.

No other spaces possess the powers of self-reflection that human beings have. The ability to self-respect offers many benefits by allowing us to plan ahead, reminisce about the past consider options, innovate, and evaluate ourselves. However, self-awareness also sets us up for a host of problems that are unlike the difficulties faced by another species. The human capacity for self-reflection distorts people's perceptions of the world, leading them to draw inaccurate conclusions about themselves and other people and prompting them to make bad decisions based on faulty information. Self-awareness conjures up a great deal of personal sufferings in the form of depression, anxiety, anger and other negative emotions by allowing people to ruminate about the pat or imagine what might be fall them in the future. The inherently egocentric and egotistical manner in which the self-processes information can blind people to their own short coming and undermine their relationship with others. The self also underlies a great deal of social conflict, leading people to dislike those who are different from them and to fight with members of other social groups. It also lead people to endanger their own wellbeing by putting egoistic goals over personal safety. For those inclined towards religion and spirituality, visionaries have proclaimed that the self- stymies the quest for spiritual fulfillment leads to immoral behavior. And, ironically, using self- reflection to help us deliberately control our own behavior can often back fire and create more problem then it solve.

People are often urged to solve their problems and improve their lives by focusing on themselves, setting more egoistic goals, enhancing their self-esteem and other, strengthening their sense of self. Although these strategies are sometimes useful, those who promote and egoistic approach to solving life's problems failed to recognize that excessive emphasis on self and ego is often part of the problem.

The Divine Self or Higher Self, as it is also known, is a belief held by Indians (Hindus) and New Age thought alike. According to these beliefs The Divine Self, is the self that exist at an even higher level then the soul, it is in every person even born, it is the essence of the universe that dwells in your being, the source of all light and life within you and your true motivation for living. The Divine self is what empowers you and makes you wonder. It is the soul light at your core that chose to be incarnate at this point of time. It is ever-aware and has been thinking since you began existing in this life time, and since your birth in other life time. Music may just serve as a medium to relate or reach to this divine self. The body and the physical realm, in which we dwell, are thought to be but a vehicle for the higher self.

In the same beliefs, the soul is closer to the personality and is an intermediary between the person and her Divine self until such time as she is able to directly experience and realize the Divine self as who she is.

Believers also claimed that you can more easily turn away from the distraction of physical world, and restore yourself in the light, love and power of this eternal self, because it will reveal the illusions, desires and attachments, that keep you trapped in a lower vibration and on a lesser, thus enabling you to find your higher path.

You are also supposed to gain a greater ability to recognize limiting, disharmonious and restricting energies and forms.

The Divine self is always to reach you, to send you the power, illumination, love and wisdom to draw higher forms, thought, feelings and situations into your life. The Divine self is wise, it knows all and is always showing you easier, better, more joyful ways of life. Siddheswari Devi was a warm person with such easy manners that if someone met her for the first time, he could not have felt that she was a stranger to him. She was also overwhelmingly generous at heart. Nobody who came to meet her at her home left empty-handed. Even in her last days after she had suffered a stroke and could not move about, she kept money under her pillow so that she could continue distributing it generously. Personal relations had a high priority in her scheme of things. Everyone who came received a warm welcome. She remained a warm-hearted, simple and lovable person with an extraordinary amalgam of innocence, courage, humor, generosity, youthful zest for life and a rare dignity.

Because of things, it's not a huge struggle through your will power to contact you Divine self. All you need to do is set yours intention and open to all the gifts of consciousness that await you as you connect with this self. Pt. Rajan Mishra said, "you know my mind is a beautiful place where what dwells is love, happiness and good memories. Anger, hatred and jealousy can't remain there for long. To me, peace matters the most. You should always strive to be exactly the way you wanted. Your role in your family, your circle, your society all impact you. Nothing is big or small, but our thinking is what it makes so. How we handle little things will be reflected in how we do the big things. I must say one should always lead a life as a very good student because lifelong learning is only going to increase your importance because things are changing very fast."

According to Pt. Goverdhan Mishra, find a calm, quiet spot to spend sometime and set your intention to make contact with your Divine self, to open to it and to receive it's energy, love, inspiration and all the transformations, awareness and gifts of consciousness it is always offering you. Silence is a vital factor in this process. It is the moment that the Divine self can import to as much of its wisdom, power and love that you can receive.

You don't have to spend a lot of time doing this meditation, in fact it is very effective to have frequent ten- or twenty-seconds meditation periods during the day. Even passing briefly during the day to get quiet and ask for energy or guidance is a wonderful way to deeper contact with your Divine self. For instance, Begum Akhtar always claimed that she had a personal equation with god and she would pray when she wanted rather than when others would ask her to. Once she decided to go for hajj instantly, in the spur of a moment that is without any plan. She just got her tickets booked and set out for the journey. On reaching her destination, she realized that she didn't have enough money, but without being bothered, she started offering the best she could, that is singing a *naat* and she believes that Allah rewarded her by taking care of the rest of the journey.

According to Pt. Ajoy Chakraborty, thousands of years ago, beyond the scope of scholarly research the *siddhis* (seers) of ancient India created a society and culture wherein religion, art and science thrived in harmony, without any competition or need of comparison. Music was known to be a Divine art inter woven with the sciences of sound psychology and mathematics. It was partially intended for pleasure and entertainment, but primarily intended to assist in man's quest for self-realization.

Shanti Hiranand ji shared that music was known to be an expression of the original sound, Brahma, scripturally referred to as the word, cosmic vibration or Aum. The *rishis* discovered the effect of physical sound on the body, emotions and consciousness. They deciphered various melodies and rhythms they could re-create the effects of the seasons and times of day on men. Ragas were created to paint a sonic picture or rouse a certain emotion (*Rasa*) or state of being (Bhava) such as tranquility, love, happiness, courage. Our music that is being discussed here has a major role to play on the development of self of an individual and vice versa.

According to Pt. Kameshwar Pathak, as you listen to Indian music, realize that you are linked to an ancient coalition of science, art and spirituality. Seek to perceive the essence of the raga as it awakens within you some profound response. Feel the indulging rhythm that unites the pulse and breath of your body with the swag of nature realize that a humanizing flood of sound is pouring over your being the calming *tanpura* drone, the raga of voice and instrument, the energising tale of drum.

Pt. Chhannulal Misra reiterated listen not only with your ear but also with your heart, mind and soul. This music is a bridge from modern life to ancient India, connecting the present time with the timeless. Allow your soul to reach for the yogic state wherein the listener, the music and the musician become one. Experience music as you never have before.

Vidushi Girija Devi shared that she considers the achievement of perfect *sur* to be the high point of her *sadhna*. Music to her was more than a mantra, that is it is both a means and an end. For sometimes she kept silence and said that Pandit Jasraj's singing has a rare spiritual quality. Kumar Gandhar was a *rishi* living out his penance in this mortal world, he really belonged to the rare celestial plane. The way he presented the *bhav* of a composition-pure & luminous.

In a TV interview before her last illness, Siddeshwari Devi confessed with dignity, 'There was a time when I used to sing for the public'. 'Now I sign to please my God- I realize how kind God has been to gift me the voice the he gave me'. She would then lower her eyes in obeisance to the power that she believed has always protected her. She wanted to die in a singing as she felt closest to God then. Begum Akhtar also had expressed a similar wish – she also wanted to die singing – which was fulfilled when she died at the peak of her glory. Before curtain call during a memorable performance. Once Balasaraswati (her full name was Tanjore Balasaraswati, a Bharatnatyam dancer) came to meet Siddheshwari Devi in her house when she was ill. The two sat on the floor, along with the harmonium, table and *tanpura*. Siddeshwari ji sang, *"Ras ke bhare tore nayan aaja sanvariya tohe garva laga loon"* (Beloved, your eyes are full of love/come to me my love, I want to embrace you). Balasaraswati sat beside her and acted out the bhav of the composition (Bandish). Siddheshwari's voice and Balasaraswati's eyes and hands moved to express the lover's emotions in all the variety that creates the complex web of love. It was like two divine forces interacting with one another through the medium of *sur, bhava* and *taal*. The same divinity we used to find when Girija ji used to sing and Pt. Birju Maharaj ji expressed different *bavas* according to the demand of emotions of *thumri*.

The analytic, philosophical and spiritual tradition of India and South Asia having long being an inspirations to people from all cultures and all walks of life, evoking thoughts of a wise and ancient culture that has proposed the hidden depths be melt the surface of life. This has also been supported by the discussion we had with Rita Ganguly ji.

Another very important aspect of our lives is our self-esteem, the feeling of self-worth that derives from the ratio of our actual successes to our estimation of our potential successes and this informed by our values, goals and aspirations. It consists of personal power, self-control, moral self-approval, body-appearance, body functioning, identity, integration like ability, lovability and defensive self-esteem enhancement. Children, whose parents are accepting of their strengths and limitations and set explicit high, but attainable standards, which they supports their children in attaining, develop high self-esteem. Parents who cope with life challenges by using an active problem-solving coping style are more likely, through their example, to help the children develop high self-esteem. High self-esteem and strong self-efficacy beliefs, entailed by the view of self as object, contribute to personal strength and resilience (Mark, 1999, Bandura, 1997). A performing art like music definitely and directly impacts the self-esteem of the individual as he attaches his achievement, failures with this art which may also become an indicator of his/her social standing. Self-esteem is also influenced by wider social factor, notably socio-economic status. Higher socio-economic status is associated with high self-esteem in vis-à-vis. Higher Self- esteem is associated with achievement, having the power and skills to influence others, acting in a way we perceive to be moral (rather than immoral) and being accepted and approve by others (rather than rejected). Thus, self-esteem derive from our own evaluations of our worth based on an appraisal of our personal accomplishments, virtues and attributes as well as from our perception of the way we are evaluated by others. Over the course of adolescence, there is considerable variability in change in self-esteem, but with the onset of adulthood, self-esteem gradually increases. Successful people have the overall goal of enhancing their views of themselves by focusing on their strengths and seeking opportunities to use these to be outstanding, whereas people with low self-esteem aim to find out about their short comings so that they can remediate these in order to be adequate and avoid failure.

But self-esteem can be improved by skill training, environmental change, cognitive therapy and capitalizing upon transitions that promote self-esteems.

Skill training may increase competence. This includes training in problem solving skills, social skills, assertive skills, academic skills and work related skills depending on the area of low competence. Where a low sense of worthiness derive from poverty or social disadvantage, environmental changes such as occupational re-training, occupational placement or social relocation to a less disadvantage area may be appropriate. Where a low sense of worthiness is due to unrealistically high aspiration, despite a realistic level of achievement, then cognitive therapy may be required to help challenge their very high standards.

Self-esteem is concerned with self-efficacy. Self-efficacy refers to beliefs which we hold about our capabilities of organizing and performing task within a specific domain to effectively lead to specific goals. If we expect to be successful and achieved desired outcomes, then this self-efficacy acts as an incentive to perform the action. These efficacy beliefs and expectation of certain consequences determine our behavior and performance, and this intern leads to certain outcomes. For example, if I judge myself to be capable of performing in Taj Mahotsav Music Concert, this is self-efficacy beliefs. The anticipated physical mental pleasure of wining audiences' acceptance and approval of other competitors, self-satisfaction are positive outcome of self-efficacy. Thus, self-efficacy and self-esteem differ in so far as self-esteem is concern with judgment about personal worth, while self-efficacy is concerned with judgment about personal capabilities, whereas self-esteem affects our general mood, self-efficacy beliefs about our ability to succeed at specific tasks or how well we perform at these tasks. Self-efficacy beliefs are constructed from mastery experience, social persuasion, vicarious experiences and physical and emotional states. Self-esteem is driven from self-enhancement maintaining a consistent view of the self, maintaining a socially approve view of the self and maintaining an accurate view of self. Self-efficacy also developed from observing others through sustain efforts. These beliefs may be strengthened if they are persuaded that they can succeed and given manageable challenges which confirm their gurus (coaches) persuasive exhortation. Finally, people's self-efficacy beliefs are enhanced by perusing goals when physically fit and in positive mood. Efficacy beliefs help in reducing worrying and negative thinking about potential threats. It regulates emotional states by facilitating problem-focused coping to alter potentially threatening environmental circumstances by enabling people to solicited social support to act as a buffer against stress and by using the self-soothing techniques such as humor, relaxation and exercise to reduce arousal associated with potentially threatening situations. It leads to better physical health and better physiological and social adjustment.

Interestingly, despite all the competition and rivalry in the professional domain, most of the artists are very encouraging and motivating towards each other. It was in the early sixties that Bade Ghulam Ali Khan visited Siddheshwari's home in Kabir Chaura. He had come to attend the Sangeet Parishad Conference held in Banaras which didn't go well as per him. His dissatisfaction was evident to Siddeshwari Devi, she called upon a personal *mehfil* at her place and invited Khan sahib to sing, who came over with his son Munawar Ali to perform. He was deeply touched by the generosity of Siddheshwari Devi who took great pains to organize everything to his taste. She knew about his love for food and organized a lavish and tasty affair. She gifted him an exquisite piece of *kim khwab* (special variety of rich Banarasi brocade) along with a token money of five hundred and one rupees. Khan Sahib knew "*maa*" did this short term reduction in negative intention, to sooth his nerves and comfort him and this was a big boost to his self-esteem. Similarly, Begum Akhtar never asked any of her disciples for 'fees' because she never wanted to discriminate between her students or make anyone feel inferior about not having or not being able to afford the education (music education here). She believed that talent and skill cannot be bought with money and money should not become a parameter to measure anyone's self-esteem with.

Positive self is useful and problem solving by taking social support, catharsis, crying which leads to immediate emotional relief and short term reduction intention, improving faith to cope with external crisis and intra-psychic conflict, meditation, relaxation, exercise, reframing (we attempt to step out of the old frame and look at our problems within the context of an alternative frame of reference that makes the emotional impact of problem less severe or finding a solution to the problem easier) humor, distraction, etc. all are mechanisms for coping anxiety, tension, stress etc.

We have better health and well-being when we evaluate ourselves positively (high self-esteem) and believe that we will succeed at tasks we attempt (high self-efficacy) with life challenges and using adaptive defense mechanism to manage inter-psychic conflict which are entailed by the view of self as agent.

Epilogue

On 16th September 2019, Sunday, I am once again sitting in Kamani Auditorium. This time my dearest guru, legendary singer of *Thumri* from Banaras Gharana, Vidushi Savita Devi is singing. An extremely beautiful singer with a magical voice, Savita Devi's arthritic knees have made it difficult for her to sit on the floor, so she now sat on a wooden bench. She went through with the *Guru Vandana "Om Namo Bhagwate Vasu devaya"* (Om, I bow to Lord Vasudev), before starting the show. Her confident and mesmerizing voice reverberated in the auditorium and there was a pin drop silence in the audience. It showed that with age, one's physical agility may go down but the liveliness need not. A blind man sitting next to me was whispering that Savita Ji's music has definitely reached the gods. I looked at him and my eyes welled up. She said from the stage, "I pay my tribute to my seniors who have left us. Their deaths brought a big loss in the field of classical music, especially *thumri*. But those we love and lose are always connected by our heart strings to infinity."

In her rendition, one can sense that emotion is more intense than thought. Still, the right understanding of the genre and wisdom were visible because emotions without thought would lead to all kinds of indecisions.

She was wearing a green Mysore silk saree and a big maroon bindi (her signature style) on her forehead for bidding farewell to the rainy season. She sang a *Kajri, 'Barkha Laga Mori Guiyan'*, in raga *'Piloo'*. She said, "*Namaskar*, it's my pleasure to sing before you. I am now 80 years old and

I am sure that most of the listeners are younger than I am and a few are of my age. I pray to the Almighty for your prosperity, happiness and good health." She continued, "My dear audience, you all have made me a celebrity, so you are most valuable asset of my life." The legends have the skill of making you very important, they are very polished and courteous.

In the beginning, she was looking a bit stressed due to her painful knee but she lubricated the stress very quickly. She started singing *thumri,* then a *dadra*. Initially, she was singing and looking at the audience and enjoying the moment but gradually I found that she was moving towards devotional lyrics. We can say that she had started her concert with an eye-opening path when personal self was present but concluded it with an eye-closed path where she was moving towards her spiritual self.

During concerts, the legends generally converse with the audience to make them focused and fully participate. She said like any other person, the artists have also gone through ups and downs in their lives but one should continuously stick to music or any art even when the going gets tough. It will make a difference to your music, your love and your life. "I had lost my 18-year-old son but I never discontinued my singing. I derive life energy from my art. The world is surviving on hope. We should be optimistic in our life." She says, "I am a devotee of Lord Krishna and Krishna says to his devotee that 'I am here! I am near you, I'm for you and I will be forever. So no need to be fearful.' If he pushes you to the edge he himself will either catch you or teach you to fly." Almost all the stalwarts are god-fearing. At the end of her concert, Savita Ji said, "Next time I come to perform, I would like to see maximum participation from the youth of our country." We all know that the countries which are more inclined towards culture have fewer incidences of crime and terrorism. We should spread this message on a global level to bring peace and harmony in this world with the help of different institutions.

In India, *Guru-Shishya parampara* is still in practice very successfully in the field of art. However, it should be more encouraged from both sides. Parents should take more interest in inclining their kids toward culture from a very early stage of life. We can't deny that *"virasat"* and 'destiny' play an important role in the making of an artist but hard labour, discipline and good education can transform a talented and creative person into a very good artist without having any cultural family background. Through good education and networking skills, they can also become a master of their destiny.

At the end I was returning with my Guru and two of her other disciples in an SUV. I told her that she sang very beautifully. She exclaimed and laughed at a perfect pitch with a twinkle in her eyes. How motivated she was at the age of 80... My inspiration!

To attain the status of a celebrity is no doubt a great achievement but to maintain that status is even greater. Success is not magical, it is the natural consequence of consistently applying the basic fundamentals. But to maintain that state requires so many other characteristics and traits along with hereditary and environmental factors. As per my observation, these stalwarts have an exceptionally good sense of aesthetic and creativity in them. They are highly emotional and sensitive, but they know how to balance their emotions. Their level of hope and optimism is very high. Needless to say, they have an in-depth knowledge of their genre and to maintain their status they work very hard and always keep thinking new things while restoring the originality. Vidushi Girija Devi used to say that original *bandish* should not be changed, but you can do experiments with improvisations.

We have to restore our traditions. Kameshwar Pathak used to say that our old songs depict that period's social structure. Hence if you want to revisit that period you should not criss-cross the originality while showing your creativity. If you want to create something, you create entirely new lyrics which show the socio-economic condition of your period, so that the coming generation can see the legacy left behind as you are blazing the trail of the past and the present.

Stalwarts are God-fearing. They always say, *"Ishwar ke marzi ke bina kuch nahi hota* (Nothing happens without the will of the God)." They have a deep faith in *Guru-shishya parampara* (tradition) wherein surrender to the *guru* is supreme. As emphasized by Pt. Rajan-Sajan Misra, surrender consists of dedication, devotion and commitment towards the Guru. In fact, surrender means being egoless, which is the first condition of learning any traditional art. Rita Ganguly believes, "your surrender increases your capacity to hone the skill as well as increases your hunger to learn more." In turn, the guru transfers their legacy for the next generation. They are very good at networking, very polished in their mannerisms, way of communication, witty in their ideas. The lyrics they chose are highly emotional, relevant to the theme of the event and aesthetically preferred. They are very cautious about their values and culture. Their sense of connectedness with the audience is very high, as has been mentioned by Pt. Ajoy Chakrabarty as well. Moreover, they are very balanced in maintaining their relationships and they also have strong bonds with their accompanists and disciples for years together. It won't be an exaggeration to state that it continues throughout their lives. They are always with them in their personal lives in good and bad times. With pupils their behavior is just like that of a parent. These leaders display a paradoxical combination of personal humility and personal will, channeling their energy, knowledge, aesthetic quotient, creativity and discipline.

Combined advantage of lineage and absence of virtually any formidable competition results in helping them maintain status as leaders in their genre which may not be easy in the current socio-economic scenario. I would like to encourage upcoming artists to work very hard under the supervision of knowledgeable guides and practice the quote by success of Jim Rohan, "don't wish it was easier, wish you were better." We can't always blame destiny and legacy for our failure. This destiny has become a popular scapegoat, a way to deal with failure, a fatalistic ruse to reconcile ourselves to all kind of uncomfortable situations. Since they are learning a new art and growing in new avenues they must be willing to become a small fish in a big pond because they are reaching higher functions.

I dream to restore the glory days of the art tradition *Thumri* genre by tracing its chronological journey and its characteristics. Successful people do what unsuccessful people are not willing to do (Jim Rohn). Hence, I have come to believe that:

Success and relations never depend on
the capability of your brain.
But, they always depend on the greatness
of your behavior and thoughts.

Something I have learnt and appreciate in this journey is the undying positive attitude of the stalwarts. Despite their age and frail health, many of them are continuously working to enhance the lineage further. It is as if they wanted to do something for themselves and the field even till their last days as mortal. I am grateful to all of them as they were ever so helpful, kind and cooperative in sharing their wisdom with me. Some of them would call me up themselves later to share some instances as they felt it could be helpful for some of the younger artists.

All these artists have shared their stories of struggle.

Even if they were not very 'happy' during that time, their psychological richness helped them in reaching their goal and appreciating their skill and life they had. A recent research (Nield, 2021) demonstrated that a 'good' life does not necessarily have to be happy. What makes a 'good life'? This is an age-old question and various answers have been offered for it. But a recent study places its emphasis on living in a way that's 'psychologically rich'. This richness can be defined by experiences that are out of the ordinary, varied, complex and perhaps also cause a shift in perspective for the person going through them. A psychologically rich life is more important than being happy or finding a sense of meaning two main areas that current psychological research tends to be concerned with, especially while evaluating a 'good life'. Unlike happy or meaningful lives, psychologically rich lives are characterized by a variety of interesting and perspective changing experiences.

All the stalwarts were happy to share their views especially when they got to know that this would be of help to the younger generation. They believed that the future and glory of the field rests with the upcoming generation and they were pleased to motivate them, guide them and hone their skills. All of them have given their blessings to the younger artists and students and wish them a holistic and fulfilling journey ahead. I also wish to give my best to the younger generation in their endeavors and urge them further to rise above their struggles and shine. Further research in this area can really be helpful in understanding additional nuance in the *natu liningre* of artists, their traits and characteristics and what makes a person a successful artist.

Author interviewing Smt. Savita Devi

Author interviewing Vidushi Girija Devi

With Pt. Channulal Mishra after the interview

With Kameshwar Pathak after an interview

Performance by participants and distribution of certificate as incentive after workshop

Performance by participants and distribution of certificate as incentive after workshop

Veteran Thumri exponent Vidushi Savita Devi is teaching disciples in her Gurukul (Siddheshwari Devi Academy of Indian Music)

Workshop conducted by the author at ARSD College, Delhi University

A musical moment with Dr. Shanti Hiranand during an interview

Interaction with Pt. Govardhan Mishra

References

1. Adlai-Gail, W.S. (1994). *Exploring the autotelic personality. Dissertation Abstracts International: Section B: The Sciences and Engineering, 55(4-B), 1684.*

2. Alkan, S., Ordulu, M.Z., SEZER, Y., Soyer, E., Aslan, D., *and* Sayek, I. (2007). Is there a correlation between extroversion personality characteristics of medical students and awareness of works of art?. *Turkish Journal of Medical Sciences,* 37(5), 311-317.

3. Ames, C., *and* Archer, J. (1988). Achievement goals in the classroom: Students' learning strategies and motivation processes. *Journal of Educational Psychology.* 80, 260-267

4. Asakawa, K. (2004). Flow Experience and Autotelic Personality in Japanese College Students: How do they Experience Challenges in Daily Life? *Journal of Happiness Studies: An Interdisciplinary Forum on Subjective Well-Being,* 5(2), 123-154.

5. Asakawa, K. (2009). Flow Experience, Culture, and Well-being: How Do Autotelic Japanese College Students Feel, Behave, and Think in Their Daily Lives? *Journal of Happiness Studies.* 11. 205-223. 10.1007/s10902-008-9132-3.

6. Baker, F.A. (2013). The ongoing life of participant-composed songs within and beyond the clinical setting. *Musicae Scientiae,* 17(1), 40–56.

7. Bassi, M., *and* Fave, A.D. (2004). Adolescence and the Changing Context of Optimal Experience in Time: Italy 1986-2000. *Journal of Happiness Studies: An Interdisciplinary Forum on Subjective Well-*

Being, 5(2), 155-179.

8. Baumgarten, Alexander Gottlieb (2007). *Ästhetik,* ed. and trans. Dagmar Mirbach. Hamburg: Meiner.

9. Bell, HM (1962). *Manual, Bell adjustment inventory* (revised student form, (P.3). California.

10. Betsur Ningamma C. *and* Mahmoudi Armin. (2010). Relationship between Adjustment and Self esteem among Adolescents. *Asian Journal of Development Matters.* 4(1). 197-203

11. Bhawuk, Dharm P.S. (2003). Culture's Influence in Creativity: the case of Indian Spirituality. *International Journal of Intercultural Relations,* Volume 27, Issue: February 2003.

12. Boden, M.A. (1998). *Creativity and artificial intelligence. Artificial intelligence,* 103(1-2), 347-356.

13. Booth-Kewley, S., *and* Vickers, R.R. (1994). Associations between major domains of personality and health behavior. *Journal of Personality,* 62, 281-298.

14. Boyce, C., *and* Neale, P. (2006). Conducting in-depth interviews: A guide for designing and conducting in-depth interviews for evaluation input.

15. Buch, M.B. (ed) (1991). *Survey of research in education,* New Delhi: NCERT.

16. Chamorro-Premuzic, T., Furnham, A., *and* Reimers, S. (2007). *The Artistic. Psychologist,* 20(2), 84.

17. Clift, S., Hancox, G., Staricoff, R. *and* Whitmore, C. (2008) *Singing and Health: A systematic mapping and review of non-clinical research.*

18. Coopersmith, S. (1987). *SEI: Self-esteem inventories.* CA: Consulting Psychologists Press.

19. Costa, P.T. *and* McCrae, R.R. (1992). *The Revised NEO Personality Inventory Manual,* Odessa, FI: Psychological Assessment Resources.

20. Cross, Ian (2014). Music and communication in music psychology. *Psychology of Music.* 42. 10.1177/0305735614543968.

21. Csikszentmihalyi, M. (1996). *Creativity: Flow and the Psychology of*

discovery and Invention. New York. Harper Perennial.

22. Csikszentmihalyi, M. (1999). Implications of a systems perspective for the study of creativity. In R.J. Sternberg (ed.), *Handbook of creativity.* Cambridge: Cambridge University Press.
23. Csikszentmihalyi, M., *and* Csikszentmihalyi, I. S. (Eds.). (1988). *Optimal experience: Psychological studies of flow in consciousness.* New York, NY, US: Cambridge University Press.
24. Csikszentmihalyi, M., *and* Schneider, B. (2000). *Becoming adult: How teenagers prepare for the world of work.* New York, NY, US: Basic Books.
25. Csikszentmihalyi, Mihaly. (1998). Finding Flow: *The Psychology of Engagement With Everyday Life.*
26. Deshpande, G.T. (1992). *Abhinavagupta.* Sahitya Akademi, New Delhi (pp. 85)
27. Diener, E., Oishi, S., *and* Lucas,R.E. (2002). Subjective well-being: The science of happiness and life satisfaction. In C.R. Snyder *and* S.J. Lopez (Ed.), Handbook of Positive Psychology. Oxford and New York: Oxford University Press (pp 63).
28. Elliot, A.J. (1999). Approach and avoidance motivation and achievement goals. *Educational Psychologist,* 34, 169 –189. doi:10.1207/ s15326985ep3403_3.
29. Elliot, A.J., *and* Church, M.A. (1997). A hierarchical model of approach and avoidance achievement motivation. *Journal of Personality and Social Psychology,* 72, 218 –232. doi:10.1037/0022-3514.72.1.218.
30. Elliott, E.S., *and* Dweck, C.S. (1988). Goals: An approach to motivation and achievement. *Journal of Personality and Social Psychology.* 54, 5-12.
31. Feist, G.J. and Barron, F.X. (2003). Predicting creativity from early to late adulthood: Intellect, potential, and personality. *Journal of Research in Personality,* Vol. 37, No. 2, pp. 62-88.
32. Ferand, E.T. (1961). *Improvisation in Nine Centuries of Western Music.* Cologne: Arnovolk.
33. Friedman, H.S., Tucker, J.S., Schwartz, J.E., Martin, L.R., Tomlinson-

Keasey, C., Wingard, D.L., *and* Criqui, M. H. (1995). Childhood conscientiousness and longevity: Health behaviors and cause of death. *Journal of Personality and Social Psychology,* 68(4), 696-703.

34. Fritz, A. (2007). The experience of flow and subjective well being of music students. Horizons of Psychology ISSN 1318-187.

35. Furnham, A., *and* Walker, J. (2001). Personality and judgements of abstract, pop art, and representational paintings. *European Journal of Personality,* 15(1), 57-72.

36. Gilani, M. *and* Hyder, Q. (2003). *Ustad Bade Ghulam Ali Khan: Sabrang: His life and Music.* New Delhi: Harman Publishing House.

37. Guilford, J.P. (1950) Creativity. *American Psychologist.* 5, (444-454) http://dx.doi.org/10.1037/h0063487.

38. Harackiewicz, J.M., Barron, K.E., Tauer, J.M., & Elliot, A.J. (2002). Predicting success in college: A longitudinal study of achievement goals and ability measures as predictors of interest and performance from freshman year through graduation. *Journal of Educational Psychology,* 94, 562–575. doi:10.1037/0022-0663.94.3.562

39. Heidegger M. Translated by Macquarrie J. *and* Robinson E. (1962). *Being and Time.* Harper and Row Publishers. Translated from German *Sein Und Zeit.*

40. Hess, L. (2009). *Singing Emptiness: Kumar Gandharva Performs the Poetry of Kabir* ISBN-10: 0534624022

41. Humes, J. (2008). The art of communication is the language of leadership. *International Trade.*

42. Jackson, S.A., Ford, S.K., Kimiecik, J.C., *and* Marsh, H. W. (1998). Psychological Correlates of Flow in Sport. *Journal of Sport and exercise Psychology,* 20, 358-378.

43. Jackson, S.A., Thomas, P. R., Marsh, H.W., *and* Smethurst, C.J. (2001). Relationships between flow, self-concept, psychological skills, and performance. *Journal of Applied Sport Psychology,* 13(2), 129-153.

44. Joshi, K. (1991). *The Veda and Indian Culture: An Introductory Essay.* Motilal Banarsidass.

45. Knepler, H.W. (1953). Communication and the Artist. *College Art Journal*, 12(2), 148-153.

46. Lubart, T. I. (1999). The Concept of Creativity: Prospects and Paradigms. In R. J. Sternberg (Eds.), *Handbook of Creativity*. London: Cambridge University Press.

47. Malloch, S. (1999). Mothers and Infants and Communicative musicality. *European Society for Cognitive Sciences of Music*

48. Manuel, P. (1990). *Thumri in Historical and Stylistic Perspectives.* South Asia Books.

49. Maslow, A. (1970). *Towards a Psychology of Being (2nd ed).* Princeton, NJ: Van Nostrand.

50. McManus, I.C., *and* Furnham, A. (2006). Aesthetic activities and aesthetic attitudes: Influences of education, background and personality on interest and involvement in the arts. *British Journal of Psychology*, 97(4), 555-587.

51. Middleton, M.J., *and* Midgley, C. (1997). Avoiding the demonstration of lack of ability: An underexplored aspect of goal theory. *Journal of Educational Psychology*, 89, 710–718

52. Midgley, C., Kaplan, A., *and* Middleton, M. (2001). Performance approach goals: Good for what, for whom, under what circumstances, and at what cost? *Journal of Educational Psychology*, 93, 77– 86. doi:10.1037/0022- 0663.93.1.77.

53. Mishler, G. (1999). *Storylines: Craftartists' Narratives of Identity.* Cambridge: Harvard UP, 1999.

54. Moneta, G. (2004). The Flow Experience Across Cultures. *Journal of Happiness Studies*. 5. 115-121. 10.1023/B:JOHS.0000035913.65762.b5.

55. Monroe, P. (ed.) (1990). *International encyclopedia of education.* New Delhi: Cosmo Publications.

56. Nield, D., (2021). *A 'Good' Life Doesn't Necessarily Have to Be Happy, New Psychology Research shows.* Retrieved from:
https://www.sciencealert.com/life-doesn-t-have-to-be-happy-or-

meaningful-many-of-us-just-want-to-be-psychologically-rich

57. Oliva, A., *and* Parra, A. (2001). Autonomía emocional durante la adolescencia [Emotional autonomy during adolescence]. *Infancia y Aprendizaje,* 24, 181-196.

58. Paintner, C.V. (2007). The Relationship Between Spirituality and Artistic Expression: Cultivating the Capacity for Imagination. *Spirituality in Higher Education,* Volume 3, issue 2.

59. Pandit, S. (1977). *An Approach to the Indian Theory of Art and Aesthetics.* Sterling Publishers. New Delhi.

60. Raghavan, V. (1982). *The Aesthetic of Ananda Commaraswamy.* The Indian Institute of World Culture

61. Rawlings, D., *and* Ciancarelli, V. (1997). Music preference and the five-factor model of the NEO personality inventory. *Psychology of Music,* 25, 120–132. Retrieved from http://shodhganga.inflibnet.ac.in/bitstream/10603/214082/7/07%20chapter%202.pdf

62. Robinson, J. (2005). *Deeper Than Reason: Emotion and Its Role in Literature, Music, and Art,* Oxford University Press, 2005, 515pp., ISBN: 0199204268.

63. Sampath, V. (2010). *My name is Gauhar Jaan; the Life and times of a musician.* Rupa Publishers

64. Scheier, M.F., *and* Carver, C.S. (1985). Optimism, coping, and health: Assessment and implications of generalized outcome expectancies. *Health Psychology,* 4(3), 219-247.

65. Schnare, B., Macintyre, P.D., *and* Doucette, J. (2011). *Possible selves as a source of motivation for musicians.*

66. Schwartz, K.D., *and* Fouts, G.T. (2003). Music prefe- rences, personality style, and developmental issues of adolescents. *Journal of Youth and Adolescence,* 32(3), 205-213.

67. Seligman, M.E.P. (1998). *Learned optimism.* New York: Pocket Books.

68. Shukla, S. 1983. *thumri ki Utpatti, Vikas aur shailiyan.* New Delhi, Delhi. Hindi Madhyam karyanvaya Nideshalaya.

69. Silvia, P.J., *and* Nusbaum, E.C. (2011). On personality and piloerection: Individual differences in aesthetic chills and other unusual aesthetic experiences. *Psycho- logy of Aesthetics, Creativity, and the Arts,* 5(3), 208.

70. Snyder, C.R. (2000). The Past and Possible Futures of Hope. *Journal of Social and Clinical Psychology,* 19, 11-28.

71. Soto, C.J., *and* Tackett, J.L. (2015). Personality traits in childhood and adolescence: Structure, development, and outcomes. *Current Directions in Psychological Science,* 24(5), 358-362.

72. Upadhyay, D.K. (2014). Understanding Learners' Perspective on Creative Music Making. *The International Journal of Indian Psychology,* 2(1), 132-143. (ISSN: 2348-5396).

73. Vallerland, R.J, *and* Bissonnette, R. (1992). Intrinsic, extrinsic and a motivational styles as predictors of behavior: A prospective study. *Journal of Personality,* 60, 599-620.

74. Vallerland, R.J., Fortier, M.S. *and* Guay, F. (1997). Self determination and persistence in a real-life setting: Toward a motivational model of high school drop-out. *Journal pf Personality and Social Psychology,* 72, 1161-1176.

75. Van Yperen, N.W. (2006). A novel approach to assessing achievement goals in the context of the 2 * 2 framework: Identifying distinct profiles of individuals with different dominant achievement goals. *Personality and Social Psychology Bulletin,* 32, 1432–1445. doi:10.1177/ 0146167206292093

76. Wallas, G. (1926). The art of thought. London: Watts.

77. Weinberg, M. Jospeh, D. (2016). If you're happy and you know it: Music engagement and subjective wellbeing, doi: 10.1177/0305735616659552 *Psychology of Music* July 29, 201603057356166595

Glossary

Abhinaya: expressive techniques used to convey a mood, theme or idea (specifically in Indian classical dance)

Adaayagi: a recital, a musical entertainment usually by a single performer and one or more accompanists

Addha: rhythmic beat pattern of 16 beats (a form of taal)

Ang: geographical region to which a particular style belongs

Bandish: composition - a strictly defined relation of words, notes and rhythm, also called as *khayaal*- a classical vocal form in Hindustani music

Baramasa: poetic form found in many northern Indian languages in which, perhaps, 12 beauties of a girl or 12 attributes of a deity might be extolled by relating them to the characteristics of each month of the year

Begum: a muslim woman of high rank

Bhajan: Hindu devotional song

Bhakti: devotional worship directed to one supreme deity, it could be through music

Bhava: aesthetic expression of sentiment

Bol-baant: a technique through which the text technically divided for vistaar (elaboration)

Bol-banaao: passage which use the words of composition in various melodic settings, designed to reveal the emotional measures inherent in each phrase

Braj Bhaashaa: a dialect of western Hindi spoken in the region around Mathura in Uttar Pradesh

Carnatic: South India classical music is called as Carnatic or karnatik

Chaiti: a semi-classical sing sung in the month of chait (March/April)

Dadra: light classical vocal form, this is also a Hindustani classical taal of 6 beats

Dhrupad: it is one of the oldest vocal genres in Indian classical music. It denotes both the verse form of poetry and the style in which it is sung

Gaana: it means a song

Gayaki: style of singing, vocal rendition

Ghazal: light classical form of music, sung with Urdu poetry

Haj: religious journey to Mecca undertaken by Muslim

Harmonium: reed organ similar to key board

Hori: a semi-classical singing genre sung on Holi festival

Invocation: an incantation used to invoke a deity or the supernatural.

Jalsa: a gathering to have some fun and frolic

Jhoola: swing and a semi-classical singing genre sung in rainy season

Jugalbandi: a duet of two solo musicians

Kajri: popular form of semi-classical singing popular in Uttar Pradesh and Bihar

Karuna: a bhava (emotion) to express compassion and empathy

Kathak: North Indian Classical dance form

Khayaal: imagination or thought, composition

Laggi: a faster, virtuosic passage in which the table often takes on solo role

Laya: the timing of musical events in terms of the interval that separated them i.e. tempo

Layakari: rhythmical play with the words in khayaal

Madhurya Bhakti: herein the lover and the beloved become one through the intensity of love. It is the closest relationship between the devotee and the lord without any sensuality.

Meend: refers to a glide from one note to another

Mehfil: evening of entertainment poetry or concert of Hindustani classical music and dance, usually in smaller settings

Miyan: a title of respect in Urdu

Mukhada: first two lines of a song

Nawab: a native governor or ruler

Pandaal: a temporary structure

Qawwaali: a style of Muslim devotional music, now associated particularly with Sufis

Raga: a melodic framework, mode

Rasa: a pervading emotional flavour, essence, aesthetic experience of a sentiment

Rasik: aesthete of Hindustani Classical music, music lover

Riyaz: practice

Sampurna jati: classification of notes that comprise of complete 7 notes

Sarangi: bowed, short-necked string instrument

Sarangiaas: those who play Sarangi

Sargam: the seven syllables as an oral or written notation

Sarod: a lute used in classical North Indian music, with four main strings.

Shanti: a rasa denoting peace, balance, inner equilibrium, wisdom and serenity

Shehnai: South Asian wind instrument which is played at marriages and other ceremonies, rites and rituals.

Sher-o-shayari: Urdu poetry

Shloka: a category of verse line developed from the Vedic Poetic meter

Shringara: a rasa (emotion) which means love, beauty and eroticism

Shruti: the smallest interval of pitch that can be heard

Sitar: a plucked stringed instrument

Swara (sur): a musical note

Taan: rapid sequence of notes usually of an equal duration

Tabalchee: those who play the percussion instrument Tabla

Tabla: a percussion instrument

Tala: the rhythmic/metric system

Taluqdar: An Indian landholder in the Mughal Empire and British Raj, responsible for collecting taxes from a district.

Tappa: form of semi-classical vocal music

Taseer: basic root of something, effect

Tawaif: highly sophisticated courtesan who catered to the nobility, excelled in and contributed to music, dance, theatre, and the Urdu literary tradition

Teentaal: rhythmic beat pattern of 16 beats (a form of taal)

Ustad: an expert or highly skilled person

Vasant: Spring season

Vatsalya: love, care and warmth of a mother

Vilambitektaal: 12 beats in slow pace

Viraha: separation leading to sadness and pain

Yashoda: the foster-mother to the god Krishna and a wife of Nanda in the Puranic texts of Hinduism

Zamindar: a landowner, especially one who leases his land to tenant farmers.

The point of the book is to understand the influence of psychology in the emergence of an artist achieving high and maintaining the status for decades. We have highlighted the role of aesthetics, creativity, surrender to Guru, self and spiritualism, translation of everyday life into music and flow experiences, all of it leading to subjective well-being and growth eventually. A special feature of the book is that apart from utilizing traditional resources such as archives, private papers, newspapers books et cetera, the book has attempted to use the experience and understanding of stalwarts to help the new brigade in the field of classical music, especially to *thumri* genre. This book is an effort to restore the art tradition especially "*thumri*-Genre.

Index

Banaras Gharana • 24, 55, 61, 63, 86, 101, 111, 240, 299

Bandhish Thumri • 1, 3, 4, 25, 26, 33, 34, 35, 36, 37, 38, 39, 40, 41, 43, 48, 52, 59, 80, 99, 145, 299, 303, 308, 314

Bol Banaao • 34, 38, 43, 94

Ghulam Ali Khan, Ustaad • 22, 27, 31, 46, 68, 69, 73, 78, 124, 127, 130, 142, 168, 187, 207, 208, 209, 210, 234, 235, 240, 241, 249, 255, 273, 297, 313

Girija Devi Ji • 26

Vidushi Savita Devi • 24, 25, 74, 89, 101, 114, 147, 176, 225, 276, 299, 308

DISCLAIMER:

The views, and quotes expressed in this book by the stalwarts, artists and interviewees are purely personal and are not intended to hurt anyone. The author cannot be held liable for any hurt or damage whatsoever.